CHUCK PALAHNIUK

Beautiful You

Chuck Palahniuk's thirteen previous novels—*Doomed, Damned, Tell-All, Pygmy, Snuff, Rant, Haunted, Diary, Lullaby, Choke, Invisible Monsters, Survivor,* and *Fight Club*—have sold more than five million copies in the United States. He is also the author of *Fugitives and Refugees,* published as part of the Crown Journeys Series, and the nonfiction collection *Stranger Than Fiction.* He lives in the Pacific Northwest.

www.chuckpalahniuk.net

Also by Chuck Palahniuk

Beautiful You

A Novel

CHUCK PALAHNIUK

ANCHOR BOOKS
A Division of Penguin Random House LLC
New York

FIRST ANCHOR BOOKS EDITION, JULY 2015

The Library of Congress has cataloged the Doubleday edition as follows:
Palahniuk, Chuck.
Beautiful you / Chuck Palahniuk.—1st ed.
p. cm.
I. Title.
PS3566.A4554B43 2014   813'.54—dc23 2013033379

Anchor Books Trade Paperback ISBN: 978-0-345-80711-3
eBook ISBN: 978-0-385-53804-6

Book design by Michael Collica

www.anchorbooks.com

Printed in the United States of America
10 9 8 7 6 5 4 3 2 1

*"A Billion Husbands Are
About to Be Replaced"*

Beautiful You

Even as Penny was attacked, the judge merely stared. The jury recoiled. The journalists cowered in the gallery. No one in the courtroom came to her rescue. The court reporter continued to dutifully keyboard, transcribing Penny's words: "Someone, he's hurting me! Please stop him!" Those efficient fingers typed the word "No!" The stenographer transcribed a long phonetic moan, a groan, a scream. This gave way to a list of Penny's pleas:

His fingers tapped out, "Help!"

They typed, "Stop!"

It would've been different if there had been other women in the courtroom, but there were none. In the past few months all women had disappeared from sight. The public sphere was devoid of women. Those looking on as Penny struggled—the judge, the jurors, the spectators—they were all male. This world was a world of men.

The court reporter typed, "Please!"

He typed, "Please, no! Not here!"

Otherwise, only Penny moved. Her slacks were bunched down rudely around her ankles. Her underthings were ripped away to expose her to everyone who dared look. She swung her elbows and knees, trying to escape. In their front-row seats the sketch artists drew fast lines to capture her grappling with the attacker, her torn clothes flapping, her tangled hair whipping the air. A few tentative hands rose among the spectators, each cupping a cell phone and snapping a surreptitious picture or a few seconds of video. Her outcries seemed to freeze everyone else present, her ragged voice echoing around the otherwise silent space. It was no longer the sound of just one woman being raped; the reverberating, shimmering eddies of sound suggested that a dozen women were under attack. A hundred. The whole world was screaming.

In the witness stand, she fought. She wrestled to bring her legs together and push the pain away. Lifting her head, she tried to make eye contact with someone—with anyone. A man pressed his palms to the sides of his head, covering his ears and squeezing his eyes shut, as red-faced as a frightened little boy. Penny looked to the judge, who sighed piteously at her plight but refused to gavel for order. A bailiff ducked his head and mumbled words into a microphone clipped to his chest. His gun holstered, he nervously shifted his weight, wincing at her outcries.

Others peeked decorously at their watches or text messages as if mortified on Penny's behalf. As if she ought to know better than to scream and bleed in public. As if this attack and her suffering were her own fault.

The lawyers seemed to shrivel inside their expensive pinstriped suits. They busily shuffled their papers. Even her own boyfriend stayed seated, gaping at her brutal assault in utter disbelief. Someone must've called an ambulance, because paramedics were soon rushing down the center aisle.

Sobbing and clawing to protect herself, Penny fought to stay conscious. If she could get to her feet, if she could climb from the stand, she could run. Escape. The courtroom was as densely packed as a city bus at rush hour, but no one seized her attacker or tried to drag him away. Those who were standing took a step or two back. Every observer was edging backward as far as the walls allowed, leaving Penny and her rapist in a growing emptiness at the front of the room.

The two paramedics pushed through the crowd. When they first reached her, Penny lashed out, still gasping and struggling, but they calmed her, telling her to relax. Telling her that she was safe. The worst was over, leaving her chilled, drenched in sweat, and shivering with shock. In every direction a wall of faces looked for blank spots where their eyes wouldn't meet other eyes filled with their mutual shame.

The paramedics lifted her onto a gurney, and one tucked a blanket around her trembling body while the other buckled straps to keep her in place. Finally the judge was gaveling, calling for a recess.

The medic pulling the straps snug asked, "Can you tell me what year this is?"

Penny's throat burned, raw from shouting. Her voice sounded hoarse, but she said the correct year.

"Can you tell me the president?" asked the paramedic.

Penny almost said Clarissa Hind, but stopped herself. President Hind was dead. The first and only female president was dead.

"Can you tell us your name?" Both medics were, of course, male.

"Penny," she said, "Penny Harrigan."

The two men leaning over her gasped in recognition. Their professional faces slipped for a moment and became delighted smiles. "I *thought* you looked familiar," one said brightly.

The other snapped his fingers, exasperated by words that wouldn't come to mind. He piped in, "You are . . . you're *that one,* from the *National Enquirer!*"

The first one pointed a finger at Penny, bound and helpless, watched by every masculine eye. "Penny Harrigan," he shouted like an accusation. "You're Penny Harrigan, 'the Nerd's Cinderella.'"

The pair of men lifted the gurney to waist height. The crowds parted to let them wheel it toward the exit.

The second medic nodded with recognition. "The guy you dumped, wasn't he, like, the richest man in the world?"

"Maxwell," the first declared. "His name was Linus Maxwell." He shook his head in disbelief. Not only had Penny been raped in front of a federal courtroom filled with people, none of whom had lifted a finger to stop the attacker, but now the ambulance attendants thought she was an idiot.

"You should've married him," the first one kept marveling all the way to the ambulance. "Lady, if you'd married that guy you'd be richer than God. . . ."

Cornelius Linus Maxwell. C. Linus Maxwell. Due to his reputation as a playboy the tabloid press often called him "Climax-Well." The world's richest megabillionaire.

Those same tabloids had dubbed her "the Nerd's Cinderella." Penny Harrigan and Corny Maxwell. They'd met a year before. That all seemed like a lifetime ago. A different world entirely.

A better world.

Never in human history had there been a better time to be a woman. Penny knew that.

Growing up, she repeated the fact like a mantra: *Never in human history has there been a better time to be a woman.*

Her world had been perfect, more or less. She'd recently graduated law school in the top third of her class, but failed the bar exam twice. Twice! It wasn't self-doubt, not really, but an idea had begun to haunt her. It bothered Penny that, due

4

to all the hard-won victories of women's liberation, becoming an upbeat, ambitious girl attorney didn't feel like much of a triumph. Not anymore. It didn't seem any bolder than to be a housewife in the 1950s. A couple generations ago, society would've encouraged her to be a stay-at-home mom. Now all the pressure was to become a lawyer. Or a doctor. Or a rocket scientist. Whatever the case, the validity of those roles had more to do with fashion and politics than they did with Penny herself.

As a college undergrad she'd devoted herself to gaining the approval of the professors in her gender studies department at the University of Nebraska. She'd exchanged the dreams of her parents for the dogma of her instructors, but neither of those outlooks was innately her own.

The truth was, Penelope Anne Harrigan was still being a good daughter—obedient, bright, dutiful—who did as she was told. She'd always deferred to the advice of other, older people. Yet she yearned for something beyond earning the approval of her parents and surrogate parents. With apologies to Simone de Beauvoir, Penny didn't want to be a third-wave *anything*. No offense to Bella Abzug, but neither did she want to be a post-*anything*. She didn't want to replicate the victories of Susan B. Anthony and Helen Gurley Brown. She wanted a choice beyond: Housewife versus lawyer. Madonna versus whore. An option not mired in the lingering detritus of some Victorian-era dream. Penny wanted something wildly beyond feminism itself!

Nagging at her was the idea that a deep-seated motive kept her from passing the bar exam. That submerged part of her didn't want to practice law, and she kept hoping that something would happen to rescue her from her own small-scale, predictable dreams. Her goals had been the goals of radical women a century ago: to become a lawyer . . . to compete toe-to-toe with men. But like any second-hand goal, it felt like a burden. It had already been fulfilled ten million times over by other women. Penny wanted a dream of her own, but she had no idea how that dream would look.

She hadn't found her dream as a well-behaved daughter. Nor had she found it by regurgitating the hidebound ideology of her professors. It comforted her to think that every girl of her generation was facing this same crisis. They'd all inherited a legacy of freedom, and they owed it to the future to forge a new frontier for the next generation of young women. To break new ground.

Until a wholly new, novel, original dream reared its lovely head, Penny would doggedly pursue the old one: an entry-level position at a law firm, fetching doughnuts, wrangling chairs, cramming for the next bar exam.

Even now, at the age of twenty-five, she worried that it might already be too late.

She'd never trusted her own natural impulses and instincts. Among her greatest fears was the possibility that she might never discover and develop her deepest talents and intuitions. Her *special* gifts. Her life would be wasted in pursuing the goals set for her by other people. Instead, she wanted to reclaim a power and authority—a primitive, irresistible force—that transcended gender roles. She dreamed of wielding a raw magic that predated civilization itself.

While she mustered her courage for a third attempt at the bar exam, Penny reported to work at Broome, Broome, and Brillstein, the most prestigious firm in Manhattan. To be honest, she wasn't a full associate. But she wasn't an intern, either. Okay, occasionally she ran to the lobby Starbucks for a half dozen last-minute lattes and half-caf soy cappuccinos, but not every day. Other days she'd be dispatched to fetch extra chairs for a big conference meeting. But she wasn't an intern. Penny Harrigan wasn't a lawyer, not yet, but she certainly wasn't a lowly intern.

The days were long here at BB&B, but they could be exciting. Today, for example, she'd heard thunder echoing amid the towers of lower Manhattan. It was the roar of a helicopter landing on the rooftop. Sixty-seven floors up, on the heliport of this very building, someone incredibly important was arriving. Penny had been standing on the first floor, juggling a flimsy cardboard box loaded with a half dozen hot venti mochas. She was waiting for an elevator. Reflected in the polished steel of the elevator doors, there she was. Not a beauty. Not ugly, either. Neither short nor tall. Her hair looked nice, clean and pooling along the shoulders of her simple Brooks Brothers blouse.

Her brown eyes looked wide and honest. In the next instant her clear-skinned, placid face was erased.

The elevator doors slid open, and a scrum of massive men, like a charging football team in identical navy blue suits, emerged from the arriving car. As if running offense for a star quarterback, they shouldered their way out, pressing back the impatient crowd. Forced to step aside, Penny couldn't help but crane her neck to see whom they were protecting. Everyone else with a free hand reached straight up, every hand cupping a camera phone, and began to shoot video and pictures from overhead. Penny couldn't see through the onslaught of blue serge, but she could look up and see the famous face in the screens of the numerous recording devices. The air was loud with electronic clicks. The static and chatter of walkie-talkies. From behind it all came the muffled sound of sobbing.

The woman on the small screens of myriad phones was dabbing at her cheeks with the corner of a handkerchief, the linen and lace already stained with tears and mascara. Even wearing oversize sunglasses, the face was unmistakable. If there was any doubt it was resolved by the dazzling blue sapphire balanced between her perfect breasts. If you could believe what you read in the supermarket checkout line, it was the largest flawless sapphire in history, almost two hundred carats. This stone had graced the necks of ancient Egyptian queens. Roman empresses. Russian czarinas. It was impossible for Penny to imagine what any woman wearing such a jewel would have to cry about.

Suddenly it made sense: The helicopter delivering some megacelebrity to the building's roof while this traumatized beauty scurried out on the street level. The senior partners were taking depositions today. It was the big palimony suit.

A man's voice within the mob shouted, "Alouette! Alouette! Do you still love him?" A female voice shouted, "Would you take him back?" The crowd seemed to draw its collective breath, growing quiet as if waiting for a revelation.

The weeping beauty framed in the small viewfinders of a hundred phones, documented from every direction and angle, lifted her elegant chin and said, "I will not be discarded." Fractured into all of those perspectives, she swallowed. "Maxwell is the greatest lover I have known."

Ignoring a new flurry of questions, the security team forced its way through the curious throng to the street doors, where a motorcade of limousines waited at the curb. In a moment, the spectacle was over.

The woman in the center of all that fuss had been the French actress Alouette D'Ambrosia. She was a six-time Palme d'Or winner. A four-time Oscar winner.

Penny couldn't wait to e-mail her mom and dad and tell them about the scene. That was one of the perks of working at BB&B. Even if she was only fetching coffee, Penny was still glad she'd left home. You never saw movie stars in Nebraska.

The motorcade was gone. Everyone was still looking in the direction it had disappeared when a friendly voice called out, "Omaha girl!"

It was a fellow clerk from the firm, Monique, snapping her fingers and waving to get Penny's attention. Compared to Monique, with her elaborate porcelain fingernails studded with flashy Austrian crystals, and her long weave, braided with beads and feathers, Penny always felt like such a plain, gray sparrow.

"Did you see?" Penny stammered. "It was Alouette D'Ambrosia!"

Monique threaded her way closer, calling, "Omaha girl, you need to be up on sixty-four." She caught Penny by the elbow and towed her toward a waiting elevator. The cups of hot coffee sloshed and threatened to spill. "Old man Brillstein has the entire crew together, and they're screaming for more chairs."

Penny's assumption was correct. It was the deposition. The palimony suit: *D'Ambrosia v. Maxwell.* Everyone knew it was a nuisance lawsuit. A publicity stunt. The world's richest man had dated the world's most beautiful woman for 136 days. Exactly 136. Penny knew the details of the case because of the grocery store checkout lines. In New York the cashiers were so slow and surly that you could read the *National Enquirer* from cover to cover while waiting to pay for your melting pint of Ben & Jerry's butter brickle. According to the tabloids, the billionaire had given the woman the world's largest sapphire. They'd vacationed in Fiji. Glamorous Fiji! Then he'd broken off the affair. If they'd been anybody else that might've been the end of the matter, but this couple had the whole world watching them. Most likely to save face, the jilted girlfriend now demanded fifty million dollars' compensation for emotional distress.

As they stepped into an elevator, a cheerful voice called across the lobby, "Yo, Hillbilly!" The two girls turned to see a smiling, fresh-faced young man in a pin-striped suit sprinting toward them. Dodging between people, he was only a few steps away, shouting, "Hold the elevator!"

Instead, Monique punched the button to shut the doors. She repeatedly stabbed the button with her bejeweled thumb as if she were sending a distress signal in Morse code. Penny had lived in the Big Apple for six months, and she had yet to see anyone press an elevator button fewer than twenty times. The doors thudded together, mere inches in front of the young lawyer's aquiline nose, leaving him behind.

His name was Tad, and he'd flirted with Penny every time they'd met. His pet name for her was "Hillbilly," and Tad represented what Penny's mother would call "a real catch." Penny herself suspected otherwise. Secretly, she sensed that he only paid attention to her because he was trying to endear himself to Monique. It was the way any man might curry favor with a pretty girl by fawning over her fat, stinky dog.

Not that Penny was stinky. Or fat, not really.

Not that Monique cared, either. With her flashy streetwise attitude she was angling for a hedge fund manager or a newly minted Russian oligarch. Unapologetic, she told everyone that her only aspiration was to live in an Upper East Side town house, munching Pop-Tarts and lounging in bed all day. Breathing a huge, fake sigh of relief, she said, "Omaha girl, you should let that poor boy put his slippery little tadpole inside you!"

Penny wasn't flattered by his winks and wolf whistles. She knew she was only the ugly dog. The stepping stone.

Aboard the elevator Monique appraised Penny's workaday outfit. Monique cocked her hip and wagged a finger. There wasn't room left on any of the stylish girl's fingers for even one more glitzy ring. Monique pursed her lips, sporting three distinct shades of purple lip gloss, and said, "G'friend, I love your retro figure!" She tossed her beaded braids. "I love how you're so okay with your big-girl thighs."

Penny hesitantly accepted the compliment. Monique was a work friend, and that wasn't the same as a real friend. Life here was different than in the Midwest. In New York City you had to settle.

In the city every gesture was calculated to dominate. Every detail of a woman's appearance demonstrated status. Penny hugged the cardboard box of warm coffees, holding it like a vanilla-scented teddy bear, suddenly self-conscious.

Monique cut her eyes sideways, recoiling in shock at the sight of something on Penny's face. To judge from Monique's grimace, it couldn't be anything less than a nesting tarantula. "A place in Chinatown . . . ?" Monique began. She took a step away. "They can take care of those crazy werewolf hairs you have sprouting around your mouth." Adding in a stage whisper, "So cheap even you can afford it."

Growing up on her parents' farm in Shippee, Nebraska, Penny had seen cooped-up hens peck one another to bloody death with more subtlety.

It was obvious that some women had never gotten the memo about universal sisterhood.

As they arrived on the sixty-fourth floor the elevator doors opened, and the two young women were greeted by the probing noses of four German shepherds. Bomb-sniffing dogs. A burly uniformed guard stepped forward to wand them with a metal detector.

"We're on lockdown above this level," explained Monique. "Because of you-know-who being in the building, they've evacuated everything between sixty-four and the roof." Sassy as ever, Monique took Penny by the elbow and reiterated, "Chairs, girl. Fetch!"

It was ludicrous. BB&B was the most high-powered firm in the country, but they never had enough seating to go around. Like a game of musical chairs, if you arrived late to any important meeting you had to stand. At least until some underling like Penny was sent to find you a chair.

While Monique ran to the meeting to stall for time, Penny tried door after door and found them all locked. The hallways were strangely deserted, and through the window beside each locked door Penny could see the chairs each associate had safely left behind at his or her desk. Here in the rarified air of the executive floors it was always hushed, but this was spooky. No voices or footsteps echoed off the paneled walls or tasteful landscape paintings of the Hudson River Valley. Open bottles of Evian had been left behind so quickly that they still fizzed.

She'd completed a four-year undergraduate degree in gender politics, and two years of law school, and now she was rounding up chairs for people too lazy or too self-important to take their own to meetings. It was so demeaning. This, no, this was something Penny would definitely not e-mail her parents to boast about.

Her phone began to vibrate. It was Monique texting: "SISTER, WHERE ARE THOSE CHAIRS?!" By now Penny was sprinting down hallways. With the cardboard box of coffees barely balanced in one hand, she was lunging at doors, grabbing knobs only long enough to see whether they'd turn. Frantic, she'd all but given up hope, hurtling breathlessly from one locked office to the next. When one knob actually turned, she wasn't ready. The door swung inward, and she was instantly thrown off balance. Falling through the doorway in a great splash of hot coffee, she landed on something as soft as clover. Sprawled on her stomach, she saw close-up the intertwined greens, reds, and yellows of beautiful flowers. Many flowers. She'd landed in a garden. Exotic birds perched among the roses and lilies. But hovering directly in front of her face was a polished black shoe. A man's shoe, its toe was poised as if ready to kick her in the teeth.

This wasn't a real garden. The birds and flowers were merely patterns in an Oriental rug. Hand-dyed and woven from pure silk, it was the only one of its kind in all of BB&B, and Penny realized exactly whose office this was. She saw herself reflected in the dark shine of the shoe: her coffee-drenched hair swinging in her eyes, her cheeks flushed, and her mouth hanging slack as she panted on the floor, out of breath. Her chest heaving. The fall had lifted her skirt, leaving her bottom stuck up in the air. Thank goodness for old-school opaque cotton panties. Had Penny been wearing a racy thong, she would have died from shame.

Her eyes followed the black shoe up to a strong, sinewy ankle sheathed in an argyle sock. Even the jaunty green-and-gold pattern of the man's sock couldn't disguise the muscles within it. Beyond that was the hem of a trouser cuff. From this low angle, her gaze followed the sharp crease of the gray-flannel pant leg upward to a knee. Meticulous tailoring and cut revealed the contour of a powerful thigh. Long legs. Tennis player legs, Penny thought. From there the trouser inseam led her eyes to a sizable bulge, like a huge fist wrapped in smooth, soft flannel.

She felt the hot wetness between her and the floor. She was wallowing on the squashed cups. A combined gallon of soy latte skinny half-caf mocha chai venti macchiato was soaking into her clothes and ruining the room's priceless floor covering.

Even in the buffed, murky leather of the shoe, Penny could see the blush in her cheeks deepen. She gulped. Only a voice broke the moment's trancelike spell.

A man said something. The tone sounded firm, but as soft as the silk carpet. Pleasant and bemused, it repeated, "Have we been introduced?"

Penny's eyes looked up through the veil of her long, fluttering eyelashes. A face loomed in the distance. At the farthest point of this gray-flannel vista, there were the features she'd seen so often in the supermarket tabloids. His eyes were blue; his forehead was fringed by a boyish ruff of his blond hair. His gentle smile put a dimple into each of his clean-shaved cheeks. His expression was mild, pleasant as a doll's. No wrinkles in his brow or cheeks suggested he'd ever worried or sneered. Penny knew from the tabloids that he was forty-nine years old. Neither did crow's-feet offer any proof that he'd smiled very often.

Still sprawled on the floor, Penny gasped. "It's you!" She squeaked, "You're him! I mean, you're you!" He wasn't a client of the firm. Quite the opposite, he was the defendant in the palimony case. Penny could only assume he was here to be deposed.

He was seated in a guest chair, one of the firm's highly carved Chippendale armchairs upholstered in red leather. The smells of leather and shoe polish were pungent. Framed diplomas and leather-bound sets of law books lined the room's walls.

Behind him was a mahogany desk that glowed crimson from a century of hand rubbing and beeswax. Standing on the far side of the desk was a stooped figure whose bald head glowed almost as red, spotted and blotched with age. In the gaunt face the rheumy eyes blazed with outrage. Thin, palsied lips revealed tobacco-stained dentures. On all of the diplomas and certificates and awards, inked in elaborate gothic calligraphy, was the name Albert Brillstein, Esq.

In polite response to her stammering, the younger man asked, unflustered, "And who might you be?"

"She's no one," snarled the man standing behind the desk, the firm's senior partner. "She shouldn't even *be* here! She's nothing but a girl Friday. She's failed the bar exam *three times*!"

The words stung Penny as if she'd been slapped. In shame she looked away from the blue eyes and once more caught sight of her reflection in the younger man's shoe. Her boss was right.

She was just a gofer. She was nobody. Just some stupid bumpkin who'd moved to New York with dreams of finding some . . . destiny. Something. The brutal truth was that she'd probably never pass the bar. She'd spend her life filing papers and fetching coffee, and nothing wonderful would ever happen to her.

Without waiting for her to get up, Mr. Brillstein snapped, "Out." He pointed a trembling, bony index finger at the open door and shouted, "Remove yourself!"

In the pocket of her skirt, her phone began to vibrate. Penny didn't have to look to know it was Monique, justifiably exasperated.

Brillstein was right. She shouldn't be here. She should be in suburban Omaha. She should be happily married to a pleasant, even-tempered Sigma Chi. They would have two babies and a third on the way. That was her fate. She should be covered in baby spit instead of expensive double-shot espressos.

Reflected in the shoe, there she was, made as tiny as Alouette D'Ambrosia had been shrunken in the screens of so many cell phones. Penny felt tears well up in her eyes and watched one spill down her cheek. Self-loathing flooded her. With her hand, she dashed the wetness away and hoped neither of the men had noticed it. Spreading her fingers against the carpet, she tried to push herself up, but the combination of whipped cream, caramel, and chocolate syrup was gluing her down. Even if she could get to her feet, she worried that the hot liquid would make her blouse transparent.

Despite their cheerful color, the blue eyes watching her were as focused and unblinking as any camera. They were measuring and recording her. He wasn't any more handsome than she was beautiful, but his jaw was firmly set. He oozed confidence.

Mr. Brillstein stammered, "Mr. Maxwell, I can't tell you how sorry I am about this rude interruption." Lifting his telephone and punching a few numbers, he said, "Rest assured that I'll have this young lady evicted from the building immediately." Into the receiver he bellowed, "Security!" Judging from the vehemence in his voice, this would be no simple dismissal. It sounded as if he planned to have her flung from the roof.

"May I offer you a hand?" asked the blond man, reaching down.

A signet ring with a large red stone gleamed on his finger. Later, Penny would discover that it was the third-largest ruby ever mined in Sri Lanka. It had belonged to sultans and maharajas, and here it was coming to her rescue. Its sparkle was blinding. The fingers that closed around her own were surprisingly cold. An equally amazing strength lifted her as the lips, those lips she'd seen kissing movie stars and heiresses, said, "Now that your evening is free . . ." He asked, "Would you grant me the pleasure of your company at dinner tonight?"

The saleslady at Bonwit Teller eyed Penny with a disdainful expression. "May I show you something?" she asked, a sneer in her voice.

Penny had run every step, all eight blocks from the subway to the department store, and hadn't yet caught her breath. "A dress?" she stammered. More resolutely, she added, "An evening gown."

The associate's eyes looked her up and down, not missing a detail. Not Penny's tragic knockoff Jimmy Choos, bought at an Omaha factory-outlet mall. Not her shoulder bag with the fraying shoulder strap and pecan pie stains. Her almost-Burberry trench did little to hide the fact that her clothes were drenched in cold coffee and sticky whipped cream. A few houseflies had found the sweet scent and followed her from the crowded train platform. Penny tried to wave them away with a cavalier gesture.

To a stranger, she must've looked deranged. The saleslady's eval-uation felt like an eternity, and Penny fought the urge to turn on her scuffed heel and stalk away from the snobbish woman.

For her part, the sales associate could've been a penthouse socialite slumming from Beekman Place. Chanel everything. Immaculate nails. No pesky black flies hovered around her per-fect French braid or roamed the flawless skin of her forehead. After taking cold inventory, the associate's eyes met Penny's. With an aloof tone she asked, "Is it for a special occasion?"

Penny started to explain the situation, but caught herself. The world's richest man had asked her to dinner tonight. He'd suggested eight o'clock at Chez Romaine, the most exclusive eatery in the city. Perhaps in the world. People reserved tables years in advance. Years! He'd even agreed to meet her there. No way did Penny want him to see the sixth-floor-walk-up, one-bedroom she shared with her two roommates. Of course, she was busting, absolutely dying to tell someone. Good news didn't seem real until you'd told at least a dozen friends. But this suspicious stranger in the dress department of Bonwit Teller would never believe her. Such an incredible story would only serve to confirm the impression that Penny was a homeless nut job, here to waste the associate's valuable time.

A fly landed on the tip of her nose, and Penny shooed it off. She willed herself to calm down. She wasn't a lunatic. And she wasn't going to run away. Smoothing the fear from her voice, she said, "I'd like to see this season's Dolce and Gabbana wrap gown, the one with the shirred waist."

As if testing her, the associate narrowed her eyes and asked, "In crepe chiffon?"

"In satin," Penny countered quickly. "With the asymmetrical hemline." All those long waits in the grocery checkout line had paid off yet again. The dress she had in mind was the one Jen-nifer Lopez had worn on the red carpet at last year's Oscars.

The woman scrutinized her body and asked, "Size fourteen?"

"Size ten," Penny shot back. She knew houseflies were landing in her hair, but she wore them like they were Tahitian black pearls.

The associate disappeared in search of the dress. Penny almost prayed she wouldn't come back. This was crazy. She'd never spent more than fifty dollars on a dress, and the one she'd asked to see couldn't cost less than five thousand bucks. A few keystrokes on her phone showed she had that much available on her credit limit. If she charged the dress, wore it for two hours during dinner, and returned it in the morning, she'd have a story she could tell for the rest of her life. She wouldn't allow herself to imagine anything beyond tonight. Tonight was a gamble. A longshot. Cornelius Maxwell was renowned for his gallant gestures. That was the only way to explain this. He'd seen her humiliated on the carpet in front of her furious boss, and he was trying to salvage her pride. It was chivalrous, really.

From what Penny had read in the tabloids, Cornelius Maxwell was famous for his chivalry.

Their backgrounds weren't all that different. He'd been born in Seattle to a single mother who'd worked as a nurse. His dream had always been to someday support her in high style, but his mom had been killed in the crash of a bus. When it happened Cornelius had been a graduate student at the University of Washington. A year later, he'd founded DataMicroCom in his dorm room. A year after that he'd be among the wealthiest entrepreneurs in the world.

Among the glamorous women first linked with him had been Clarissa Hind, an unlikely candidate for the New York state senate. With his financial backing and political connections, she'd won. Before her first term was complete, she'd set her sights on becoming the youngest senator the state had ever elected to Washington, D.C. It didn't hurt that the media idolized the couple: the statuesque junior senator and the maverick high-tech billionaire. Between his money and her determination, she won by a landslide. Fast-forward to three years ago, when Clarissa Hind had fulfilled not just her own dreams but the dreams of millions of American women. She'd been elected the first female president of the United States.

Throughout it all Corny Maxwell had stumped tirelessly on her behalf, always praising her, always supporting her in public and private. But the two had never married. A miscarriage was rumored. There was even gossip that she'd asked him to be her running mate, but once the election was over, they'd issued a joint press release to announce that they were dissolving their relationship. Sharing the podium at a press conference, the madam president-elect and her dashing consort had affirmed their continued affection and respect for each other, but their romance was complete.

Penny knew that such success involved hard work and sacrifice, but the paparazzi photos made it look seamless and effortless. President Hind had been her inspiration for becoming a lawyer. Dared she dream? What if Corny Maxwell was looking for a new protégée? It wasn't impossible that he saw some innate potential in her. Tonight might be an audition, and if she passed it then Penny Harrigan might find herself being groomed to take a major role on the world stage. She was about to enter the world's most exclusive sorority.

Her reverie was interrupted by a large housefly buzzing into her mouth. There, daydreaming in the dress department of Bonwit Teller, Penny began to cough and hack.

It was just as well. She was getting too carried away with her fantasy, and the future had a way of breaking your heart if you expected too much. Just look at C. Linus Maxwell, who smiled through one failed romance after another. Following Clarissa, he'd been involved with a member of the British royal family. A

19

princess, no less, and not one of the ugly, inbred ones. She was no slouch. Princess Gwendolyn was beautiful. She was third in the line of succession, only two heartbeats away from becoming the queen. Again, it seemed like an ideal match of European aristocracy and Yankee high-tech know-how. The world waited for them to set a date. When the king had been felled by an anarchist's bullet, it was Corny who supported the weeping princess at her father's funeral. And when a freak accident, a plummeting satellite of all things, had killed the heir apparent, Gwendolyn's brother, her coronation was assured.

By all rights Corny Maxwell should be a prince living the high life in Buckingham Palace, but history repeated itself. The tycoon and the aristocrat had parted amicably.

Twice he'd sidestepped marriage to one of the most powerful women in the world.

If you believed rumors, he felt threatened by women whose status began to rival his own. The tabloids despised him. But Penny suspected, as did most people, that C. Linus Maxwell would forever be an orphan still looking for the lost mother on whom he could shower his adoration and riches.

None of Maxwell's ex-flames seemed the worse for their love affair with him. Clarissa Hind had vaulted from shy political neophyte to leader of the free world. Gwendolyn had been something of a heifer, pretty but overweight; during their relationship she'd slimmed down, and the royal had been a fashion plate ever since. Even Alouette had struggled with her own demons. The tabloids were full of her drunken, drug-addled misadventures. Maxwell had gotten her clean. His love had accomplished something that a dozen court-ordered addiction treatment programs had not.

There in Bonwit Teller, Penny's phone began to vibrate. It was Monique. No longer carping about chairs, Monique had texted, "CALL ME!" Everyone at BB&B must've heard the news by now. A part of Penny wished no one had found out. It was going to be embarrassing to be linked in people's minds with President Hind and Queen Gwendolyn and Alouette D'Ambrosia. Penny surfed her memory for the romances that had occurred in the interim. There had been the Nobel Prize–winning poetess. The heiress to a Japanese steel fortune. The newspaper chain baroness. To date, none of their feet had fit the glass slipper. Penny tried not to think about it, but what she did between this moment and midnight might determine the rest of her life.

Before she could respond to Monique's text, the sales associate had returned. A swath of red chiffon was draped over her arm. One penciled eyebrow arched skeptically, she crooned, "Here you are . . . a size ten." She motioned for Penny to follow her toward the dressing room.

President Penny Harrigan. Mrs. C. Linus Maxwell. Her mind reeled. In tomorrow's *Post* her name would be set in boldface among the celebrity names on Page Six. Tomorrow, this snooty woman would know she wasn't a liar. Everyone in the city would know her name.

Whatever the case, she'd wear this dress very, very carefully.

It was three o'clock. Dinner was at eight. There was still time to have her legs waxed, her hair done, and to telephone her parents. Maybe that would help make the situation seem more real.

Scurrying after the saleslady, Penny asked nervously, "You do offer a full money-back return policy, don't you?" And she crossed her fingers that the zipper would go all the way up.

Kwan Qxi and Esperanza were the ideal roommates with whom to share a cramped studio apartment in Jackson Heights.

Months earlier, as Penny's mom had helped her pack for the big cross-country move to New York, the wise older woman had sagely insisted, "Get a Chinese and some kind of Latin to share the lease."

Penelope's folks might sound, at times, like backward, race-baiting monsters, but they really had their daughter's best interests at heart. In a multicultural, racially diverse household, they reasoned, there was less chance of girls poaching one another's makeup. Cosmetics were expensive, and sharing them could spread deadly staph infections. This was sensible advice. Herpes and bedbugs were everywhere. Theirs were salt-of-the-earth words to live by.

Despite her parents' corn-fed good intentions, the three young roomies from a trio of widely divergent cultures had had more in common than they'd ever imagined. In no time they'd been sharing their clothes, their secrets, even their contact lenses. Not much was declared off-limits. So far, this casual familiarity hadn't been a problem.

Esperanza was a fiery high-breasted Latina whose dark eyes sparked with mischief. She often feigned exasperation over the simplest tasks—changing a lightbulb, for instance, or washing a dish—shouting, *"Ay, caramba!"* because such a patently stereotypical outburst never failed to make Penny bray with laughter. Clearly, she wasn't too uptight to poke fun at herself. The fact that Esperanza could toss a gaily embroidered sombrero onto the living room floor and then stomp a lively hat dance around the brim proved that she'd evolved far into the post–politically correct future of personal identity.

Kwan Qxi, so quiet, so implacable, Kwan Qxi was the counterpoint to the hot-tempered señorita. The Asian moved soundlessly about the crowded apartment, dusting the baseboards . . . trimming her bonsai . . . folding the trailing end of the toilet paper roll into origami surprises for the next user, in general always transforming chaos into order. Her placid face and manner acted as a balm on Penny. Her dense curtain of dark hair was a wonder compared with the frizzy, doo-wop ponytail that Penny wore most days.

In the final hours before the dinner at Chez Romaine, Penny begged both girls to contribute their best skills to perfecting her appearance. From Esperanza, she wanted eyelids painted to glow like Havana sunsets. From Kwan Qxi, she wanted hair that hung like great harvest sheaves of heavy silk. Her roommates pitched in tirelessly, coddling her like flower girls attending to an anxious bride. Together, they primped and dressed her.

Resplendent in the gown, Penny was a vision. To complete her look, Kwan Qxi had unearthed an elegant pendant. It was bright green jade carved into the shape of a dragon, with two pearls for its eyes. A true family heirloom. Esperanza dug out her own favorite earrings, each shaped like a tiny, rhinestone-encrusted piñata. Whether or not her roomies accepted her story about dinner with the world's richest man, both girls were teary-eyed at the sight of Penny's stylish transformation.

Someone buzzed from the street door. The taxicab they'd ordered had arrived and was waiting.

At the last moment, Penny held her breath and went to retrieve a small, gray plastic box she'd long ago hidden in the bathroom. The box held her diaphragm. *An ounce of prevention.* She hadn't needed it since the winter formal, her senior year as an undergraduate. Still searching the bathroom cabinets, she wondered whether such a long period of disuse might've damaged the birth control device. Would the latex have dried out and become brittle, like condoms were known to do? Might it have cracked? Or worse, would it have grown furry with mold? She snatched the gray box from the jumble in a drawer and held her breath as she opened it. The box was empty.

Tapping her foot in mock outrage, Penny confronted the

two girls in the kitchen. She held the empty box like an accusation. Printed on its label was her name, Penelope Harrigan, and the name and address of her family practitioner in Omaha. Placing the box on the counter, next to the rusted, cheese-encrusted toaster oven, she announced, "I'm going to shut off the lights and count to ten, okay?" The faces of both girls were unreadable. Neither blushed nor sheepishly evaded her gaze. "No questions asked," she said. A swipe of the wall switch plunged the room into pitch darkness. She began counting.

A faint, wet sound was followed by a gasp. A giggle.

Penny counted, ". . . eight, nine, ten." The lights blazed, revealing the open box, filled with a familiar pink shape. The diaphragm glistened, fresh and dewy, beaded with someone's healthy vaginal moisture. Clinging to it was a single tightly curled pubic hair. Penny made a mental note to rinse the thing off if she'd need to use it later in the evening.

It never failed. The taxi was late getting to Chez Romaine. Traffic had been backed up in the tunnel, and it was impossible to get a cell phone signal. That was just as well. The cabbie kept glancing in the rearview mirror, saying he was sorry. Saying she looked terrific.

Penny knew he was only being nice. For as much money as she'd spent that afternoon, Penny told herself, she'd darn well better look good. To the saleslady's chagrin the dress had fit perfectly, hugging her young body. Her new Prada shoes, another last-minute splurge, also looked amazing. But Penny was sensible enough to realize that she'd never be a ravishing beauty.

At least there were no dirty houseflies buzzing around her. That was an improvement. Anything was an improvement over living in the Midwest.

Nebraska had never been a good fit for Penny. As a young woman in Omaha, or even when she was a small girl growing up in Shippee, Penny had always felt like an outsider. For one thing, she'd looked nothing like her sturdy, pear-shaped, splay-footed mom and dad. Where they were densely freckled and ginger-haired members of the Irish Diaspora, Penny had a peaches-and-cream complexion. As pale as birch bark. They'd both thought she was crazy for kiting off to New York City.

Moments before, when she'd first climbed into the cab, she'd called Omaha to spill the big news. When her mother's voice had answered, Penny had asked, "Are you sitting down, Mom?"

"Arthur!" her mother had shouted away from the receiver. "Your daughter's on the line."

"I've got some pretty exciting news," Penny had said, barely able to contain herself. She looked to see whether the driver was watching her. She wanted him to eavesdrop.

"So do I!" her mother had exclaimed.

There was a click, and her father's voice had joined the conversation. "Your mother grew a tomato that's the spitting image of Danny Thomas."

"I'll send you a picture," her mother had promised. "It's uncanny."

Her father said, "What's your big news, cupcake?"

Penny had hesitated for effect. When she'd spoken, she'd made sure her voice was loud enough for the cabbie to overhear. "I have a date with C. Linus Maxwell."

Her parents hadn't responded, not right away.

To save time, Penny's dad drank his morning coffee while sitting on the toilet. Her mom dreamed of owning a waterbed. Every birthday they sent her a Bible with a twenty-dollar bill tucked inside. That was her parents in a nutshell.

Penny had prompted them, asking, "Do you know who Mr. Maxwell is?"

"Of course we do, sweetheart," her mother had replied flatly. "Your father and I don't live in Shippee anymore!"

Penny had waited for their shouts of joy. For their gasps of disbelief. For anything.

Finally, her father had said, "We love you no matter what, Pen-Pen. You don't have to invent wild stories to impress us." He was calling her a liar.

It was at that point the cab had gone under the river. The connection was broken. Her roommates hadn't believed her either, but they'd fussed over her, helping with her eye shadow and lip liner as if they'd been bridesmaids. Tomorrow they'd all believe her. Normally she'd never take such pains with her appearance. She hadn't primped just because Maxwell would see her. Tonight the whole world was watching. Penny would walk into that restaurant a complete nobody, but by the time dessert was served she'd be a household name. Even her hero, President Hind, would know Penny's name.

Stalled in the traffic beside her, Penny noticed two men seated in a black sedan. Like the bodyguards who had escorted Alouette D'Ambrosia, both wore tailored, navy-blue suits and mirrored sunglasses. Their stern, chiseled features betrayed no emotion. Neither turned his head in Penny's direction, but she knew from long experience that the pair of them were covertly watching her.

From her earliest memories, she'd been aware of similar strange men following her. Sometimes they'd trailed behind her in slowly moving cars or sat parked at the curb outside her grade school. Other times, they'd strolled purposefully in her wake, always at a discreet distance. There were always two, sometimes three men, each dressed in a plain dark suit and wearing mirrored sunglasses. Their hair was clipped short and neatly combed. Their wingtip shoes were highly polished, even as they'd trailed her like two-legged bloodhounds across rain-wet Cornhusker football fields and the sandy beaches of Lake Manawa.

Many a winter afternoon as the twilight faded, these chaperones would shadow her steps over lonely farm fields, weaving between the dead, wind-blasted stalks of corn as she trudged home from school. One man might lift his lapel and whisper into a microphone pinned there. Another sentinel would raise his arm and appear to signal to a helicopter that was also tracking Penny's every step. Sometimes a great slow-moving blimp would hover above her, day after day.

Ever since Penny could recall, these chaperones had haunted the edges of her life. Always in her peripheral vision. They were always in the background. Chances were excellent that tonight, they'd be among the diners at Chez Romaine, albeit seated at inferior tables, ever watchful.

She'd never felt in the least bit threatened. If anything, she felt coddled and safe. From her first inkling that she was being followed, Penny assumed the men were agents of Homeland Security. All Americans, she told herself, enjoyed this same brand of diligent supervision. So enamored was she of her bodyguards that she'd come to accept them as guardian angels. A role they'd fulfilled more than once.

One grim winter's eve she'd been picking her way homeward through acres of rotting silage. The eventide sky was dark as a bruise. The chill air smelled heavy and ominous with decay. In a twinkling, a killer funnel cloud descended, churning the landscape into a dirty froth of fertile topsoil and airborne dairy cattle. Razor-sharp farm implements clattered around her on all sides. Fist-size chunks of hail pelted her young scalp.

Just as Penny thought she'd be killed, some force had knocked her facedown in the furrows and a gentle, insistent weight pressed itself upon her body. The tornado spent its fury in a moment. The weight lifted, and she could recognize it as one of the anonymous watchers. His pin-striped suit soiled with mud, he removed himself from her backside and walked away without accepting a word of thanks. More than just a passive guardian, he had been a hero. This stranger had saved her life.

Years later, when Penny was in college, a beer-saturated Zeta Delt had dragged her down some stairs into a dirt-floored cellar. It was during a high-spirited Pledge Week mixer. In retrospect, she recognized that she might've promised the young man more than she was willing to deliver. Frustrated, he had thrown her to the ground and straddled her, a knee planted on either side of her struggling torso. His muscular hands began the savage task of shredding her brightly flowered afternoon frock. He fumbled with the zipper of his chinos, producing an angry red erection. Dire as this situation seemed, Penny remained a lucky girl.

Thank goodness for the agents of Homeland Security, Penny thought, as a gray flannel–suited stranger stepped from the shadows near the cellar walls. He delivered her attacker a violent karate chop to the windpipe. With the would-be rapist gasping, Penny had raced away to safety.

Even after she'd said good-bye to her home state, the guardian angels had kept tabs on her. In the Big Apple, she saw them, the neon lights glinting off their sunglasses as they watched over her from a discreet distance. At Bonwit Teller. Even at BB&B they wore their sunglasses indoors, and still they guarded her. As the agents of Homeland Security, she assumed, they guarded all Americans. All of the time.

While she'd been lost in thought, traffic had begun to thaw. Even now her cab was pulling to the curb in front of the Chez Romaine canopy. A valet stepped forward to open her door. Penny paid the cabbie and took a deep breath. She checked the time on her phone. Fifteen minutes late.

She did a last-second check of her dress and arms. No flies.

In the pages of the *National Enquirer,* Jennifer Lopez or Salma Hayek never walked a red carpet without an escort. Penny Harrigan had no choice. There was no sign of Climax-Well. A cadre of photographers was corralled behind a velvet rope, but they didn't give her a second glance. None of them snapped her picture. No one with a microphone stepped up to say how nice she looked and ask about her dress. Another car arrived at the curb, the valet opened another door, and she had no choice except to proceed through the restaurant's gilded entrance, alone.

In the foyer, she waited for the maître d' to notice her. He did not. No one noticed her. Elegantly dressed men and women lingered, waiting for their cars to arrive or to be seated. The din of laughter and conversation made her feel even more invisible, if that was possible. Here, her dress was barely good enough. Her jewelry drew bemused stares. The same way she'd wanted to run from the haughty saleslady at Bonwit Teller, Penny again longed to turn and flee. She'd wrap the gorgeous red gown in its original tissue paper and take it back tomorrow. Men like Maxwell didn't date girls like her.

Still, something nagged at her. She wished she'd never bragged about this date. Her roommates . . . her parents . . . even the taxi driver had thought she was a liar. She had to prove she wasn't. Even if one gossip columnist saw her with Corny Maxwell or a shutterbug snapped their picture together, she'd be vindicated. This thought pushed her the length of the foyer, toward the door to the main dining room. There, a flight of carpeted steps led downward. Whoever entered would draw every eye in the vast, crowded space.

Standing on the top step Penny felt as if she were on the edge of a high cliff. Ahead of her beckoned the future. Behind her, the rich and powerful were already bottlenecked, backing up like gridlocked traffic in the streets. Someone cleared his throat loudly. Below her, the room was packed. Every table was occupied. A mezzanine held even more watchful diners. Where Penny found herself, on the stairs, was like a stage, visible from every seat.

In the center of the room, one man sat alone. His blond hair caught the light from the chandelier. Open on his table was a small notebook, and he was studiously jotting notes in it with a silver pen.

A stranger's breath touched Penny's ear. An officious voice behind her whispered, "Pardon me. Young lady?" The speaker sniffed loudly.

Everyone in the restaurant was watching the lone man scribbling, but watching in that discreet New Yorker way: ogling him over the tops of their menus. Spying on his reflection in the silver blades of their butter knives.

More insistently, the officious voice at Penny's shoulder whispered, "We must keep this space open." He said, "I must ask you to step aside."

Frozen, Penny willed the solitary diner to look up and see her. To see how pretty she looked. The crowd forming behind her grumbled, restless. She couldn't move. The doorman, the parking valet, someone would have to lift her and carry her out like a sack of potatoes.

At last, the man writing in his notebook looked up. His eyes met Penny's. Every head in the cavernous room turned to follow his gaze. The man stood, and the noise of so many people dwindled. As if a curtain were rising at the opera, every voice fell silent.

Without breaking eye contact, the man crossed to the bottom of the stairs and began to climb toward her. Still two steps down, he stopped and offered his hand. As she had once been below him on the office carpet, reaching up, now he was beneath her.

She reached out. His fingers felt as cold as she remembered.

Just as she'd seen in the *National Enquirer,* C. Linus Maxwell escorted her. Just as he'd escorted so many exquisite women. Down the remaining steps. Across the hushed room. He pulled out her chair and seated her. He took his own seat and closed his notebook. Only then did the voices that surrounded them begin to rise.

"Thank you for joining me," he said. "You look lovely."

And for once Penny actually believed she might.

In the next instant, his hand lashed out. As if to slap her face, he leaned forward, swinging his arm so fast it blurred. She winced.

When she opened her eyes, his fist filled her vision, huge, hanging there, his knuckles so close they almost touched the tip of her nose.

"I'm sorry if I scared you," he said, "but I think I caught him." Opening his fingers, Corny Maxwell showed her the crushed little corpse of a black housefly.

The next morning, Penny was standing outside the locked doors of Bonwit Teller for a half hour before they opened. She couldn't afford even a day's credit card interest on what the evening gown had cost. Even if this made her late for work, she had to return the dress right away.

The fairy tales never showed Cinderella getting up at dawn to return her gown and her shoes, terrified that some wary salesclerk would notice a flaw and refuse to credit her account with a full refund.

Despite the extraordinary food and wine, dinner had been less than magical. The stares had never let up. It was impossible to relax and have fun in a fishbowl. Maxwell wasn't the problem. He'd been attentive, almost too attentive, hanging on her every word. Several times, he'd even opened his notebook and written a few words in a quick, spidery shorthand, as if he were taking dictation. It felt less like a romantic tryst than a pleasant job interview. He'd volunteered almost no information about himself, nothing she didn't already know from gossip columns. In her nervousness, Penny had chattered without taking a breath. Desperate to fill any possible silence, she'd told him about her parents, Myrtle and Arthur, and their suburban life. She'd reminisced about the long hours in law school. She'd rambled on about the love of her life, her Scotch terrier, Dimples, and how he'd died the year previous.

Throughout her monologue, Maxwell had smiled calmly. Thank goodness the waiters had occasionally arrived, giving her a moment to shut up and catch her breath.

"If madam will allow . . . ," a waiter said with a white-gloved flourish of his hand, "the kobashira sushi is a house specialty."

Penny smiled winningly. "That sounds delish."

Max shot her a questioning look. "You do know that's raw aoyagi scallops, don't you?"

She didn't. In fact, Maxwell might well have just saved her life. Unknown to him she had a severe shellfish allergy. One succulent bite and she would've slumped to the floor, swollen and lifeless. Penny's alarm must've shown on her face, because he'd immediately revised her order, saying, "The lady will have the Chicken Divan."

Thank God that someone was paying attention. Her runaway mouth resumed its nervous monologue.

She knew she sounded pathetic. Still, Penny couldn't stop herself. No one here had ever expressed any interest in her, not in New York City. She'd gone from being her parents' little miracle to being miserable and invisible. Most nights she'd force herself to walk around the streets until the neighborhood fell quiet and she felt exhausted enough to go to bed. She'd wander around the Upper East Side, alone except for the doormen who stood behind glass in the elegant lobby of each building and watched her pass. These stately town houses and sumptuous co-op apartments, these were what everyone aspired to. In some way she was trying to train herself to want them also. The truth was: She didn't. Penny only pretended to want the jewelry in the windows at Cartier and the furs at Bloomingdale's.

She didn't want merely the trappings of success. Penny craved actual power. Even to her own ears she sounded *crazy* ambitious.

Above all, Penny didn't want what other women professed to want. They seemed possessed, the way they swarmed to the same mundane things. And that worried her; she felt shut out of some hive. If she didn't crave the correct movie heartthrobs and scented candles, she worried that something was horribly wrong with her.

Daily, she caught sight of lady attorneys and execs furiously crunching numbers and barking demands into phones. None seemed to possess some progressive enlightenment. Theirs no longer seemed like the road less taken. Penny sought a career path beyond the knee-jerk strictures of gender identity politics.

Over the dessert course, Penny Harrigan admitted that she didn't know what she wanted.

Becoming a lawyer wasn't her life's dream. As a teenager in high school she'd been told by everyone—her parents, her teachers, her minister—that a person needed a long-term goal and a plan for achieving it. Everyone said she needed to devote

33

her life to something. She'd chosen a career in law as blithely as if she'd plucked the vocation, unseen, from a hat. President Hind notwithstanding, being an attorney was no more appealing to Penny than wearing a sable coat and walking two afghan hounds in diamond collars to hear Verdi at the Met. No, to be honest Penny said she didn't know what she wanted, but she knew something . . . soon, some glorious destiny would reveal itself to her.

Maxwell hadn't asked about any of this, but he listened intently. He watched as if he were memorizing her. At one point, between the appetizers and the salad, he took out the small notebook in which he'd been jotting notes when she arrived. He opened it to a blank page. He removed the cap from a silver fountain pen and began to write, seemingly transcribing her fears. Penny couldn't tell for certain, because his handwriting was cramped, almost microscopic. Scribbling continuously, he was either remarkably rude, or Maxwell was enormously empathetic and caring.

Having her words recorded made her feel self-conscious, but it couldn't silence the overflow of her pent-up anxiety. She'd never expressed this to anyone, but her life seemed to have stalled. After twenty-five years of getting good grades and behaving politely, she'd reached a terrifying dead end. The full extent of her potential. Even as she talked Penny was aware that she'd most likely never see this man again. That made him a safe confessor.

Her relief was evident. Under his rapt gaze Penny glowed. She preened. Emboldened by his attention, she shook her head to make the piñata-shaped earrings dance. She lifted one hand to her bosom, trailing her fingertips over the sinuous curves of the jade dragon. Both accessories reminded her how blessed she was with girlfriends.

Max's blue eyes seemed fascinated by her every gesture. He

smiled but didn't interrupt. His eyes never left hers, but his hand continued to write.

He almost looked in love. This was more than infatuation. More than love at first sight. Maxwell seemed enchanted by the sound of her voice. With his entire body, he seemed to lean forward with yearning. Something in his expression said that he'd been searching for her his entire life.

Penny wanted this kind of attention from the world. She wanted people everywhere to know her name and to love her. There, she'd admitted it aloud. But she couldn't do anything that would justify such massive public acclaim. She just needed a mentor, a teacher, someone to discover her.

Standing outside the locked department store doors, Penny held the garment bag high, lest it drag on the sidewalk. She recalled each delicious course of the meal she hadn't enjoyed. She'd been too afraid of dropping food into her lap. One itty-bitty stain, and she'd spend the next five years paying for her own sloppiness. When the store's doorman turned the locks she rushed straight to the department where she'd bought the gown.

Waiting at the register was the saleslady who'd helped her less than twenty-four hours before.

Offering the garment bag, her voice as firm as she could make it, Penny said, "I'd like to return this."

The saleslady took the bag by the hanger. Laying it on the counter, she unzipped it and inspected the red satin folds.

"When I got home I tried it on," Penny said. With one hand she made what she hoped was a dismissive gesture. "It isn't at all what I had in mind."

The saleslady tossed and smoothed the skirt, peering at the seams, the hem. She asked, "So you didn't actually wear it?"

"No," Penny replied. She held her breath, terrified that a snagged stitch or perspiration stain would expose her as a liar.

The unsmiling woman pressed, "Not even for a quick dinner?"

Penny was certain the woman had found a wine stain. A smudge of chocolate mousse. Or she'd smelled perfume or cigarette smoke in the fabric. It might've been Penny's imagination, but suddenly the sales floor seemed crowded with shoppers, sales associates, even a security guard, all of them eavesdropping on her interaction. "No," Penny insisted. Now she was sweating.

"Not at Chez Romaine?"

"No," Penny squeaked.

The saleslady fixed her with a stern look and said, "I need to show you something." Tucking the dress back inside its garment bag, she reached below the counter and brought out something. It was a newspaper: today's *New York Post*. There on the front page was the headline: "Nerd Prince Plucks New Cinderella from Obscurity."

And next to those huge words was a color picture of Penny sitting elbow-to-elbow with Maxwell. There was no denying it: She was wearing the dress.

"If you don't mind me saying so, miss," the saleslady said, her expression damning, "this is unacceptable!"

Penny was so, so busted. In her head she did a quick calculation. Based on the price and her current credit card interest rate, she'd have the dress paid for sometime around her fortieth birthday.

"For this kind of publicity," the woman admonished, "the people at Dolce and Gabbana ought to be *paying you* to wear their clothes." Leaning forward like a conspirator, she said, "Prada. Fendi. Hermès. They'd die for this much ink." She winked. "Let me contact a few people on your behalf. If you're going to be accompanying Mr. Maxwell, you could earn a fortune by promoting certain designers."

That might be a problem. Maxwell had asked whether he could call her, but in Penny's experience that was strictly a courtesy. It never guaranteed a second date. They hadn't made definite plans. She didn't say it now, but she might never see him again.

Looking around the dress department, Penny saw that strangers were gravitating toward them. Men. Women. Some wearing uniforms. Some in fur coats. Everyone was clutching the same morning edition of the *Post*. And they were all beaming at her.

This saleslady who'd been so unfriendly only the day before, now her face broke into a shy smile. Her eyes sparkling and alive, she sighed. Placing one hand flat against her chest as if to calm a rapidly beating heart, she said, "Please forgive my unprofessional behavior, but . . ."

Even under the woman's heavy makeup, Penny could see that she was blushing.

Offering the day's *Post,* she asked, "Would you autograph your picture for my daughter?"

C. Linus Maxwell didn't call. Not the next day. Nor the day after. A week went by.

Penny went to work and shrugged off Monique's excited interrogation about Chez Romaine.

After work, Penny went to the Jackson Heights branch of Chase Manhattan and rented a safe-deposit box. It required two keys to open. She watched as the bank clerk inserted his key and turned it. She used her own key, and he left her to open the metal box in the privacy of a small room. Once he'd taken leave, Penny picked something small and pink from her handbag and placed it in the box. Quickly, she locked it and summoned the clerk. Her share-and-share-alike roommates wouldn't get another chance to borrow her diaphragm.

Back at the apartment, she returned the earrings and necklace. Every time her phone chimed with a call or text, she caught Kwan Qxi and Esperanza watching her expectantly. But every time the message was from her mom or dad. Or it was the sales associate at Bonwit Teller announcing that she'd scored some dazzling Alexander McQueen gown or pair of Stella McCartney heels for Penny's next night as Cinderella.

In the checkout line at the grocery store, she stood waiting to buy her ice cream, trying to ignore the tabloid headlines that glared out at her. "Cinderella Gets the Brush-Off!" Another front page showed a huge picture of her buying ice cream, under the headline, "Rejected Cinderella Stuffing Herself!" It was surreal. Here she was buying butter brickle ice cream while she looked at a photo of herself, taken the day before, buying ice cream. To make matters worse, in the more recent photos she already looked fatter! Everyone in the store recognized her and stood ready to pat her on the shoulder and console her. The cashier waved her through without paying, telling her, "No charge, honey." To be an object of pity in New York—the city without pity—that's how far she had fallen.

A few days later she could barely get her pants to button. Too much free comfort food. That's why she was taken aback when Tad asked her to lunch at the Russian Tea Room. There, seated at an intimate corner booth in that swank setting, he made her laugh with his rollicking stories about Yale panty raids. Tad recited his curriculum vitae in its entirety, obviously insecure about how he'd compare with her recent billionaire beau. He boasted about rowing as captain for the Yale team. As proof, he wore a bright green Yale sweatshirt. Boring as he was, Penny was still pathetically grateful. Tad's prattle and bluster distracted her from her current public humiliation and crushing woes. Tad was passably handsome—better looking than bland, blond Max—and there was the possibility that a roving *Post* photojournalist would snap a pic of the pair of them and run it under the heading, "Cinderella Bounces Back!"

To her own surprise, Penny found herself holding Tad's hand across the white linen tablecloth. She'd only wanted to give onlookers the impression that she and Tad were canoodling, but . . . something magical was happening. Vibes. Mojo. Juju. Her fingers and his were already entwined, deeply. She wondered whether she could get to the bank, to access her safety-deposit box before closing time.

Penny wasn't a prude. She wasn't some prim, tongue-clucking schoolmarm type. To her, intimacy outside of marriage wasn't sinful . . . she'd simply never seen the margin in casual sex. During her coursework in gender studies she'd learned that roughly 30 percent of women are entirely nonorgasmic, and that seemed to be the case with her. Fortunately, there were other pleasures in life. Salsa music, for example. Ice cream. Tom Berenger movies. It made little sense to court herpes, venereal warts, viral hepatitis, HIV, and unwanted pregnancy in pursuit of unattainable sexual fulfillment.

Nonetheless, Tad's fingers smelled so good. She'd been wrong about him. So wrong. The ambitious young lawyer had wanted her, not Monique. His eyes said as much. Maybe she was also wrong about sex. With the right guy, maybe she could find pulse-pounding release.

"Penny," he stammered.

"Yes." She swallowed. To calm herself, she rested her gaze demurely on the basket of cheesy bread sticks. When she dared look back at him, she repeated, "Yes, Tad?"

His grip tightened. *The Tadpole*. Their simple lunch was becoming everything that her fabled dinner at Chez Romaine had not been: passionate . . . sultry . . . freighted with erotic suggestion.

Stashed deep in her handbag, Penny's phone chimed. The sound caught her off guard.

"Penny," Tad continued, "I've always loved . . ."

Her phone chimed again. Penny tried to ignore it. Her whole body stiffened.

Tad rallied his courage. "If you're no longer dating . . ." His lips puckered and he leaned close. Closer. She could smell the delicious Veal Prince Orloff on his breath.

Penny dodged the kiss. The incoming call was impossible to ignore. "Sorry," she quipped as she retrieved the phone.

According to the ringtone it was Max.

It was unfair. As Penny tried to tell people, C. Linus Maxwell was more than an Internet whiz kid. So much more! He ran a multi-national group of corporations that led the world in computer networking, satellite communications, and banking. Adamantly, she would describe to Monique how Maxwell's enterprises employed more than a million people and served hundreds of millions. Every year his charitable foundation alone poured a billion dollars into each of a dozen high-profile causes, fighting hunger, curing disease, promoting women's rights. As President Hind could attest, gender equality was a dream close to Maxwell's heart. He ran schools in Pakistan and Afghanistan, where young girls could strive toward a brighter future. He financed the political campaigns that brought female leaders into the highest positions of every nation.

That, Penny told everyone, all of that pride and altruism made Maxwell so much more than a wealthy nerd.

What she told herself was that she enjoyed being with him.

It was a hard sell. Especially to herself.

At the office, Monique asked, "Omaha girl, are you wearing a diaphragm?" She gave her head a sassy swivel, making her beaded braids rattle. Without waiting for an answer, she said, "Because if you are—take it out! Burn it! Flush your birth control down the toilet and *let that man knock you up!*"

It was none of Monique's business, but after a month of dating, Penny still hadn't gone to bed with him. Late at night, her parents would call. Penny suspected that they were hoping to catch her in flagrante with Maxwell. Sleepily, she'd answer, "What time is it?"

On the telephone, long-distance, her mother shouted, "How can you not love him? He's so rich!"

On the extension, her father added, "*Pretend to love him!*"

"Your dad and I have never met Maxwell," her mother gushed, "but we already think of him as family."

Penny hung up. She unplugged the phone and went back to sleep. She didn't want to be a pushover. She'd seen too many of her sorority sisters walk down the aisle. Too many of those marriages had devolved into a grim lifetime of mandatory "date nights." Like life sentences in a prison where the conjugal visits were few and far between. Rich or poor, she and Maxwell were still two people who needed the mutual passion to share a lifetime together.

The fact never left her mind: None of his famous romances had lasted longer than 136 days. That couldn't be by accident. They had all lasted exactly 136 days.

And it wasn't as if Maxwell had pressured her for sex, either. He was so detached, so pleasant, but he was so distant that Penny wondered whether Alouette D'Ambrosia had been lying when she'd claimed he was the greatest lover she had ever known. The French beauty must've been with better men, hotly passionate men. Maxwell wasn't exactly aggressive. He did little more than watch and listen and jot notes in his little book. At yachting parties, women whom Penny didn't even know glared at her. Pencil-thin supermodels sneered at Penny's normal hips. They wagged their high-cheekboned heads in disbelief. The men leered at her. They assumed she had some erotic skill that bewitched Maxwell. Their lecherous stares suggested the scenes of unbridled sodomy and expert fellatio they envisioned. How funny it would be to tell them all that the world's richest man had taken her skiing in Bern and to bullfights in Madrid, but he'd never taken her to bed.

Penny wasn't a virgin, not when she and Maxwell had first met. She'd had sex with boys in college, a few. But only one at a time. *Only* boys. And *never* from behind! She wasn't a pervert, and she wasn't a slut. Her boyfriends were mostly Sigma Chis who played at being gentlemen by opening car doors for her. They'd brought icy orchid corsages and had pinned them to her dress with nervous fingers. In her experience every man thought he was a natural dancer, and every one thought he was good in bed. The truth was that most men only knew one dance step—usually the pogo—and between the sheets they were like a monkey in a nature film poking at an anthill with a stick.

She'd had intercourse, but she'd never had an orgasm. Not an *orgasm*-orgasm, not the kind of earth-moving orgasm that made your teeth go numb, the kind she'd always read about in *Cosmopolitan*.

No, when Penny graduated from law school she wasn't a virgin, but neither was she looking to settle down.

———

In Paris, at an exclusive dinner party on the top deck of the Eiffel Tower, Penny had her chance to meet Alouette D'Ambrosia in person. With a private supersonic jet at their constant disposal, Paris seemed no farther away than midtown Manhattan. Maxwell could zip her almost anywhere in the world for a quiet supper, then return her to her squalid apartment in Jackson Heights by midnight. Seeing the same troop of resentful and lustful faces of the international jet set night after night, at parties and movie premieres, made the world seem even smaller. Even at the top of the Eiffel Tower, with glittering Paris at her feet, Penny sipped a glass of champagne, too timid to engage with other movers and shakers. The night air was warm, but Penny felt a chill down her spine, exposed by the plunging back of her Vera Wang gown. Maxwell, usually so attentive, had been called away, and she sensed hostile eyes upon her. Looking around, she wasn't wrong. Like twin lasers, they flashed from across the tower's open terrace. It was the movie star, the winner of four Academy Awards. She'd been nominated this year, and she was the front-runner to win a fifth Oscar in a few weeks. Here was the woman Penny had seen fractured in the tiny screens of countless cell phones. Now there was only one of her, and she loomed huge.

A confrontation was imminent and every guest was gleefully watching as Alouette strode closer. Circling, she was clearly stalking her prey. The actress moved like a panther in a curve-hugging black leather catsuit. Her lovely nostrils flared. Teeth bared, she was seething.

The Bonwit Teller saleslady had done as she promised and introduced Penny to haute couture designers who dressed her to look fabulous, but compared to this approaching man-eating predator she felt like a bag lady. As always, she fought the urge to flee the battlefield. If only Maxwell would return. Monique would know how to fight off a furious Amazon. Jennifer Lopez or Penelope Cruz would be ready to kick some French ass. All Penny could think to do was turn her back and brace herself for the impending impact.

"Little mouse," a voice said. The heavily accented voice, recognizable from so many films.

The sharp points of long fingernails clutched Penny's shoulder and slowly pulled, turning her to face the speaker. Those impossibly soigné features were now distorted with hatred.

"Are you frightened, little mouse?" Alouette D'Ambrosia thrust her chin forward. "You should be very frightened. You are in grave danger."

Penny tightened her grip on her glass of champagne. If push came to shove, she'd throw the sweet, sparkling wine in the actress's eyes. Then run like heck.

"Whatever you do . . . ," Alouette said. As she wagged a long manicured finger in Penny's face, she warned, "Do not sleep with Max. You must *never* have sex with Maxwell."

The crowd was visibly disappointed as the film star turned away. As she slinked across the room people stepped aside. Before anyone spoke, she'd stridden into an elevator and disappeared.

It was clear to Penny that Alouette was wildly jealous. This French goddess was still very much in love. Penny laughed to herself. She, plain Penny Harrigan, was the envy of the world's most enticing sex symbol. In another minute Maxwell was back and standing beside her. As usual, he was scrawling notes in his little book. He could be such a space cadet.

When Penny didn't speak, he asked her, "Are you okay?"

She described the scene he'd missed. How Alouette had approached her. How the actress had threatened her.

A strange look crossed Maxwell's bland face. It was something Penny had never seen, anger mixed with another emotion. Possibly love. The warm wind tousled his blond hair.

Whatever it was, she couldn't resist. Whether it was physical attraction or the prospect of enraging Alouette, Penny couldn't resist the idea of sleeping with Max. She took his hand in hers. "Let's not fly back tonight." She brought the cold hand to her lips and kissed it, adding, "Let's stay over and go back to New York in the morning."

In bed, Maxwell's touch was so exact it was almost clinical. The way he used his fingers, they were almost calipers, there only to measure her. Like a doctor or a scientist, his fingertips gripped her as if he was testing her blood pressure. Often he'd pause midcaress, lean over to reach the bedside table, and scribble a note in his mysterious, spidery shorthand.

That first night in Paris, Penny found herself slightly drunk, naked in his bed while he knelt between her spread legs.

The bedside table held a strange combination of objects. There were faceted crystal bottles, like perfume bottles, each holding a different vivid color of liquid. They looked like massive rubies, topaz, and emeralds. They reminded Penny of the huge sapphire she'd seen on the neck of Alouette D'Ambrosia. Among these colorful bottles were plain glass beakers and test tubes of the same sort Penny had always associated with high school chemistry classes. There was a small cardboard box, like for facial tissues, but it appeared to be full of latex gloves, and one sprouted from the top, ready for the plucking. One flask held an assortment of wrapped condoms. Maxwell's notebook was tucked among these items. Of course it was. That notebook was almost an appendage. The final object Penny could identify was a small digital recording device, something a busy executive might dictate his thoughts into. The nearest item was a bottle of champagne.

Maxwell was already erect, but he hardly seemed aware of his aroused state. Only inches away from Penny's nakedness, he was leaning half off the bed. First he uncorked the bottle of champagne and poured some into a beaker. It fizzed pink. Pink champagne. He handed the beaker to Penny. Lifting the bottle, he made a toast: "To innovation and progress." They each drank from their respective bubbly.

"Don't guzzle all of it, my dear." Maxwell snapped his fingers to indicate he wanted the beaker back. He poured in a smidgen more champagne and set the bottle aside. With great deliberation, he picked among the crystal flasks. From some he poured dribs and drabs of richly colored syrup into the beaker of pink wine. He paged forward and back in his notebook as if consulting a coded recipe.

As he worked intently, Maxwell mused, "People are so misguided. They will devote themselves to the study of everything except what is of most importance." His lips curled into a wry grin. "I have studied the infinitely finer points of the sensual realm. I've learned from physicians and anatomists. I've dissected many cadavers, both male and female, to understand the mechanics of pleasure."

Sloshing the beaker to thoroughly mix its contents, Maxwell gave Penny a frowning look and asked, "Have you ever enjoyed an orgasm?"

"Of course," Penny answered quickly. Too quickly. It was a lie, and it sounded like a lie.

Maxwell smirked. He continued, "I've apprenticed myself to the world's most accomplished sex experts." There was no boasting in his words, just a determined resoluteness. "I've studied with tantric shamans in Morocco. I devoted myself to

46

mastering the kundalini energy. To understand the coefficient of friction between different types of skin, I consulted the world's leading organic chemists."

Penny let her eyes roam over his naked body. She knew from the *National Enquirer* that he was forty-nine years old. He was old enough to be her father, but his lean frame looked almost insectlike. Each limb was as defined and well proportioned as that of an ant or a hornet. His pale, hairless skin was as perfectly tailored as his clothing, without a wrinkle or sag visible. She searched his shoulders and hands for freckles or moles but found none. The way he talked about his sexual quest, she expected to find his nipples pierced. His torso busy with tattoos or the scars of consensual torture games. But there was no such evidence. This was a child's pristine skin stretched to cover the musculature of a man's body.

"My own secret recipe," he said, offering the beaker for Penny to sniff. The wine, mixed with mysterious extras.

It bubbled less, but it still looked like pink champagne. It smelled sweetly delicious. Like strawberries. Penny peered doubtfully at the full beaker and said, "You want me to drink this?"

"Not exactly," Maxwell said. From a drawer in the table he produced something that looked like a squeeze toy. It was an ovoid ball made of soft red rubber, roughly the size of a grapefruit. One end of the ball sprouted a long, white nozzle of some sort. "A vaginal syringe," Maxwell said, holding it up for her inspection. He demonstrated how the nozzle unscrewed from the ball, revealing a threaded hole in the rubber. Into this hole he poured the pink champagne concoction. As he screwed the nozzle back into place, Penny realized what he had in mind.

"It's a douche?" she asked nervously.

Max nodded.

Penny squirmed uneasily. "You don't think I'm clean?"

Maxwell stretched his hands into latex gloves, saying, "You don't want to get this stuff on your skin."

She didn't like the sound of that. Wasn't he planning to squirt this pink stuff inside of her?

"Don't worry." He chuckled softly. "It's just a very mild neural stimulant and euphoric. You'll love it." He rubbed the thin nozzle between her legs.

The nozzle slipped deep into her. "Enjoy yourself," he said, and began to compress the rubber ball. The syringe.

Penny could feel the cold, effervescent bubbly filling her.

With his free hand, Maxwell held her in place, stroking her belly in slow circles. His entire body was as chilled and hard as his fingers.

When the bulb was empty Maxwell withdrew it. He used a soft, clean towel to wipe away the pink trickle that escaped her. "Good girl," he told her. "Just hold it inside for a minute." He was biting the plastic wrapper off a condom and rolling it down his erection. "You're doing very well."

Penny tried not to imagine dignified President Hind subjecting herself to a similar magic champagne cleansing.

Still kneeling between her spread knees, he said, "I love you because you're so average."

If that was a compliment, Penny had heard better.

"Please don't be hurt," he said softly. "Look at yourself. You have a textbook vagina. Your labia majora are exactly symmetrical. Your perianal ridge is magnificent. Your frenulum clitoridis and fourchette . . ." He seemed at a loss for words, pressing a hand to his heart and sighing deeply. "Biologically speaking, men treasure such uniformity. The proportions of your genitalia are ideal."

Under his gaze, Penny felt less like a woman than like a science experiment. A guinea pig or laboratory rat.

It didn't help that Maxwell added, "Women in your age

48

group and economic stratum are the target consumers for most of the world's manufactured goods."

Something, perhaps the douche, made Penny's teeth feel as if they were dissolving in her mouth. The bones in her legs were melting.

"This will heighten your amusement." He spread his knees, forcing her legs farther apart. His erection reared over her, already sleeved in one condom. Rolling a second condom over the first, Maxwell spoke idly.

As he spoke, he again eyed the array of sparkling bottles on the bedside table. Selecting one, he put a few drops of something clear into the palm of his hand. To this he added a few drops from a second and third bottle. "The pH of your skin is slightly acid. I'm mixing exactly the right lubricant for your erotic needs."

He slowly wiped the oily handful around her vulva, careful not to dip his fingers too far inside. The last of it he spread on his erect sex organ.

Penny giggled, limp as a rag doll.

From the table he plucked something. It was the mini digital recorder. Pressing a button, he said, "If you don't mind, I'd like to record our session for my research." A tiny red light glowed on the device. Dictating into it, Maxwell said, "Based on the test subject's somewhat *playful* behavior, it's safe to say the vaginal wash is having its full effect."

And now he mounted her, thrusting his hardness against the pressure of the fluid. He was driving it higher into her. Stirring and churning the mixture.

Penny gasped. She cried out, as much from discomfort as pleasure. She felt wetness escape her and soak into the bedclothes. She felt the liquid expanding inside her. In vain she squirmed, trying to escape the sensation. As the pleasure grew, seizing control of her, Penny understood why Alouette had been so bitter and enraged. Whatever the pink fluid consisted of, Maxwell's pumping buttocks and probing cock seemed to force it into her bloodstream. Gradually her legs felt so relaxed she would swear they were floating. The feeling spread to her arms. Her breasts seemed to swell. Her mind stretched to accommodate a joy she'd never known existed.

She was only vaguely aware of Maxwell. While his hips bucked slowly into her, his bland stare observed the reactions on her face. He licked his fingers and softly tweaked her nipples, as focused as a safecracker. Without missing a thrust, he lifted the pen and scribbled a note in his book.

He petted her inner thighs and clitoris. With his hips, he made infinitesimal adjustments in the angle and speed of his thrusts. Gauging her reaction, he calibrated the depth of each stroke. Addressing the recorder, he said, "The test subject's pelvic floor has relaxed in extremis." He reached one latex-gloved hand around to the small of her back, brailling her spine until he found what he was seeking. On that one small spot, his fingertips intensified their massaging.

"Just so you understand what's happening," Maxwell explained, "I'm using two fingers to compress your anterior Hibbert artery. It's a simple tantric technique a yogi in Sri Lanka was kind enough to teach me." He talked like a tour guide, chatty and slightly patronizing. "By restricting the deeper blood flow to your groin, I'm numbing your clitoris." Whatever he was doing, he didn't need to look. His fingers knew their task. His eyes continued to hold hers.

"Your feedback is very important to this process," Maxwell said. His voice sounded fuzzy, but Penny tried to concentrate. "Do you understand?" he asked. "Nod your head if you understand."

Penny nodded.

"You must ready yourself. Do not be frightened." He said,

"Do not be afraid of crying out. You must let the pleasure pass through you." He leveled his eyes gravely. "If you hinder the flow of satisfaction, it could kill you."

Penny nodded. She was barely in the world. As pleasure drowned her, there was no past and no future. Nothing existed outside of this moment of peaking sensations. There was no world other than the energy surging in her body.

"In a moment, when I release the pressure, the blood will rush to your uris major, and you'll experience more satisfaction than you ever dreamed was possible." With that warning, Penny felt the fingertips retreat from her spine. Something, something bright and enormous flared within her.

"Cry out!" commanded Maxwell. "Don't contain your ecstasy. Don't be a prudish fool, Penny. Cry out!"

But Penny could not. A long scream of obscenities built in her throat, but she kept her teeth clenched. Her limbs thrashed and twitched beyond her control. A torrent of animal gibberish and profanities threatened to boil out of her mouth, and the digital recorder was running. She choked back the howls. A cold hand touched the side of her neck and lingered there.

Maxwell announced, "For the record, the subject's pulse is rapid and irregular." He was speaking for the recorder. "Her respiration is extremely shallow, and all signs would indicate that she is entering an erotically induced coma."

Penny sensed that she was dying. Her view of him frosted and grew dark around the edges.

Maxwell reached for something on the bedside table. With the latex-gloved pad of his thumb he lifted one of her drooping eyelids and shined a bright penlight into her iris. "Pupil dilation is sluggish," he announced. Throughout this entire ordeal his hips continued to pump, steadily planting and withdrawing his steely erection.

"Why should sex be any different?" ranted Max. "Everything—

films, music, painting—is calculated to manipulate and excite us."
He licked two fingers and scissored them against Penny, flickering fast touches against her engorged lady-parts. Such small tricks flooded Penny with more pleasure, wiping her mind clean. Whatever she'd been thinking, it was instantly forgotten. "Drugs are designed to be as effective as possible," he said. "Why shouldn't we devote the same attention to the details of sex?"

Penny shook like a criminal being electrocuted. Her limbs jangled, and her flesh jiggled like a nervous puppet. Her tongue jutted from her mouth and lapped at the air.

"Stay with me," he coached sternly. "You're going into shock."

Penny felt something rest against her forehead.

"The subject's temperature is falling . . . ninety-eight-point-five degrees. Ninety-seven-point-five . . ." It was a temporal thermometer. A cold mouth pressed itself over hers. These were Maxwell's lips. His lukewarm breath filled her throat and inflated her lungs. "The subject has stopped breathing," he announced. His lungs once more filled her lungs. Just as his penis was filling her. "I am attempting to resuscitate the test subject." Throughout all of this, Penny was dimly aware that he was still fucking her with the same cadence of long, smooth strokes. He was monitoring the pulse in her neck. "Use my breath," he demanded. "Use the breath I'm putting inside you to cry out. Express your exaltation." In a flat, expressionless voice he said, "Do not die while you have so much pleasure still awaiting you. . . ."

Now Penny knew why the tabloids called him "Climax-Well."

That would be the first and final time Penny would see him naked. There was plenty of sex to come, too much perhaps, but none of it would involve Maxwell's sexual organs.

Once Maxwell had excused himself to use the bathroom, Penny rewound the recorder and tried to find her outcry. To erase it. The filth that had poured from her mouth was totally degrading. To her own ears she sounded like someone possessed by a demon. Out of her mind. The voice was less hers than it was the howl of some animal in heat baying at a primordial moon.

If Climax-Well could be believed, it was that beastly outburst that had saved her life. With it, she had allowed the tension of a life-threatening orgasm to pass through her without lasting damage. A woman's purpose, he claimed, was not to be a vessel, but to be a conduit. For her to survive, all things must pass through her.

Between marathon sessions of arousal culminating in mind-shattering orgasms, Maxwell lectured Penny. He slipped a wet finger into her, matter-of-factly saying, "This is your urethra." Rotating the finger, he said, "And this . . . this is your urethral sponge, often called the 'G-spot.'"

The walking tour his fingers took sent shivers through her body.

He oiled his hands with a pink, rose-scented gel and slipped two fingers into her. "When I massage the rear wall of your vaginal vault . . ."

Unseen, he must've done so, because Penny twitched and shivered with uncontrolled joy. Whatever Max was doing, she drove her hips against his hand, wanting more.

"That," he explained, "is your perineal sponge, a mass of erectile tissue that connects through the pudendal nerve to your clitoris."

Penny didn't need to look to know that her clit was stiffening. Untouched, it was achingly engorged and throbbing.

Massaging whatever he'd found, Max was stimulating her clitoris by remote control. "The perineal sponge is the reason women can achieve orgasms while having anal sex." He slipped a third and a fourth finger inside. "Good girl, your vagina is 'ballooning.'" During arousal, he explained, the inner vagina expands, lengthening to create a dead end beyond the cervix. Now his entire hand was inside.

Penny looked down to see only his smooth, pale wrist disappearing into her. At the sight of it, she moaned.

Maxwell's eyes had a glazed, faraway look, not focused on anything. Through his hand, he was clearly exploring a hidden world. "This, I believe, is your cervix," he said. "If I apply a steady pressure . . ."

Penny's fingers went involuntarily to her mouth, and she bit down on a knuckle, whimpering. She closed her eyes, embarrassed by the mewling that rose from deep in her throat. It was terrifying being coaxed this far beyond her own rational control. It was as frightening as she'd always imagined a heart attack would feel, but she never wanted it to stop.

His voice muted with admiration and wonder, Maxwell said, "This is exceptional. Do you always ejaculate this much?"

Penny opened her eyes and peeked. A rivulet of shimmering juice was erupting from near the top of her pussy. It flowed down Maxwell's arm until it dripped from his elbow. "Sorry," she whispered, instantly ashamed.

"But why?" asked Maxwell, twisting his hand deep inside her.

"I'm peeing on you."

He laughed. With his free hand he collected a smidgen of the liquid. He rubbed it between two fingers, brought the fingers to his nose and smelled it, tasted it with the tip of his tongue. "Enzymes," he pronounced, "from your Skene's glands. That's why it vents from your urethra instead of your vulva." He brought the wet fingers near her mouth and asked, "Would you like to taste yourself?"

Excited as she was, purring and thrashing like an animal,

Penny couldn't bring herself to lick his fingers. She didn't have to.

He shoved them into her mouth. Gagging her. Choking her. The taste of her own sensual emissions was metallic and salty. For a short eternity she couldn't speak or breathe.

Maxwell's voice was reproachful. "I thought you said you were wearing a diaphragm."

She wasn't. Her diaphragm was in Jackson Heights—securely locked in a safe-deposit box at Chase Manhattan. Penny wasn't trying to get pregnant. She just hadn't planned to have sex tonight.

The fingers withdrew from her mouth, allowing her to draw a new breath.

"Don't think you can trick me, Miss Harrigan." The fingers within her were still roving, mapping that hidden world. "When and if I ever marry anyone it will be for love. I had a vasectomy many years ago."

Penny wanted to explain, but she was exhausted. Instead, she lay back, sinking deeper into pleasure as he petted the glans of her clitoris. He described how the short clitoral shaft descended into her skin. Using gentle pressure, he traced the shaft to where it divided into two legs which he called "crura." These legs, Maxwell explained, wrapped around the vaginal cavity.

He said more, a long, rambling travelogue about a land Penny had never visited. A history lesson about the world contained inside her.

Maxwell explained how physicians from the time of Hippocrates until the 1920s had always been formally trained in how to bring their female patients to "paroxysm." Using fingers and oil, it was standard practice for doctors and midwives to treat hysteria, insomnia, depression, and a host of conditions common to women. *Praefocatio matricis* it was called. Or "suffocation of the mother." And even the great Galen recommended that the vagina must be vigorously manipulated until it readily expressed the accumulation of fluid.

Vibrators, he claimed, were among the first household appliances to be powered with electricity. In 1893, a man named Mortimer Granville built a huge fortune when he invented a battery-driven vibrator. A full range of such sex toys were commonly sold through national mass-circulation magazines and the Sears, Roebuck catalog. It wasn't until they appeared in the crude pornographic films of the 1920s that vibrating dildos became shameful.

Galen. Hippocrates. Ambroise Paré. Penny couldn't keep the names and dates straight in her mind. After the sixteenth century, she fell asleep. She dreamed of plummeting from the top of the Eiffel Tower. She was falling because Maxwell had pushed her.

When she woke, Maxwell's side of the bed was empty. The bathroom door was closed, and from the far side of it came the sound of running water.

Was it Betty Friedan or Gloria Steinem? Penny couldn't remember, but she thought one of them had written about the "zipless fuck," an ideal kind of physically satisfying sex that left no emotional obligations. Sex with Maxwell might very well be what the author had in mind. It left Penny weak, feeling as if she'd suffered the flu. That was only for a few minutes; beyond that she was ravenous. They ate and fucked and ate and fucked. Endlessly. Ziplessly.

It was official. Until now, Penny Harrigan had never experienced an actual orgasm. Not like the thrilling sensations that Maxwell coaxed from her eager body. For once, the descriptions of fireworks and convulsions she'd read so often in *Cosmo,* they seemed like understatements instead of exaggerations.

Stroking her pubis, Maxwell said, "I would like to shave you. It would make the testing more accurate." She'd acquiesced. No biggie. She'd been shaved before, and waxed, to be bikini-ready for spring break. "This time," he warned her, "it will never grow back." He used a special formula passed down through millennia of Uzbek tribesmen, a lotion of aloe vera and pureed pine nuts that would forever leave her as smooth as a child.

Penny looked forlornly at her shorn curls lying among the bedsheets. She told herself she'd never liked being bushy.

The aspect of sex that Maxwell seemed to enjoy most was finding ways to coerce her to greater satisfaction. That seemed his sole source of pleasure. Whenever Penny asked whether he wanted to come, he'd simply shrug and say, "Maybe next go-round." Beyond their first encounter he never so much as removed his shirt. Soon he came to don a white lab coat to protect his clothing.

For a beauty like Alouette, a woman accustomed to driving men to fits of lust, Maxwell's failure to come must've been maddening. Penny tried not to think of the French beauty who'd threatened her life, but that wasn't easy. Alouette had enjoyed 136 days of intimacy with Maxwell. Gwendolyn had enjoyed 136 days. The *National Enquirer* never lied. Unless she'd miscounted, Penny figured she had 103 days to go. If the sex kept up like this, she doubted whether she could live that long. But what a great way to die!

If she could just find the recording of her howling, find and erase it, Penny's happiness would be complete. The bathroom door remained shut. Behind it the water continued to run.

Retrieving his recorder from the bedside table, she rewound the memory. Hitting Play, she heard, ". . . don't be a prudish fool." Penny felt like a hypocrite, but she never wanted another human being to hear the insane gibberish that had spilled from her mouth. Again, she hit Play. This time she heard a scream.

With the shower running full-blast, she hoped Maxwell hadn't heard it in the bathroom.

Someone was screaming in French. Not that Penny could understand French, but she could guess based on her own experience. It was Alouette under the influence of pink champagne and secret ingredients. She fast-forwarded and hit Play. "Stay with me, Penny," the recording said.

Even as she listened, spellbound, the device in her hands issued a shrill ringtone. It wasn't only a recorder; it was a telephone! Penny was so startled she almost dropped it; instead she tossed the phone back onto the table, where it continued to ring and ring. When she checked the caller ID it said, "Private."

Penny leaped from the bed. She knocked at the bathroom door. "Max, it's your phone!" She tried the knob, but it was locked. She could hear the shower, his voice singing a song she couldn't identify. After a couple more rings, curiosity got the better of her. She put the phone to her ear and said, "Hello?"

Silence.

The bathroom door opened and Maxwell stepped out with a towel wrapped around his waist. Water dripped from his hair. At the sight of her answering his phone, his eyebrows drew together in fury, and he snapped his fingers, gesturing for her to hang up.

"Hello? Corny?" asked a voice. It was a familiar voice. A woman. "Max," she said. "This isn't my fault." She pleaded, "Please don't hurt me."

Penny handed the phone to Maxwell. She could still hear the voice on the line talking excitedly, loudly. Begging. He put it to his ear and listened. Gradually his eyes wandered to the floor. The longer the caller talked, the more his angry expression changed to one of brooding concern.

"That shouldn't be an issue," he said. "The active ingredients don't fall within any of the federal schedules for controlled or hazardous substances." He listened, shaking his head. "Well, then appoint a new chairman to the FDA. Give that job to someone who *will* fast-track the products."

The caller was someone Penny had seen on television. It was a voice that brought to mind a sensible, shoulder-length haircut. A blue suit. A pearl necklace. A woman speaking behind a forest of microphones.

Talking into the phone, but eyeing Penny, Maxwell said, "I'm in the final testing phase right now. We're timing mass production for a summer rollout. By next month we'll be in a half million retail outlets." He turned his back to Penny and stepped through the bathroom door. "You know what's at stake here. Don't make me take any actions you'll regret." The door shut. Possibly to mask the conversation, the shower came back on at full blast.

Unless Penny missed her guess, the voice, the woman calling, she was the president of the United States. President Clarissa Hind.

Penny wondered what brilliant new invention they were almost done testing.

This constant sexual cavorting, this would be the pattern of their days and nights. Max always had some toy, some potion, some glorious lubricant he wanted to introduce her to.

He'd drive her to climax until her back ached and her legs wouldn't work, and he'd gently bully her, saying, "We're almost done. Just one more adjustment." Saying, "We've got to stay on a schedule here. . . ."

He'd probe with one hand buried inside her. "I'm searching for your pudendal plexus. It should be right *here*."

On other occasions, totally stymied, he'd use his free hand to shake open a folded anatomical chart, like a road map, on the bed beside her. He was a southpaw and kept those fingers planted in her vagina as if marking his place in a book. *You Are Here.* One hand inside her, he'd use the other to smooth the creased paper and trace one finger along some route while muttering to himself, "The *nervi pelvici splanchnici* branches *here* near your *nervi erigentes....*" Discovering his destination, he'd wiggle something deep within her, exclaiming triumphantly, "Penny? Did you know your coccygeal plexus is displaced two centimeters to the anterior?" Feeling along blindly, he'd add, "Don't worry. It seems to be within normal variable parameters."

Every so often he'd withdraw whatever pleasure instrument he was testing. He'd lay its length against a corner of the night table and bend the metal or plastic slightly. Or he might use a pair of pliers or vise grips he kept in the bedside drawer. Worse was when he'd just swing the instrument a mighty whack against the table, whack after whack, marring the elegant furniture until he'd achieved the desired curve.

When that happened the bedroom seemed like those sepia-toned photographs Penny had seen of Thomas Edison's Menlo Park laboratory. Or Henry Ford's workshop. For her part, Penny felt less like a girlfriend than a lab assistant. Like Dr. Watson or Igor. Or Pavlov's dog. As Max tinkered away, bringing her to new convulsions and seizures of pleasure, despite her moods, despite her growing detachment and resentment, Penny half expected him to shout, "Eureka!"

Maxwell would hover over his task, as focused as a Swiss watchmaker or brain surgeon. Often he'd request his valet or butler to wheel a tray of sterile instruments up bedside so Max need not look away from the procedure at hand. "Calipers!" he'd bark, extending one hand, and the attendant servant would slap the tool into his open palm. "Blot me!" Max would command, and the underling would use a fold of paper towel to swab the beads of perspiration from Max's forehead.

At times Max crouched between her knees, a penlight clenched between his teeth, a jeweler's loupe squeezed in one eye, tinkering. His face slack with concentration. "I chose you," Max explained, "because you have never experienced an orgasm. A man can tell. You remain asleep, and no one has yet to awaken you. You are so typical of the women I am trying to help."

"'For too many years,'" Max recited, "'women have been excluded from the full pleasure available to them in their bodies.'" He was reading from a printed sheet of paper. A press release. "'I believe, as do many medical professionals, that a large proportion of chronic mental and physical ailments beset women because they accumulate stress that might otherwise be easily and quickly released with the right tools. . . .'"

Even to Penny's unsophisticated ear, the speech sounded like a string of euphemisms. According to Maxwell, it had to. It was selling sex. Even more controversially, it was selling women the means to better sex than they had ever enjoyed with any man. To some listeners, this announcement would sound like gobbledygook, like an outdated advertisement for a feminine hygiene spray. But to other listeners, namely men who valued only their own greedy sexual needs, this speech would sound like the end of the world.

The two of them were sitting in bed. Lately, they were always in bed. Penny never donned more than a bathrobe, and that was only to accept a gourmet meal brought by the majordomo.

"'That's the reason,'" Maxwell continued, "'we're proud to introduce the Beautiful You line of personal care products. . . .'"

C. Linus Maxwell was preparing to expand his vast corporation and enter the field of empty vaginas in a big way. All of the jewel-toned gels and liquids on his bedside table. The magic pink champagne douche. The fluids engineered to modulate the coefficient of friction. He would be bringing them all to the lonely female consumer.

The packaging would be pink, but not obnoxiously. The whole line would be marketed under the umbrella name Beautiful You. Thumbing the buttons on his smart phone, Maxwell showed Penny a prototype of the advertising, the words *Beautiful You* curved in curlicue white letters. A tagline along the bottom of each ad read, "Better Than Love." The douche, Maxwell explained, would ultimately be sold as a dissolvable powder in a small envelope, which could be mixed with water or champagne. It was only one of several shockingly innovative personal care products. Soon every woman would be able to enjoy mind-bending orgasms at a moderate price.

All of the research and erotic training Maxwell had done with swamis and witch doctors and courtesans—all the sex secrets of the ancient world—he was about to market them to the modern woman. Every gal from Omaha to Oslo would soon be savoring the pounding cut-loose orgasms Penny had only recently discovered. It was stunning to imagine how this might change the world. As Maxwell's former loves had demonstrated, given the right sexual satisfaction women could flower, lose weight, kick drugs. Every woman's personal fulfillment was only weeks away.

Just in the past few days, sequestered in Maxwell's Parisian penthouse, Penny had dropped eight pounds. She slept like a baby. She'd never felt more relaxed and at ease.

In secret, she was a little proud that she'd made her own contribution to the project. Max was still tweaking some recipes. Polishing off any rough edges. In the near future, girls just like her, average girls without stellar bodies and luscious faces, they would have access to the kind of bone-melting pleasure that only movie stars currently enjoyed.

As she scrolled through photos of prototype sex toys, lubricants, and nightgowns, Penny asked, "Why 'Beautiful You'?"

Maxwell shrugged. "The publicity wonks said it tested the best. Plus, it translates into any language."

Young or old. Fat or short. Billions of women would learn to love the bodies in which they were alive. Beautiful You would be a blessing to all womankind. Penny knew that if the mass-marketed products worked half as well as the prototypes he'd been demonstrating on her, C. Linus Maxwell would quickly double his fortune. Kidding him, she asked, "Don't you have enough money?"

There it was again. That sad smile flitted across his lips. "It's not about the profits," he told her. "Not at the price point I have in mind."

It was about his mother, Penny guessed. Wasn't it every boy's dream to fete his long-suffering mom? Maxwell's had slaved away to give her boy a head start in the world, and then she'd died before he could show his gratitude. It was a little creepy: the idea that he was honoring his mother by showering women with great sex . . . but his motives were noble and touching.

A thought struck her. It was none of her business, but she asked, "Do you still miss her? Your mom?"

He didn't answer. He went back to silently reading his press release.

Impulsively, she leaned over and pecked him on the cheek.

"What's that for?" he asked.

"For being such a loving son."

And there it was again. The wan, furtive smile of a lonely little orphan.

———

"It's not like Spanish fly. There's no comparison," he insisted.

The two of them were making a rare public appearance. They were dining in a chic restaurant in the St.-Germain neighborhood of the sixth arrondissement. As usual their candlelit table was the center of attention. Even the aloof Parisians were shamelessly eyeballing them.

The fabled aphrodisiac known as Spanish fly, Maxwell explained, was the emerald-green blister beetle, *Lytta vesicatoria*. When the dead insects were dried and ground to a fine powder, they could be mixed into a beverage. The tainted drink would cause severe urinary tract inflammation. That was the legendary effect that supposedly prompted women to beg for intercourse. In actuality, the effect was about as exciting as an internal case of poison oak.

"This," Maxwell said, rolling a pink capsule between his fingers, "this is different."

He'd removed the new invention from his pocket only a moment earlier. Like all his other toys, the pink pill was a product from the new Beautiful You line. About the size of a robin's egg, it looked like a piece of candy. Like something that should be nestled in an Easter basket. It was the color of bubble gum.

Penny took it from his hand. "So I'm supposed to swallow this?"

Maxwell laughed at her innocence. He shook his head, saying, "No, my dear, it's a vaginal suppository perfectly formulated to heighten female desire."

He observed Penny rolling the pink bead between her fingers. "Note the slight stickiness of the outer coating." He said, "It's a layer of silicone impregnated with a mild herbal stimulant. If a penis were to enter the vaginal cavity and encounter the bead, both partners would share the pleasure of the effect."

Penny squeezed it between her fingers. It felt soft. In the

palm of her hand it was surprisingly heavy. She smiled slyly, lifted the napkin from her lap, and daubed daintily at the corners of her mouth. She asked a passing waiter, "*Excusez moi,* where is your *toilette?*"

On her return from the bathroom, Penny saw her nemesis: Alouette. She was seated at a discreet corner banquette, tucked away where she'd draw no public notice. Alouette's face looked gaunt, her cheeks more hollowed than Penny recalled. The actress's eyes looked sunken.

Somehow the week's bedroom ordeals had calmed Penny and filled her with a quiet confidence. She strode brazenly to her rival's table. The pink bead was inside her, working whatever magic Maxwell had designed into it. Penny regarded the haggard woman and said, "Alouette, you're looking well."

"No, I'm not," the actress shot back. "I look like shit, and it's all Max's fault."

Penny narrowed her eyes. "Are you following me?"

Alouette sighed. She drew the fingers of one hand through her long, rich hair.

Penny couldn't help but notice that strands came off between those fingers. Already, a scattering of fallen hair dusted the table and the booth's upholstery.

"My impulse had been to save you, little mouse," Alouette began. "But now I see that you've let him reduce you to a stupid slut."

Penny winced at the harsh word.

"Despite my warning, you've allowed Maxwell to bewitch you." Alouette's eyes filled with pity. She spoke without rancor in her voice. "You were someone, before. How quickly you've thrown your dreams away and become just your hungry *conass.*"

Penny turned to leave, but Alouette asked, "Tell me. Has he given you the black bead yet?"

"What black bead?" Penny asked warily.

But the actress merely smiled. "This should be amusing," she sneered.

Back at her own table Maxwell didn't rise to seat her. Instead he gestured for her to come to him and hold out her hand. He took it and held it warmly for a moment. He kissed the back, placing something in her palm, and when Penny opened her fingers, there it was: a black bead. It looked identical in size and shape to the first bead. Only the color was different.

"Pink for the vagina," Max announced. "Black for your lovely anus. It's best to keep things simple; the entire Beautiful You line of products will use that same color-coding system."

Dutifully, Penny made a second trip to the toilets.

Before she'd returned to the table the beads were already having their effect. Maxwell seated her, and then returned to his chair opposite. They perused their menus.

The sensation began like a sweet burning within her groin. Then a delicious cramping. This increased until it felt as if something ravenous, with wonderfully soft teeth, were gnawing on her insides, devouring her from within.

She gasped with a sound that caught people's attention. Coiffed heads turned to stare. To save face she put her napkin to her mouth and faked a cough. It was better that people think she had tuberculosis than know she was enduring a string of multiple orgasms.

"Don't worry," Maxwell said, "there will be no permanent damage. The silicone coating is very soft."

Something twisted and wrestled, embedded far beneath her skin.

"Both of the beads are earth magnets," Max explained. "I could not give them to you at the same time because the attraction between them is so strong." He lifted his pen and made ready to jot notes. "The ancient Peruvian tribe the Chichlachies called them 'married stones,' because once they find each other they're almost impossible to separate."

As he described it, the black bead was planted against the anterior wall of her rectum. The pink one was lodged against the posterior wall of her vagina. The stones, even coated in silicone and inserted in her two very different orifices, the stones had found each other. Even now, the thin muscular wall between her two cavities, with all its rich network of nerve endings, it was being crushed and kneaded by the two strong magnets. They ground that most sensitive spot between them.

Savoring her reaction, the gloating genius waved to flag a waiter. "Only your sensitive perineal sponge separates them. You are helpless. Your entire erogenous nervous system is under assault."

To keep from crying out, Penny bit down on her meticulously manicured finger. Her nipples grew so erect that her breasts seemed ready to levitate from the cups of her push-up bra.

"You are still a young girl," Maxwell said. He studied her reaction intently. "If you can't cope with the full potential of a woman's body, I understand." He was mocking her, daring her to endure this trial in public. As elegant twosomes dined and chatted near them, orgasmic waves of sexual energy swept over Penny.

A waiter stepped up to their table and asked, "Would you care to order, madam?"

Her pelvis felt as if planets were colliding, milling together inside of her. Great seas were heaving, eroding her sanity. She crossed her legs tightly, in a vain attempt to clamp down the rising gusher.

A bemused tone in his voice, Maxwell told the waiter, "Tonight the lady would love to indulge in a thick steak." Addressing her, he added, "Or would a helping of juicy tongue be more to your liking?"

Even with shuddering full-body spasms of ecstasy coursing through her, Penny felt the toe of Maxwell's shoe slide up the inside of her leg. From her ankle to her knee, its smooth hardness traveled until it was prodding her crotch. It reminded her of the moment they'd first met: her sprawled on the carpet, seeing her own disheveled face reflected in the polished toe of his handmade footwear. She couldn't speak. With shaking hands she touched the skirt of her gown and found it soaked. The napkin in her lap was likewise drenched. Mindless of the waiter, she shoved Max's foot away and struggled to stand. Clutching the backs of chairs, disturbing their moneyed occupants, she stumbled back toward the toilets. Her legs shook, weakened by spasms of pleasure. When she was almost to the door, Penny's knees buckled, and she fell. She was so exhausted. Her hair hanging in her face, she crawled the final steps and took refuge in the tiled sanctuary. Safely hidden in a cubicle, she hiked up her damp skirt and plunged two fingers into herself. She could feel the pink bead but couldn't capture it. The silicone was too slick.

Arching her back, Penny slid two fingers into her anus and tried in vain to find the black bead.

A voice behind her said, "You cannot extract them by yourself." It was Alouette. The cinema star had followed her into the toilet cubicle. She stood, coolly assessing Penny's erotic dilemma. "Last year," Alouette confessed, "I was caught in this very same toilet. It was a busboy who saved my sanity. That brave teenage boy. As if it were a snake's venom, he sucked the black bead from my derrière."

Thrusting her exposed pubis forward, Penny begged, "Please," her voice nothing more than a whimper.

Alouette appraised the bared vulva and whistled softly. "So this is Maxwell's attraction to you, little mouse. Your pussy is the most beautiful I've ever laid eyes on." She wet her lips. "Glorious."

Penny's secretions dripped to the floor, where they'd begun to pool.

"Let yourself go," Alouette advised. "Only the intense flow of your feminine juices can flush the love stone from its seat!" Alouette knelt on the tiled floor and gripped Penny's hips in her hands. Planting her movie star mouth tightly over the younger woman's dripping vagina, she began to suck. Penny bore down, riding that lovely face as if it were a saddle. She could feel Alouette's fingers exploring inside her rectum.

Gradually the flood of stimulation receded. Alouette lifted her mouth from Penny's groin and spit the pink bead into the toilet bowl. Deprived of its partner, the black bead slipped out easily, pinched between the actress's fingers, and she held it for Penny's inspection before letting it plunk into the water. The two magnets clicked together with a frightening force, and Alouette flushed them away. Appraising the damage done to Penny's *masque,* she said, "Do not thank me, little mouse. One day you will wish I had let you die from the pleasure." As she went to a mirror and began to repair her own smeared lipstick, she said, "It is already too late for you. Soon you will be like the rest of us, his slave."

When they weren't banqueting on delectable food among illustrious people, they were being chauffeured back and forth between Maxwell's penthouse in Paris and his château in the Loire Valley. There she wandered the echoing salons, examining the priceless antiquities that had belonged to so many celebrities before Max. There was something so isolating about being famous. She wandered the château's formal parterre gardens while security patrols armed with machine guns watched her from the roof, and closed-circuit cameras documented her every step.

Penny had chewed her knuckles raw to stifle her shrieks of ecstasy. She thought that if she overindulged for a few months, an overdose of pleasure would leave her satisfied for life. She might momentarily reflect on some larger issue, like famine in the Sudan, but then Max would covertly slip some thrilling new product into her and her mind would become a blank. Euphoria erased everything. She had no energy left over to fret about her stalled legal career or the ominous future of her aging parents in Nebraska. Or global climate change. She was grounded entirely in her body, in the present moment of glorious sensation. No past or future existed, and Max could keep her there. Under his touch the world collapsed. Nothing existed beyond Paris, beyond his bed, beyond her own pulsating clitoris.

She was getting everything she'd ever been taught would make her happy—Gucci clothes, great sex, her name a household word—and every day she felt more miserable. It didn't help that people expected her to be ecstatic. No one wanted to hear the problems of a disappointed Cinderella; she was supposed to live happily ever after. But this . . . none of this was the great life's mission she'd been hoping to find.

Almost eagerly, she counted down. Only eighty-seven days left.

At her age Penny knew she ought to be living large, making herself available to people, and having misadventures. She longed to get smashed at one of the noisy blowout parties that her friend Monique was probably throwing at right this very moment. She would even settle for a Sigma Chi mixer with beer kegs and frat boys using their permanent erections to menace coeds.

In the penthouse or château, when they were alone together, Max never wanted to talk. He only wanted to test his tantric thingamajigs on her. She told herself he was under pressure.

With Beautiful You only a month away from rollout, everything had to be perfect. Still, she tried to leaven his mood. She told him jokes. She complimented him on his cars, his hair, his clothes, but he shrugged off the flattery.

Even the fabled shopping of the French capital wasn't much fun. Not after she'd been in and out of the elegant boutiques for weeks. Top designers vied for Penny to wear their clothes. No matter what she tried on they told her she looked fantastic. They even offered her kickbacks to wear their labels at high-profile events. It was all so phony. She knew she looked awful, and that they only wanted the publicity. Her neck was too short and thick. Her breasts were too small. Her breasts weren't even the same size. Her hips were too wide. The mirrors in the ateliers didn't lie.

Before she'd gotten famous, people in New York had openly insulted her body, but at least they'd been telling her the truth.

The only part of her anatomy that was beautiful was her privates. And Penny could hardly ask Christian Lacroix to design a gown that would highlight those.

Out shopping, she looked for gifts that might amuse Max, but that was a steep order. What did you give the man who had everything? Who'd *had everyone*? The only thing that seemed to please Maxwell was when a prototype or a new formula brought her to higher crescendos of pleasure. The greater her excitement, the greater his. Realizing that, Penny resolved to give him a gift in the only way possible.

One night, when a particular device—a toy like a pinecone engineered to expand inside her, based on some pre-Columbian doohickey—when it failed, Penny didn't let on. It felt nice, but that was all. Penny worried that she might be getting jaded. Perhaps she was suffering some sort of pleasure-center fatigue. When she sensed Max's disappointment, she couldn't help but amp up her performance. She flopped around the bed like a sea lion and flapped her arms. She barked like a dog and crowed like a rooster.

At the height of her well-intentioned albeit faked orgasm, Maxwell told her, "Stop."

He looked at her, his jaw set. He tugged the silken cord that tethered the toy and it slipped from between Penny's legs. Like a sulking child, he wrapped the cord around the device, saying, "Don't imagine that you can ever lie to me. A scientist is first and foremost a keen observer. Your heart rate never rose above a hundred and five beats per minute. Your blood pressure hasn't budged since we started."

Clearly disappointed, he set the failed device on the bedside table. "What I treasure most about you is your honest, unfiltered feedback." He pressed a button to summon the butler. "Let's forget tonight. Tonight is wasted."

Maxwell retrieved the remote control and brought the television to life. The noise of gunfire and squealing tires filled the spacious bedroom. Not taking his eyes off the screen, he said, "You must never, ever again fake it with me."

His eyes never leaving the TV screen, he said, "If I wanted fake results I'd still be testing on prostitutes."

Later that night, something snapped Penny awake. A muffled noise. She held her breath, listening to the silence of the penthouse bedroom. The air-conditioning stirred the drapes in the window. Max stretched beside her, asleep against the satin sheets, his bedside clock reading three eighteen a.m. Before she could drift back to dreamland, the sound came again: a male voice, mumbling.

Maxwell was talking in his sleep. In words that were hardly

more than groans, he said, "Maybe." Perhaps it was two words: "Feed me." Penny couldn't be certain. She raised herself onto one elbow and leaned closer. He mumbled again. "Need me," he said.

She leaned closer. Too close. As if in warning, his voice hoarse with panic, now he cried, "Phoebe!" And the force of his frantic outburst stunned Penny. The word rang in her mind. *Phoebe.* After that he was silent.

It would appear that the still waters of C. Linus Maxwell ran deep. Within the pale skinny chest of that scientist beat a real heart. If he could only share his secrets, Penny thought wistfully, maybe then their relationship could rise above fantastic sex and blossom to become a true romance.

It never ceased to amaze her how Maxwell could act so petty. Outwardly, he remained a geeky, science-obsessed boy of a man. A distant tyrant, withholding his heartfelt emotions and affections. His skin was odorless and as cold as metal, like a robot from some science fiction movie. But when he stimulated her . . .

When Max stimulated her, the feeling was like hearing a big-name tenor at the Paris Opera House, or like dining alfresco on some scrumptious Italian thing. Even if Max didn't love her, when he stimulated her glands Penny couldn't help herself. Despite his coldness and cruelty, she felt herself fall temporarily in love with him. When his Beautiful You tools stirred the passion within her, Penny gazed into his remote blue eyes and desired nothing in the world but him. It was as if he'd cast a spell over her.

Penny wanted to believe that making love was more than just fiddling with nerve endings until harum-scarum chemicals squirted around limbic systems. Real love, she knew, was something lasting and soulful. It sustained and nourished a person. The "love" that Max engendered seemed to evaporate as her orgasms petered out. Despite their delightful effects, the Beautiful You products generated merely a powerful love substitute.

Her darkest fear was that the world's women wouldn't know the difference.

The next day, inspiration hit. She phoned her mother in Omaha.

"How's Paris?" Her mother asked this teasingly. "Please tell me you've missed your period!"

"How do you know I'm in Paris?" Penny challenged.

Long-distance, her mother clucked her tongue. "Honey, you're on the front page of the *National Enquirer* every day with the Eiffel Tower behind you!"

Penny shuddered. For weeks she'd been phoning into work sick. She'd told Brillstein she had hepatitis C. Unless everyone at BB&B lived under rocks, they had to know she was lying.

"They're calling you 'the Nerd's Cinderella,'" her mother shouted. She always shouted on long-distance calls.

"Mom?"

"Did you see that picture they ran last week of President Hind?" her mother shouted. "She looks terrible!"

Penny ventured, "Maybe she has hepatitis."

"And that Alouette D'Ambrosia looks even worse." Penny's mother cautioned, "Don't let Maxwell get away. The ladies who break off with him all go to hell."

Penny tried to steer the conversation. "That's the reason I'm calling, Mom. Do you have any back issues of the *Enquirer*?"

"Name a date," her mother said proudly. "I have every issue going back as far as 1972."

"You're kidding."

"It's my life's work," her mother boasted.

"I'd like to surprise Max," Penny said, "but I don't know much about him—you know, his childhood, his likes and dislikes."

"Why don't you just use the Wiki-thing?"

"Wikipedia, Mom. That's no good, either." Her voice heavy with resignation, Penny explained that "Climax-Well" employed teams of hackers who did nothing but comb the Internet and manage his public image. He controlled every detail that could be found. "I'm looking for little anecdotes from before the Internet age."

Her mother sounded doubtful. "It's the *Enquirer,* honey, not *The New York Times.*"

"Please, Mom."

"What did you have in mind?"

Penny thought a moment. "The names of his childhood pets. Old hobbies. Maybe something sweet about his mother; was her name 'Phoebe'?"

"She's dead."

Penny insisted, "I know, but it would be sweet to find an old nickname. A favorite flavor of ice cream. A lullaby. Something along those lines."

Penny's mother sounded energized, thrilled to be recruited on such a project. "I'll head down into the basement right now."

"Thank you, Mom."

The truth was, once Penny had faked one orgasm she found herself questioning all of them. She'd stopped trusting her own physical reactions. With every nightly session, she worried that she was under- or overreacting to his ministrations. She'd never loved Maxwell, but she'd loved what he could generate in her body. Now even the orgasms were losing their hold over her.

She wondered whether this was how his affair with Clarissa Hind had ended. And Princess Gwen. And Alouette.

Only sixty-seven days were left.

Whether or not she did it intentionally, Penny continued to fake it occasionally. On those nights not even the steamy memory of Alouette's hot mouth clamped between her legs could bring on a climax. A few times, she convinced him. More often, she couldn't. He knew more about her body than she did.

The times she was caught—betrayed by her baseline heart rate, the pH of her sweat excretion, her skin lividity—Maxwell would summarily extract the prototype. He'd rip the applicable pages out of his notes and make a big show of tearing them into bits and sprinkling them into the trash can beside the bed. He'd open his laptop and begin reviewing the first generation of marketing materials for Beautiful You.

Once, to defuse his silent anger, Penny looked pointedly at his notebook and asked, "Are they all in there?"

"Who?" Max asked, not looking up from a screening copy of a television commercial. To Penny, these videos all looked the same: manically smiling women, their eyes gleaming, running home from the store or the post office carrying the same bright pink box printed with the curlicue Beautiful You logo. The voice-over tagline at the end of each commercial was a dulcet female purr saying, "A billion husbands are about to be replaced!"

"All of your former lovers," Penny clarified. "Are they all in there?" She nodded at the notebook filled with his spidery shorthand. "The president, the princess, the steel heiress?"

She knew they were. Maxwell collected data like a magpie.

"That's only the latest of many notebooks," said the man who was scrolling down through mock-ups of print ads that would run in every women's magazine in the world. The Beautiful You logo in Basque, French, Hindi, Afrikaans, Mandarin Chinese. "Are you certain you want to hear this?" he asked coldly.

She wasn't sure, but she nodded.

"I have, indexed and cross-indexed, the forensic specifications of seven thousand, eight hundred, and twenty-four females, ages six through two hundred seven." Turning to meet her gaze, he added, "Before you phone the child welfare authorities, my encounter with the six-year-old occurred when we were both that age and playing 'doctor' in the basement of her family home in Ballard." The centuries-old subject was a mystic who lived high on Mount Everest.

He smiled. "I've trained myself with the abilities to please any woman," Max said flatly. He wasn't bragging, not in his own mind. "Young or old. Fat or thin. Any race. From any culture. I can quickly and efficiently bring any woman to greater levels of orgasm than she has ever dreamed possible."

Turning back to his computer screen, he continued. "I've collected data about the sexual responsiveness of high school girls, college coeds, young professionals. I have studied the erotic tricks of Tajikistan temple prostitutes . . . German sex therapists . . . Sufi belly dancers. The women you know of, the rich and powerful, are only the tip of my sexual iceberg. By the time I bedded them I was already very well rehearsed in a thousand ways of providing pleasure."

Penny realized that with numbers like that, very few of his partners had gotten more than a few minutes of Max's attention. "Is that why you pursued Clarissa Hind?"

"No, the purpose of women such as Clarissa and Alouette was not research. It was testing. Testing and connections. Not to mention advertising. I've found it very useful to know the president and the queen of England on such an intimate level. And the prestige of knowing them has lured many more test subjects into my grasp."

"Subjects like me?" Penny asked, at once honored and revolted by the idea.

Maxwell looked at her kindly. He was sitting cross-legged on the bed, the laptop open in front of him. "No, my good girl. You were my victory lap."

He'd pioneered the most extraordinary collection of erotic tools in the history of the world. He knew they worked. In fact, some worked too well. The pleasure they generated might kill an average Jane Doe. This final round of trials was intended to blunt the power of the most dangerous toys. Now the Beautiful You collection could enter the world without fear of lawsuits.

"Before you feel yourself ill-used," he continued, "please remember that you've gotten great enjoyment from our time together. You've been feted by the world press. And your wardrobe has grown to become quite impressive."

Penny couldn't deny any of his statements, but she could understand why a woman like Alouette would file for fifty million dollars in compensation for emotional distress.

"If it helps your pride, my girl," Maxwell said, "you should know that you've saved innocent lives." He pecked away at a few keys, bringing up a new selection of adverts. "However," he added, "I do use the term 'innocent' loosely."

Within hours of each marathon session of erotic bliss, Penny felt her muscles tighten and flare with soreness. It felt as if she'd climbed to the peak of Mount Everest or swum the English Channel. Some episodes, the more extreme, left her feeling as if she'd rebounded from polio. More sex was out of the question until she'd recuperated; Maxwell knew that. He didn't push. Some of the positions they achieved required her legs to be as limber as a circus contortionist's. A pulled muscle or ruptured tendon would delay further testing for weeks.

A battalion of physical therapists streamed through the

penthouse. To aid in her rapid recovery, masseurs stroked her for hours with scented oils, working their muscular, intuitive hands deep into her. Acupuncture specialists performed miracles by pricking her with their thin needles. Only when she was fully revitalized did Maxwell approach her with the next piece of equipment or aphrodisiac. He inflicted his sweet, consensual torture and left her gasping and aching, and once again the recovery team would nurse Penny back to health in time for another round of crippling pleasure.

"I do not want fatigue to dim your senses," Max told her. As a burly Turkish brute fingered the inside of her aching thighs, Max stood by fully dressed in a twelve-thousand-dollar bespoke suit and examined her nude body for bruises. "It is of the utmost importance that you be fully rested and responsive when we engage in our experiments."

He stepped closer to the massage table, where she lay faceup, glistening with oil. Her labia were ruddy and distended from the sensual abuse they'd taken the previous night. Bowing low over her body, he placed his lips against her inflamed clitoris.

Penny winced.

"The lactic acid must dissipate. You are still too tender," Max declared. "We will postpone further trials for two days."

Over the past few weeks, Penny had lost track of how many Beautiful You products he'd tested on her body. A few had proved mediocre, lackluster, unremarkable. But most had left her drained and limp with satisfaction. Fearful for her own safety, she'd even asked Max to dial back the effects of some. She was young, a fit, healthy girl just out of law school. On an older woman or someone with a preexisting health condition, those most effective products could prove fatal.

On the evenings when recent erotic play had left her too damaged for more, Penny lay in bed and asked Max to read to her from his notebook of test results. Freshly massaged and sipping a glass of Côtes du Rhône, she'd curl in her nest of satin sheets. Max would sit on a straight-backed chair beside the bed. Attired in a tuxedo and white bow tie, he'd lick a fingertip and page forward and back in his book until he found just the right test subject.

"'Date: June seventeenth, the year 20—,'" he read. "'Test site: the Mall of America in Minneapolis, Minnesota. Product: Beautiful You item number two sixteen, the Veggie Play Shaper, a food processor that quickly turns any raw vegetable into an erotic tool.'" In his flat, robotic voice, Maxwell described standing at a folding table as a stream of shoppers moved past. A few lingered, watching as he inserted uncooked carrots and zucchini squash into a plastic housing. With a single deft movement, he pressed a lever. Unseen blades within the device shaped the vegetable and out popped a phallus engineered for maximum fulfillment. As curious shoppers coalesced into a crowd, Maxwell demonstrated how the internal blades could be adjusted to make the resulting sex toy longer or shorter, thicker or thinner. Other blades carved channels and ridges that would excite the vaginal opening. His audience giggled and gasped with amusement, but they didn't leave. A voice near the back of the crowd called out, "Will it work on eggplants?"

Maxwell assured them it would.

"How about potatoes?" asked another shopper.

Max asked for a volunteer.

Reading to Penny, seated on a straight-backed chair beside her bed, his legs crossed primly at the knee and his notebook balanced atop them, he said, "The test subject, number seventeen sixty-nine, gave her name as Tiffany Jennifer Spalding, a twenty-five-year-old mother of three and homemaker. Height: a hundred and seventy centimeters. Weight: sixty-one kilos."

There in the Mall of America, he dialed the adjustment

knobs. "How thick do you like it?" He grinned lecherously. "Your potatoes, I mean."

She blushed. "Not too big around. Medium."

"Smooth or textured?"

Tiffany Jennifer tapped a finger against her temple and thought for a moment. "Textured."

"Ridges or nubs?"

She asked, "Can you do both?"

The crowd held its collective breath as he lifted the device's top and wedged the tuberous vegetable into the chopping chute. Like a magician performing a trick onstage, he ceremonially asked his volunteer to press the blade-activation lever. "Is this your first time?" he asked.

She nodded, trembling. Reality slowed to sex time.

To steady her, he slipped an arm around Tiffany Spalding's waist. He placed both her hands on the lever, then laid his own atop them. "You must shove it quickly and smoothly." On the count of three, they pressed together and the onlookers gasped.

Maxwell lifted the safety panel to reveal a perfect phallus. Sleek and slightly curved, it didn't suggest the rude Idaho spud that had gone into the top of the device. With sufficient sanitary precautions and a thorough cooking, he assured the onlookers there was no reason it couldn't go from the farm field to the bedroom to the family dinner table. For a young mother on a tight food budget it would pay for itself in a matter of weeks.

"Now," he boasted, "you can have your good times and eat them, too!"

Several people laughed. Everyone applauded. Money in hand, they surged forward to buy. No one recognized him. They never did. The disguise he donned for such occasions was simple and effective. Even when his false mustache fell off during cunnilingus, as it often did, test subjects never realized whom they were cavorting with. It was too impossible that C. Linus Maxwell, the richest man in the world, was the stranger fishing his prosthetic facial hair from their bedclothes.

Still reading in his Paris penthouse, Maxwell edged his chair closer to the bed. Holding the open notebook with one hand, he reached between the sheets with his other until his fingers found Penny's weary groin.

"The Veggie Play Shaper sold briskly. Even when the stock was gone, one shopper lingered." Test subject number 1769 had asked, "What about me?" Her voice descended to a sex-drenched murmur.

In the penthouse bedroom, Maxwell's fingertips carefully traced the soft contours of Penny's overtaxed pussy. With small circling motions, he provoked moisture to rise from deep within her.

Test subject 1769 still clutched her sculpted potato. Eyeing him from beneath her fluttering lashes, she said, "You're quite the pitchman." She wore Avon Pink Palace lipstick and held the potato suggestively near her mouth. From her skin tone, Maxwell estimated she was seventeen days from estrus. According to his notes, she asked, "Do you have anything else I might be interested in? Another labor-saving device?"

His voice still droning on, even and monotone, Max dipped his fingers, milking at Penny's hot wetness. Unlike earlier in the day, she didn't wince. In fact, she groaned and rolled her battered pelvis against the weight of his hand.

"'Test subject seventeen sixty-nine,'" Max read aloud, "'proved to be a willing and eager participant in preliminary evaluation of the champagne douche product. . . .'"

There was more. Maxwell kept reading for hours. But as his hand worked its customary magic Penny was no longer listening.

On another night of recovery, Maxwell pulled a chair to the side of the bed where Penny lay. That night, from among the recollections of geishas and singsong girls and courtesans, he read to her about a nondescript homebody recruited almost at random. "'Test subject thirty-eight ninety-one,'" he read. "'Place: Bakersfield, California, the auditorium of Hillshire Elementary School. Time: seven p.m., October second, 20—.'"

To prove product number 241, he was on the prowl for a larger woman. Vaginal tissue was wonderfully absorbent, and to exploit that aspect of it, Maxwell had invented the Burst Blaster, a vibrator containing as many as four internal cavities. Each functioned as a reservoir which could be filled with fluid, and the operator could program the device to release measured amounts during use, be it coffee for a quick pick-me-up, or cough syrup for something more euphoric. Even antibiotics. Or an essential oil for extra lubrication as needed. The tip of the vibrator would spout at the desired time. To prove its efficacy, he approached a lone mother and initiated small talk. To cut her from the pack of other mothers, he complimented her appearance. The strategy proved successful, and soon he'd sequestered her in an otherwise unoccupied kindergarten classroom.

"'There among the caged gerbils,'" he read, "'I wooed the test subject.'"

Her eyes closed, listening, Penny sighed. She knew product number 241 very well. Its caffeinated secretions had helped her stay present on many long nights of endurance testing.

"'Despite her body mass index, the test subject had exhibited an enthusiastic response to the device.'" As usual, Maxwell's voice was monotone. His delivery deadpan. "'Once application of the appliance began, the subject inexplicably shouted the name Fabio at regular intervals.'"

Penny smiled at his apparent failure to grasp the cultural reference.

"'The test subject's heart rate accelerated rapidly to a hundred and fifty-seven bpm,'" Max read. "'Her skin conductivity increased dramatically.'" He paused to turn a notebook page. "'It must be noted here that the scientist conducting this experiment had great difficulty in maintaining full possession of the product. Test subject thirty-eight ninety-one displayed enormous pelvic strength and was determined to usurp the device and complete the procedure on her own.'"

Penny pictured this. Some lonely woman wrestling with pale, scrawny Maxwell over control of a squirting sex toy. A caged gallery of hamsters and rabbits docilely witnessing these antics.

"'It was at the zenith of her climax—respiration twenty-five breaths per minute, blood pressure one seventy-five over one-oh-two—that test conditions were radically altered.'" Deciphering his own faded shorthand, Maxwell read, "'While application of the product was an unqualified success, the testing location failed to provide adequate privacy.'"

Someone had walked in on them.

"'The elders of the church school,'" Max affirmed, "'entered unannounced. Apparently alerted by the din of our procedure.'"

In a scientific aside, he noted, "'For the record, the test subject must've boasted an exceptionally large *corpus spongiosum*. Upon the entrance of additional parties to the scene, she expelled a copious stream of ejaculate from her urethra, thoroughly drenching them.'"

He briskly rapped his hairless knuckles against Penny's hypersensitive clitoris, a technique that drove her near to madness. Penny giggled softly. The poor test subject in Bakersfield, she'd spewed fluids all over the leaders of her religious charter school. Penny hoped it was worth the short-lived pleasure Maxwell's toy had provided. But knowing firsthand the power of the Burst Blaster, Penny suspected the woman had never regretted her furtive encounter.

The majordomo entered the penthouse bedroom carrying a silver tray. Lolling among the satin pillows and soft folds of the sheets, Penny accepted a flute of champagne. Taking a sip of the icy, thrilling wine, she tossed her head and gestured toward the book that lay open across his knee. "Read me another," she begged.

Injury and exhaustion weren't the only factors that impeded Maxwell's testing. When Penny's monthly period arrived, he took it in stride. Seeing her shake with cramps, her stomach bloating, Maxwell came to her aid with tablets of morphine and tiny cordial glasses of sweet sherry. She dozed in a twilight half-sleep, unaware of anything except him sitting near her, reading aloud from his notebook.

"'Test subject number thirty-eight twenty-eight,'" he announced. "'Location: Lower Manhattan, Zuccotti Park. Date: September seventeenth, 20—.'" He described seducing a young idealist who'd arrived only days before from Oklahoma to participate in the Occupy Wall Street event.

"'She gave her age as nineteen,'" he continued, "'a fact I asked that she confirm with her driver's license, as I had no desire to skew any statistical patterns with data garnered from not fully formed, preadult genitalia.'"

The scene had been late at night. While the majority of protesters slept, Maxwell had introduced the test subject to Beautiful You product number 223, the Love Lizard. It was a simple but brilliant telescoping tongue extender. A silicone tongue prosthesis calibrated to augment reach during oral coitus and engage vigorous contact with the cervix.

Even now, her mind drifting in drugged torpor, Penny recalled the clever novelty device and how it enabled Maxwell's relatively stunted oral appendage to access her to an astounding depth. At the memory of his attentions, she writhed with unfettered lust.

"'In a symbolic act of political street theater,'" Maxwell read, "'the test subject requested that the scientist conducting the experiment chain her spread-eagled to the security gates of the Bank of America Building.'"

The image played vividly in Penny's drugged imagination. The girl was nude in the moonlight, her smooth limbs bound wide apart. Test subject 3828 offered herself as this youthful sacrifice on the altar of capitalism. Maxwell knelt at her feet and adjusted the tongue extender to its full functional length. He cupped his gaping mouth over her pubis.

"'The trick was to wag the tongue,'" he read, "'as if singing. To avoid tiring the muscles of the mandible, don't hold the jaw rigid. After only a brief application of the product, the test subject expressed her approval by shouting, "I'm giving my body to you, the ninety-nine percent!"'"

Maxwell recounted how such outcries had lured a throng of bearded radicals, all eager to participate in the test. "'With only a brief tutorial,'" Maxwell recited from his notes, "'all present were able to successfully operate product number two twenty-three.'"

To Penny the boundaries between fantasy and reality evaporated. Awash in morphine dreams, she felt herself tongued by legions of hirsute political activists. Maxwell's voice threaded through a hallucination where a team of New York riot police arrived on the scene. Faceless behind the Kevlar shields of their helmets, they unsheathed their batons and menaced the test subject's nude, shameless form.

"'Once testing was complete,'" Maxwell concluded, "'the subject appeared self-conscious and professed to having ingested an unspecified amount of the drug commonly known as LSD. She requested the shackles be unlocked and asked for a sum of money sufficient to cover one-way airfare to Tulsa. . . .'"

Olympic training camps. Unsuspecting book clubs. Quilting circles. It was in all of these places Max found test subjects, and it was into this elite sisterhood that Penny had entered.

After Maxwell's umpteenth reprimand for faking an orgasm, Penny found herself doing the opposite. She held back her reaction to his efforts. No matter how Maxwell labored to please her, she began to withhold her usual squealing confirmation of his genius. Clearly she was punishing him, but Penny didn't care. She'd grown resentful. In Max's world she felt like nothing more than an instrument whose only purpose was to register the degree of his success.

One night he was testing a pair of nipple clamps on her, subjecting her to low-voltage fluctuations that shot sine waves of excitement up and down her spine, branching out along her arms and legs. Sparks of electric ecstasy shot out the ends of her fingers and glowed from the crown of her head like a halo. Throughout the entire pleasing ordeal, Penny willed herself to remain quiet. She tried to distract her own attention with thoughts about the few bar exam questions she could still recall. She willed herself to silently recite the Gettysburg Address, word for word.

Without a warning, he deactivated the batteries and made a point of unceremoniously removing the clips from her nipples. Before he spoke, Maxwell wrapped the wires in a tidy bundle and set the apparatus aside. Only then did he confront her. "You're angry at me, aren't you?"

"Don't blame me," Penny replied. "This gadget of yours must be a dud."

"A dud?" He snorted a laugh. Squinting at the notes he'd jotted in his book, he said, "Miss Harrigan, your pulse was a hundred and eighty beats per minute. Your anal temperature was a hundred and three degrees Fahrenheit. If this 'gadget' were any more effective, it would give you a coronary or a fatal brain embolism."

The last time Penny saw Alouette D'Ambrosia in person was at a cocktail party in the Rue St. Germaine. The actress had been escorted by a handsome novelist, Pierre Le Courgette, the winner of that year's Nobel Prize for literature. They made a striking couple. She lost track of them, but near the end of the get-together Alouette approached her. Glancing around nervously the French beauty asked, "Where is Max?" Without waiting for an answer, she whispered, "I was wrong not to confide in you. We must be allies, you and I. If we are not, we are both in gravest danger."

This was the first time the two women had met since the incident with the married stones. The Frenchwoman looked starved, like a leathery husk of her former self. There wasn't a whiff of booze on her breath, but she was obviously agitated. The heavy sapphire that hung around her neck glowed against her flushed cleavage. "He will spoil you for other men." Maxwell had entered from a door at the far end of the salon. As usual, his head was bowed as he took notes in his book. He'd yet to catch sight of Alouette as she insisted, "The sisterhood of us, all his castoff lovers, we are his harem around the world."

Tensing as Maxwell grew nearer, she said, "I am nominated for a new Oscar, so I must be there, but next month we will talk more deeply, no?"

Penny stammered, "I'd like that." The sensation of Alouette's lovely mouth against her came to mind unbidden.

"You will not like what I have to say," warned the actress. Nevertheless, the look she gave Penny was warm. "We will be bosom friends, no?" As Maxwell wandered closer, she kissed Penny on both cheeks and hurriedly returned to her own escort.

Without taking his eyes off her undulating body, Maxwell pulled open a drawer of the bedside table. He lifted out something and held it to one eye like a mask. It was a video camera, and he panned slowly up and down her nakedness.

Penny wasn't afraid. On some level she knew she was safe. If these images were ever made public Maxwell stood to suffer more embarrassment than she did. Many mornings she would wake to find him preparing a new device for her enjoyment. While softly twisting a new toy into her, he'd explain the ancient sex magic rituals of the Sudanese tribesmen. There were more basic tools. Soft pink versions of medical clamps that would spread her buttocks and hold them apart for his leisured convenience.

Scanning her through the lens, he said, "Good girl, don't struggle. There is no film in the camera." He assured her, "I merely want you to feel as if you're under observation." Whether or not he was actually documenting her, Penny savored the fact that someone was paying her so much regard. She wondered whether all of his test subjects had loved the attention as much as (or even more than?) the physical sensations he prompted.

———

During the day sunlight fell on the bed from tall windows, and Penny snuggled under the smooth sheets, naked, nibbling on a brioche, sipping a latte, and studying her old textbooks on tort law. These days the fashion houses brought their clothes to her. The designers themselves fitted her. If she insisted, Maxwell took her out to the symphony or the theater; otherwise she seldom left the penthouse.

Beautiful You would launch in another month, and she wondered whether Max would have further need for her. She didn't delude herself. As demonstrated by his elaborate coldness he'd never loved her. It had been sufficient to have someone who could read her needs so intuitively. Often Max dismissed the team of massage therapists and treated her himself. He could stroke her tense muscles and know exactly her mood. He listened as closely to her breathing as he did to the words she spoke.

Maxwell had come to know her so well that Penny seldom needed to speak.

Here was a man who found her intensely fascinating, and who delighted in guiding her to peaks of aliveness she had never dreamed existed. He savored and appreciated her.

Billions of people were watching him—the wealthiest, arguably the most powerful man in the world—and he was watching Penny. The gaze of his camera, the scratched shorthand of his notes, they imbued her life with even more value. Under his watchful eye she felt secure. Cherished. But, no, not loved.

Two weeks before the rollout of the Beautiful You product line, Max abruptly froze in the middle of lovemaking. With a resigned slowness he carefully withdrew the current apparatus from her and laid it on the bedside table. Pulling off his latex gloves, he said, "You're of no further use to me." He lifted his notebook. "The integrity . . . the authenticity . . . the *truth* of your reactions have become too compromised."

As he made his notes, he checked the time on his wristwatch. "My jet is already prepped. You'll find that your clothes and personal items have all been packed, and your luggage is already aboard, waiting for you."

Maxwell turned to her, her head still cradled in the white satin pillow. He pressed two fingers to the side of her neck and timed her pulse. "The pilot is instructed to take you anywhere in the world you desire." Penny had no chance to protest. She had yet to even close her legs.

He wrote down the last statistics of her heart rate and temperature. "I've deposited fifty million dollars in a numbered Swiss bank account for you. I will wire you the details for accessing it, if you agree to never contact me again." To underscore his commands he looked at her. "You must never speak of our experience together or I will block your access to those funds."

A forever of silence passed. Despite his icy demeanor she sensed Max's little-boy heart was breaking.

"Do you understand?" he asked finally.

Blinking back tears, pulling her knees together, Penny didn't answer. She was surprised by the suddenness of the rejection.

"Do! You! Understand?" he shouted. The fury of his words broke her shock and she nodded her head.

"Test subject unresponsive," he muttered over his work. There was no mistaking it. His voice sounded choked with grief.

Penny curled onto her side, facing away from him. It was over. It had been a dream to be Cinderella, but now it was time to wake up.

"Please know that you've made a significant contribution to the development of the Beautiful You line," his voice continued, a droning. "As a token of my appreciation I've placed a small gift aboard the jet. I hope it will meet with your approval."

Penny felt the bed shift. His weight left the mattress. She listened as his bare feet crossed the carpeted floor. "You will leave my house within the hour." The bathroom door closed.

It had been exactly 136 days.

Aboard the Gulfstream, Penny found a small ribbon-wrapped box in the only seat that wasn't heaped with heavy suitcases and garment bags. She'd been hustled from the penthouse so quickly that she wore nothing except a floor-length chinchilla coat and a pair of Prada high heels. Alone in the quiet cabin, she lifted the gift and held it in her lap as she fastened her seat belt and the pilot announced takeoff.

After they were airborne, she slipped the ribbons from the box and lifted the lid. Inside was a thin gold chain. When she lifted it out, a ruby swung from the lowest point. It was the ruby that Maxwell had always worn in a ring, reset as a pendant, the third-largest Sri Lankan ruby ever mined. Sharing the box was a bright pink plastic dragonfly. Its wings were thick and soft, printed with the curlicue Beautiful You logo. Penny inspected its antennae and the underside of its plastic body.

The dragonfly-shaped souvenir was a sex toy. The massproduced version of a prototype Max had tested on her several times. She'd never grown tired of the effects the little flapping wings had generated. Those unfettered sessions were among her most intense memories, and the sight of the device made a blush rise in her cheeks.

A trust fund of fifty million dollars. Enough clothes to fill a department store. No, Penny told herself, she hadn't been too mistreated. As she fastened the chain around her neck and felt the weight of the frigid ruby between her warm breasts, she slipped the plastic dragonfly into the pocket of her coat and began to plan the first day of her new life. Within reach, an open bottle of champagne bubbled in an ice bucket. The flight attendant poured her a glass and turned off the cabin lights at Penny's request.

As she sipped the dry sparkling wine, she felt a twinge of sadness in remembering how, just months before, the taste had been a special treat. Between the multiple pounding orgasms and the champagne, life with Max had spoiled her rotten.

She was spoiled but not despairing. If anything, she felt excited about the future. Tonight she'd need something more than champagne to help her fall asleep.

Once she was sure the flight crew wouldn't see, she opened the front of her coat and slipped the dragonfly between her legs, settling it snugly in place. She'd watched Max do this dozens of times. As a special selling feature, he'd designed the toy to automatically warm itself to the perfect temperature. Even without looking she felt the button that activated it.

She wondered how he would fill his time once Beautiful You was launched. Maybe he was already planning new additions to the product line. Maybe he'd find another girlfriend with "ideal" genitals on which to test his prototypes. Someone who didn't hesitate in expressing her arousal.

Girlfriend was the wrong word. More like *guinea pig*.

In the inky blackness high above the Atlantic, Penny poured herself a second glass and lay back to enjoy the delicious pulsations between her thighs.

Her first weeks back in New York were a blur.

The money Maxwell bestowed on her came in the form of an annuity. She couldn't withdraw the entire lump sum, but she could live very well off the accruing dividends for the rest of her life. Prudently, she invested in a small town house on the Upper East Side. When the realtor had shown her the sunny tiled kitchen, the elaborate scrolled-ironwork elevator, and the carved marble fireplaces, Penny had written a check for the full asking price. It had plenty of closet space, which Penny's burgeoning wardrobe almost filled to capacity.

On her first day back at BB&B, she found someone to share the house.

Despite her self-professed identity as a crunchy bohemian, Monique was thrilled to give up the squalid studio she shared with two ethnic roommates under the Kosciuszko Bridge. Before Penny could entertain any second thoughts, Monique was dragging cardboard boxes from a taxi into the town house's elegant foyer. The smell of sandalwood was inescapable, but Monique's weird sitar music helped to fill the emptiness. To celebrate their first night together the transplanted neohippie cooked a curried tofu feast. Afterward, the two young women flopped on the sofa in the media room. Each with a bowl of popcorn in her lap, they watched the Academy Awards ceremony being broadcast live.

As the camera in the Kodak Theatre panned the crowded audience, Penny couldn't help herself. She searched for Maxwell's pale boyish face and limp blond hair. There, seated on an aisle, was Pierre Le Courgette, Alouette's boyfriend. Of course he would attend; she was a shoo-in to win best actress. Other faces Penny recognized, powerful people who had snubbed her or leered at her. It was hard to believe she'd rubbed elbows with them. That part of her life was fading like a sexually charged dream. She'd allowed Maxwell to isolate her in a fantasy of addictive pleasure and no emotional attachment, but now she was free.

Between being constantly examined by Maxwell and judged

by the thoroughbred jet-setters they met in public, Penny had shed any sensitivity she'd had about getting ogled. She might occasionally hear it, the clicking of paparazzi camera shutters, but she no longer reacted. She'd come to assume that every eye was always on her, and she carried herself with a new relaxed poise.

Whether it was this new self-confidence or the new clothes, she often caught men staring. Whenever she walked down Lexington Avenue, she almost didn't recognize her own reflection in the windows of Bloomingdale's. Striding along was a leggy Amazon. Gone was the layer of baby fat. Her hair swung in a shining wave.

In retrospect, Penny was glad the City of Light had never heard of butter brickle ice cream.

In the media room, she and Monique fought good-naturedly over the remote control. Both shouted jibes at the screen, where lesser-known cinematographers and producers expressed their verbose gratitude. The winner of best documentary was ushered offstage, and the network cut to a commercial.

The television showed a group of delighted, smiling young women gathered around a table. In the center of the shot the prettiest of them blew out the candles on a birthday cake as her friends pressed gifts upon her. To comic effect, every gift turned out to be a bright pink box emblazoned with a very curlicued white logo. *Beautiful You*. The girls rolled their shoulders and giggled. As if sharing some glorious secret, they pursed their lips and leaned to whisper in one another's ears. The birthday girl squealed as if the pink boxes contained nirvana.

To Penny, it was unlikely that girls like these—thin, doe-eyed, clear-skinned—would have any problem finding men who'd romance them. They were the last women who'd need to buy Maxwell's throbbing whatchamacallits.

Suddenly Penny envisioned a billion lonely wives or single

women abusing themselves in isolated resignation. In ghetto tenements or tumbledown farmhouses. Not bothering to meet potential partners. Living and dying with no intimate companions beyond their Beautiful You gadgetry. Instead of being either whores or Madonnas, they'd become celibates who diddled a lot. To Penny that didn't seem like social progress.

The television commercial ended with the familiar tagline; a dulcet female voice intoned, "A billion husbands are about to be replaced . . ."

"They have a store on Fifth," Monique said through a mouthful of popcorn. "I can't wait until it opens tomorrow."

Penny thought of the flagship outlet. Already a line of women was forming and it snaked for two blocks, down almost all the way to Fifty-fifth Street. The building's facade was skinned in pink mirror, so anyone trying to peek inside saw only a flattering rose-colored reflection of herself.

Penny hoped the eventual products were better made than the one Maxwell had left for her aboard the Gulfstream. She'd fallen asleep to its soothing pulsations, but as they'd been descending into LaGuardia she'd blinked awake to find it broken. The two wings of the plastic dragonfly had fallen off, and the pink-silicone body had split down the middle. It was almost as if the thing had hatched. Metamorphosed, she'd thought. But it was caterpillars that turned into butterflies. Butterflies just died. They laid their eggs on cabbage leaves and died. As the pilot had prepared for landing, Penny had discreetly picked the shattered scraps of silicone out of herself and stuffed them into her coat pocket.

Resolutely, she decided to find a real, live, flesh-and-blood lover before she'd resort to standing in line on Fifth Avenue.

Monique called, "Pay attention, Omaha girl!" and began to pelt Penny with salty, buttery kernels of popcorn.

On television, Alouette sauntered across the stage to accept her award as best actress. Her floor-length gown swirled around her toned legs. Her shoulders bare and thrown back, her breasts held high in her strapless bodice, she was the perfect image of self-assurance and accomplishment. It was thrilling to watch.

"God, I love her," Monique sighed. "Is that bling for real?"

Glowing in the center of the actress's cleavage was the huge sapphire.

The camera zoomed in on Maxwell seated ten rows back, on the aisle. The lovable dork, he appeared to be playing a handheld electronic game. As his thumbs danced over the keys on a little black box, he seemed to be ignoring Alouette's triumph onstage.

In vivid contrast, the audience of big names applauded with genuine admiration. Standing behind the clear Plexiglas podium, the French beauty beamed, graciously accepting their accolades. A few people stood. Then everyone was standing. A tidal wave of adoration. As the applause subsided, leaving room for her to speak, a shadow of pain seemed to drift across Alouette's delicate features. Her lips and brow tightened almost imperceptibly. It passed, and her smile returned. Even under her makeup her face looked flushed, and rivulets of sweat flattened strands of hair to her cheeks.

She looked a little dazed, Penny thought, but who wouldn't be?

The actress began to say, *"Merci,"* but winced again. *"Alors,"* she cried out. She gasped for breath. Hugging the golden award to her chest, she took a step toward the wings, but looked uncharacteristically wobbly in her stiletto heels.

Taking a second step, she stumbled and fell. The golden Oscar landed with a clunk and rolled a few feet. A murmur of concern rippled through the auditorium.

"Somebody help the lady!" Monique shouted at the television screen.

As she lay on the stage, trying to raise herself onto her elbows, Alouette's legs began to tremble. A palsy began at her feet, but quickly traveled upward to her knees until both legs were shaking from the waist down. Her ankles moved slowly apart. Positioned toward the audience, her legs gradually spread, stretching her skirt taut between them. Even as Alouette reached down, gripping the hem and trying to keep it at a modest level, the tension on the fabric was too great. It sprang up, collecting above her crotch. She wasn't wearing underthings, Penny realized. You never did with a gown that clingy and formfitting.

"Are you seeing this?" asked Monique in a whisper. One hand hung frozen in the air, midway between the bowl of popcorn and her gaping mouth.

To Penny, the five-time Oscar winner clearly looked deranged. She twisted her head violently from side to side, lashing the stage with her long hair. Her eyes rolled up until only the whites showed. Her chest heaved, and her back arched, thrusting her hips into the air as if to meet a phantom lover.

In heavily accented English, she was screaming, "No!" Shrieking, "Please, no! Not here!" It seemed as if the suffering movie star was staring directly at C. Linus Maxwell.

None too soon, the network cut to a commercial.

Instantly, the panting woman lying on her back, shoving her bare pubis at an audience of millions, was replaced by a new bevy of giggling twenty-somethings brandishing bright pink shopping bags.

Everyone at BB&B was talking about it. Alouette D'Ambrosia was dead. According to the front page of the *Post*, she'd suffered a brain aneurysm onstage and died before an ambulance had arrived.

The rumor was that after the broadcast had cut away to an emergency break, the cameras had kept rolling. In front of that vast audience of industry swells, Alouette had acted like an animal in heat, going so far as to violently abuse herself with the gold-plated statuette. Penny couldn't believe that. Or she didn't want to. The extra footage was reportedly on the Web, but she couldn't bring herself to view it. If anything, the shocking episode only reinforced her impression that Alouette had been seriously mentally ill. It was a sad idea, but she'd likely relapsed into abusing drugs and alcohol.

Whatever the case, it was tragic. In more ways than one. Brillstein had hoped to make Penny an associate. He'd planned to appoint her as lead counsel to represent the plaintiff in the palimony lawsuit filed on behalf of their client, Alouette. It would've looked great: the defendant's most recent lover championing his jilted lover on the witness stand. Such a strategy would've made Alouette look injured and deserving. BB&B would've won the case, but not before the firm had oodles of billable hours to their credit. With the actress dead, her lawsuit was dead. BB&B would have to find a new rainmaker, and Brillstein would need to find a new shop window in which to showcase Penny's lawyering talents.

Brillstein wasn't the only person watching out for her at BB&B. Tad was back in the picture. Tad Smith, who'd always called her "Hillbilly." He was the young fresh-faced patent law specialist whose private man-parts Monique referred to as "the tadpole." After Penny's Beautiful You transformation in Paris, Tad hardly seemed to recognize her. Now a boldly beautiful eyeful, utterly unashamed to be seen by all, she was no longer anyone's fat, stinky dog. If he still had a hankering for Monique, he never asked about her. Instead, he invited Penny to lunch.

He escorted her to La Grenouille and regaled her with anecdotes about his days editing the *Yale Law Review*. After lunch they'd hired a carriage and ridden through the park. He bought her a handful of helium balloons from a street vendor, a simple romantic gesture that Maxwell—despite all his brainpower—would never think to do.

Tad didn't even tease her about being "the Nerd's Cinderella." The *New York Post* had long since moved on to other stories. Alouette's death, for instance. A forest fire in Florida. The queen of England had collapsed in convulsions during a meeting to negotiate duties on consumer goods manufactured in China. As their carriage clip-clopped down Fifth Avenue, Penny tried to ignore the pink-mirrored building that loomed ahead at Fifty-seventh Street. A line of shoppers waited to enter. The line trailed into the distance as far as she could see.

"Look," Tad said. "Is that Monique?"

Penny followed his gaze to a girl cooling her heels on the sidewalk, her arms folded across her chest. All of the people waiting in line were women. In the carriage seat she slumped her shoulders and slid down. She cringed with disappointment and resignation, pulling the balloons low to hide herself.

Tad shouted, "Mo!" He waved until the girl's eyes found them.

"Can you believe this?" Monique yelled. "This is worse than when I bought my BlackBerry!" The midday sun sparkled on her rhinestone-studded fingernails and the bright tribal beads braided into her hair.

Tad asked the driver to halt at the curb.

As before, Penny felt ignored, relegated to being her glitzy friend's stinky mutt. She looked up, pretending to only now notice her housemate. She knew Monique had a list of Beautiful You products that she was anxious to cart home and try. The online buzz posted by early adopters was positive. Beyond positive—it was raves. Despite the fact that a huge inventory had been stockpiled before the launch, the offshore factories were having trouble keeping up with orders. The praise spread like wildfire. Media wags speculated that so many women were calling in "sick" and staying home to indulge themselves that the gross national output would take a short-term dip.

Penny resented how male newscasters treated the story like a dirty joke, reporting it with winks and an implied "hubba hubba" in every pause.

"Save yourself the money," Tad shouted to Monique. "Jerald in copyright law has a crush on you." The horse shifted, restless. A taxi behind them honked.

"Haven't you heard?" Monique shouted in response. "Men are obsolete!"

The declaration drew a small cheer from the assembled women.

Monique played to the crowd. "Anything a man can do to me, I can do better!" She snapped her fingers dismissively, making the crystals glued to each nail flash in the sunlight.

This evoked a louder cheer. Jeers and whistles sounded in her support.

The taxi honked again. The line of shoppers began to move.

"Can a sex toy buy you dinner?" challenged Tad, clearly flirting.

"I can buy my own dinner!" With another step, Monique and the women nearest her were swallowed up by the big pink store.

As if she needed proof that she was back in wild-and-woolly New York City, Penny was attacked her first month there. Standing on an otherwise deserted subway platform, she was headed uptown after a late night at work. She was idly musing whether to order Thai food or pizza when two arms grabbed her from behind. They crushed the breath from her, squeezing at her chest and throat, and her vision pinholed to a narrow awareness of the fluorescent lights overhead.

She was on her back, her Donna Karan slacks stomped down around her Jimmy Choos. Later, what she'd remember most about her attacker was his stench of stale urine and peach wine coolers. What she'd never understand was how quickly it had happened. One moment she'd been deciding on lemongrass chicken, and in the next she'd felt the stranger's erection ramming to enter her.

Maxwell flashed into her mind. Not that the attacker was either curious or clinical, but how the assault was so impersonal.

Even as Penny felt herself yielding, felt the angry hardness rip into her, she also heard the man scream.

Faster than he had fallen on her, he jumped to his feet, his hands cradling the filthy penis that hung from the open front of his ragged trousers. He kept on yelping, tears streaming from his eyes as he looked down and examined himself.

Her first impression was that the man's fly zipper had snagged some tender fold of skin. Before she could rally her strength to scream or run away, she saw a large bead of blood swell from a puncture wound in the glans of his penis.

The stranger's attention shifted from his bleeding self, his eyes rising to glare at her. His voice timorous, he whined, "What have you got in your snatch, lady? A Bengal tiger?"

Penny watched as the drop of blood grew to a steady stream. She edged backward, sliding herself away from where the blood dribbled to form a growing pool on the subway platform. She saw that he'd been wearing a condom, and the latex of it had also been torn.

In another beat, a train arrived, and the man was gone. That was all she could tell the policeman who responded to her 911 call.

The doctor she'd gone to for the necessary STD tests said

she showed no signs of infection but insisted she come back for further tests in six weeks. The doctor, a sympathetic older woman with frizzy, graying red hair, insisted on giving her a pelvic exam and swabbing for DNA evidence. While she told Penny to place her feet in the stirrups of the examining room table, the woman donned a pair of latex gloves. She said to exhale while she inserted a speculum.

While the doctor clicked a penlight and began her careful inspection, Penny asked for a pelvic X-ray.

"That's usually not necessary," the doctor assured her.

"Please," Penny insisted. A wave of dread was fueling her request.

"What are you worried about?" asked the doctor, still squinting through the speculum, rotating the beam of the penlight.

Penny explained about the man's lanced penis. The hole torn in his condom.

"Well, there's nothing here that might account for a puncture wound," said the doctor. "Your first impression was probably correct: He got it caught in his trouser fly." She began to slowly withdraw the speculum. "Serves the bastard right."

They ordered the X-ray.

The X-ray came back showing nothing.

Penny told herself it was nothing. Probably just the sharp metal teeth of the man's own zipper. It was only after that fact that Penny realized the worst part. Her guardian angels, in their tailored suits and mirrored sunglasses . . . for the first time in her life, they hadn't come to her rescue.

At work, Penny was cramming like crazy to pass the bar. Brillstein was still searching for the perfect class-action case for her to helm, but that wouldn't happen unless she was an attorney.

Until then, she still had to juggle the occasional coffee run and wrangle extra chairs for big meetings.

It didn't help that Monique kept calling in sick. Since the day she'd lugged home two bright pink shopping bags, the girl had been barricaded behind her locked bedroom door. From what Penny could tell, she didn't even emerge to eat. Day and night, a faint buzzing came from behind the door. When Penny knocked the buzzing stopped.

"Mo?" Penny waited. The buzzing was all too familiar. She knocked again.

"Go away, Omaha girl."

"Brillstein asked about you today."

"Go away." The buzzing restarted.

Penny went away.

Around Wednesday, Monique stumbled into the kitchen, squinting against the sunlight as if she'd been trapped for months in a collapsed coal mine. Fumbling in the fridge for a carton of milk, she grumbled. "Damn cheap piece of junk." She drank from the carton. Gasping before another swig, she added, "I can't wait to buy a replacement."

Penny looked up from the textbook she was highlighting. "It broke?"

"I guess," Monique said. "At least, the wings came off."

Penny stiffened. She was sitting, the breakfast table in front of her covered with books and legal pads. "Was it the dragonfly?"

Guzzling milk, Monique grunted in the affirmative. All the bright Austrian crystals had been chipped off of her fingernails. Her braids were kinked and tangled in disarray.

Warily, Penny asked, "Did it split down the middle?"

Monique nodded. "I was asleep."

Penny made a note to talk to Brillstein. This might be just the high-profile case she needed. With the land-office way Beautiful You was selling, if even a small percentage of the products were defective it might warrant a recall. If she could prove real damages and assemble a pool of plaintiffs, women from around the world who'd been hurt in any way by the shattered dragonflies, she might have an enormous class-action lawsuit. The idea wasn't without precedent; it seemed that every time a new tampon or form of birth control came to market women died. Toxic shock. Ruptures of the vaginal wall. Men engineered these innovations, but it was always women who paid the price.

Alouette, for example. She'd been among Maxwell's stable of lab rats. What was to say her embolism wasn't the long-term result of some stimulant-infused silicone coating? It wasn't impossible that the queen of England and the president of the United States might be compelled to testify. Penny could see herself as another bold Erin Brockovich. This was a case that would make her career.

Sure, Maxwell would be furious. He might cut off the payouts from her trust fund, but the income and prestige from winning a huge settlement might yield more than that loss.

Highlighting passages in a text about patent law, Penny said, "I was afraid you'd died in your bed."

"Only about three thousand times," Monique quipped.

"Have you used the douche?" asked Penny.

Monique was peeling the top off a cup of yogurt and stirring it with a spoon.

"When you do," Penny continued, "read the directions. Make sure you use imported champagne, not domestic sparkling wine. Definitely do not use brut. And the temperature must be between forty and fifty degrees Fahrenheit." She wondered whether this was how Max had felt when he was coaching her.

Jotting a citation in the margin of a page, she felt like Maxwell. Without meeting Monique's curious gaze she said, "When you use product number thirty-nine, start with the oscillations at fifteen bpm and slowly dial them up to forty-five bpm. After that, you'll maintain the best effects by alternating between twenty-seven-point-five and thirty-five-point-five."

Monique was impressed. She'd yet to eat a spoonful. She kicked a chair back from the table and lowered herself into the seat. "What's product number . . . ?"

Penny completed the sentence. "The Happy Honey Ball." She asked, "Do you know where your urethral sponge is?"

"In the bathroom?" Monique ventured. "On the shelf next to the tub?"

Penny gave her a wilting glance. "Did you buy a pair of those awful Peruvian married stones?"

"Of what?"

"Good," Penny confirmed, remembering the miserable scene where Alouette had come to her rescue in the restaurant. "Don't."

Monique set her yogurt on the table, careful not to cover any of Penny's study materials. "You sound as if you designed this stuff."

Penny thought, but didn't say, *I sort of did invent them.* Her resentment toward her housemate dwindled. Life was too short. A few days of physical indulgence wouldn't kill Monique. It was pleasure without affection; she'd recognize that and outgrow it. "Listen up," Penny said. "When you use the Daisy Love Wand, keep in mind the coefficient of friction and only use it with the Glassy Glide Cream."

The expression on Monique's face was one of complete bewilderment. "This shit," she marveled, "is going to change the fabric of society."

Tearing a blank page from her legal pad, Penny went to work with a pen. "Don't worry," she said. "I'm writing this all down."

That same day she went to Tad's office and asked him to lunch. As boyfriend material Tad had more moxie than skill. He was fun and spontaneous, often sneaking a quick kiss and trying to slip his finger inside her while they rode crowded subway cars. Over hot dogs on a park bench she broached the subject. Maybe she was hypersensitive to it, but it seemed like half the women on the street were toting the bright pink shopping bags of Beautiful You. Even if half those bags were just being reused to carry sack lunches, they'd become the new status symbol for liberated, take-charge females in Union Square.

Penny mused that Max's greatest accomplishment wasn't the toys themselves. It was the idea of combining ladies' two greatest pleasures: shopping and sex. It was like *Sex and the City*, but the four playgirls didn't need Gucci belts or troublesome boy toys. They didn't even need to sip cosmos or share girl talk.

"Theoretically speaking," she began gradually, evading Tad's gaze, "what if there was a fantastically successful new consumer product? It was making its inventor a fortune."

Tad listened attentively, his thigh almost touching hers.

She tried not to think about what went into making hot dogs.

Since Maxwell's toys had gone on sale, New Yorkers seemed so laid-back. At least the half who'd made the trip to the big pink store and forked over their cash. The only tension seemed to be in the grinding teeth and toe tapping of the shoppers who were waiting. The line was longer every day. Today the *Post* carried a front-page article about a woman who'd tried to cut into the front of the queue. The frustrated shoppers already waiting there had beaten the interloper almost to death.

"Just suppose," Penny ventured, "a potential client had been crucial in the testing and development of these successful new products."

The pink bags really were ubiquitous. A city bus drove by,

the side covered with the slogan "A Billion Husbands Are About to Be Replaced."

Penny didn't especially want to tell Tad the gory details about what she'd done with Maxwell, but there were larger principles at stake.

"Let's say the person in question is a woman," she proposed, "a young innocent woman, and she allows a man to experiment on her with a number of sex-toy prototypes?"

"Hypothetically speaking," Tad confirmed, a burr in his voice. His eyebrow arched quizzically. "That sounds hot."

"Hypothetically speaking," Penny redirected, "do you think the test subject might have a claim to part ownership of the subsequent patents?"

Tad licked a dab of mustard that threatened to drip from his dog onto the pant leg of his Armani trousers. "Is the plaintiff over the age of twenty-one?"

Penny discreetly picked at the chopped onions on her own wiener. "A couple years."

"Is she someone you know personally?"

Penny nodded glumly.

"Is she very pretty?" he teased. "With flawless skin and a brilliant legal mind?"

Penny protested, "Don't be patronizing. She's not a slut. This girl could really use some sound legal advice." It might've been her imagination, but some of the ladies with bright pink bags appeared to be limping. She worried that demanding partial credit for the Beautiful You products meant she'd be culpable if they—the Dragonfly in particular—were found to be faulty and dangerous. A cut of the profits might also mean a share of the actionable blame.

Tad looked at her. His features darkened with concern. "Is the client ready to go into court and publicly describe the testing process?"

Penny swallowed. "Would that be absolutely necessary?"

"'Fraid so." He asked, "Are there any corroborating witnesses?"

Penny thought. There had been the flight crew of Max's private jet. The household staffs at his château and penthouse. And his various chauffeurs and admin assistants who at times, when she lost all control of her flailing, had been drafted to hold her spread-eagled on the bed. None of them could be subpoenaed as anything but hostile witnesses. Brightening, she said, "But there are handwritten records that we can subpoena."

"What kind of records?"

Penny considered all the names that might be in Max's notebooks. The anonymous women as well as the sex workers and the world leaders. "Would it complicate the process if those notes might be considered a threat to national security?"

"You mean," Tad asked ruefully, "if they depict the president of the United States in some compromising situations?"

He was way ahead of her. Tad Smith had a sunny, take-charge outlook on life, and Penny found that she enjoyed pulling in harness with this hopeful go-getter.

When she didn't speak, he did. "If the plaintiff will make a deposition, we can file it and begin the discovery process." He took a sip of soda. "If we get the defendant's written records and they match the deposition, your theoretical client would have a very winnable case."

Penny didn't ponder her reaction. She didn't need to. "What's our first step?"

It wasn't two days before Penny was summoned to Mr. Brillstein's office. BB&B, it seemed, had a leak. Some insider had tipped off higher-ups to the possibility of a pending lawsuit, and her boss wasn't happy. To make everything worse, the president was in town to address the United Nations, and that meant traffic in the city was gridlocked. Armed squads of antiterrorism guards were patrolling the subways with bomb-sniffing dogs. The few citizens whose tempers weren't on edge were the placid, relaxed ladies with their bright pink bags. Watching them stride, calm and unfazed, down the streets made even Penny want to get in line on Fifth Avenue.

Conversely, the male residents of the city—more specifically the hetero ones—were grouchier than ever. Not a man could compete with Maxwell's lifetime of erotic training, and the effects of his tantric studies could now be bought with a bright pink Beautiful You credit card.

Tad's idea was to immediately start by fishing for plaintiffs. They'd run a series of television ads to identify consumers who'd bought the faulty Dragonfly device and found that it broke while they were using it. Those numbers poured in by the millions. Around the world, users had fallen asleep while enjoying the deep pulsations, then awakened to find the toy in pieces. In every statement they collected the details were the same: The wings had snapped off; the body had split. Just like what Monique and Penny had experienced.

It would be difficult to prove real damages, because no one was so much as scratched in the process. Many of the women had gone to see their doctors, but no fragments of the toy could be found lodged internally.

In Tad's office, Penny stuffed her case notes into a file folder. The manila folder she stashed in her Fendi tote bag to take home. That done, she hurried to Brillstein's office on the hushed, wood-paneled sixty-fourth floor, the carpeted inter sanctum where she'd first met Max.

Outside his door, she knocked. A familiar voice said, "Come in, please." It was a female voice. Penny turned the knob, stepped through the doorway, and came face-to-face with someone she'd seen on countless newscasts. The woman's cheekbones were high and widely placed. The combination of these and her small, pointed chin gave the impression that she was always smiling. Her golden-brown eyes glowed with a warm compassion.

Penny's cantankerous boss sat behind his polished desk.

President Hind turned her serene smile on Brillstein. "Would you be so kind as to leave Miss Harrigan and me alone for a few minutes?"

"Miss Harrigan," she began.

"Penny," the younger woman prompted.

The president motioned for her to take a seat. She was roughly the same age as Penny's mother, but much more put-together. Her tailored suit fit as snug as a uniform. She wore a silver-filigree brooch on one lapel like a badge. She waited for Penny's boss to leave the room. Shutting the door, she locked it. The president motioned for Penny to sit in a red leather wing chair. She took the chair facing that, and the two sat toe-to-toe like old chums enjoying a chat.

"My dear," she said, her tone placating, "I'm here on a matter of gravest national security." She spoke as if giving a speech in the Oval Office. "Please do not pursue any legal action against C. Linus Maxwell."

Penny listened, dumbfounded. It was impossible to picture this resolute leader subjecting herself to Max's torrid exercises. Penny could scarcely imagine this well-dressed, articulate woman reduced to the chicken scratchings in a notebook. Clarissa Hind had been her role model, but the courageous leader

Penny had always imagined bore no resemblance to the person who now glanced furtively at the locked office door and spoke to her so softly.

"As a fellow attorney," continued the president, "I can empathize with your desire to see justice done, but this showdown must not be undergone in a public forum. Trust me when I say that millions of people, worldwide, will presently be put in danger by the legal actions you're about to embark upon. For you to organize this class action or contest Maxwell's patents would jeopardize their lives as well as yours."

She was no longer the pretty woman smiling on the cover of the *National Enquirer*. Three years in the Oval Office had etched wrinkles across her forehead. The president said, "I understand that you were attacked on a subway platform a few weeks ago." Her tone sounded tentative, hushed with sympathy. "That must've been terrifying, but, my dear, don't assume that it was a random crime. Whoever was hired, Max's motive was not to harm you." The president's eyes were earnest and pleading. "Maxwell was simply demonstrating his own power. For the rest of your life you must always assume that no matter where you are, he can reach out at any time and destroy you."

It struck Penny that the president was seated in the same chair Max had occupied when she had cowered at his feet. Today the carpet showed no stain to bear witness to the flood of coffee drinks. Penny thought back to the last time she'd heard this same subdued voice. Suspicion sharpened her own voice into a dart.

"How much is Max paying you?" Penny spat the accusation. "You helped him. When I answered by mistake in Paris, that was you on his telephone." She waited for a denial that didn't come. "You persuaded the FDA to approve the distribution of his . . . personal care items." Penny was livid. "People are being sold defective, dangerous sex toys, and you're helping."

The older woman continued, unfazed. "In exchange for your cooperation I'm prepared to mentor you as my political protégée."

Penny understood their plan. To avoid being exposed, Max and the president were offering her a slice of the global political pie. They would groom her to inherit their corrupt dynasty. A weaker person might've accepted, but she felt nothing but disgust for their bargain.

"It doesn't matter what office you eventually run for," the president offered. "If you side with us you'll get virtually every vote cast by women between the ages of eighteen and seventy."

Politics aside, Penny knew it was an insane promise. "You can't guarantee that," she said.

"I can't," countered Hind, "but Max can." The president lifted her wrist and slid back the sleeve of her suit jacket to check her watch. "I'm due to speak at the UN. Can we continue this discussion in the car?"

The gray Manhattan streetscape oozed by outside the limousine windows. President Hind shut her eyes for a moment and kneaded her temples with her fingertips, as if she were suffering a migraine.

"First he makes you famous," the president said in a weary voice, "so famous that you can't show your face in public." From that first paparazzi snap, she claimed that Maxwell had hired the press to hound Penny. He'd stoked the public's curiosity. He'd created the circumstances that left her trapped at home. Hind smiled ruefully, knowingly. "Eventually, the only place you feel safe is at his penthouse. He isolates you. He becomes the only person you can trust, and he provides the only comfort you know."

The tabloids that seemed to vilify him? According to President Hind, Max owned them all. He'd acquired them a few years back, when journalists started to dig a little too deep. With this arrangement, as secret owner, he could publish red herrings. He libeled himself with outrageous stories, providing a smoke screen to hide the real truth while undermining the credibility of all news media.

"Even if you discover the truth about Maxwell," the president warned, "you'll never be able to make it public. No one believes anything they read about him, not any longer." Apropos of nothing, Hind muttered as if to herself, "I never wanted to be the president of *anything*."

En route to the United Nations building, the president's cell phone rang. Settled into the leather seat, partitioned from the driver by a soundproof panel, Penny held her tongue and looked out the tinted window.

"I'm trying to reason with her," Hind told the caller. "Please don't take any action." She paused a moment, eyeing Penny. "No, I'd never tell her. And even if I did, she wouldn't believe me."

Without hearing a word on the other end of the discussion, Penny knew the caller was Max.

The motorcade moved through the streets, unhindered by traffic lights or competing vehicles. As they passed Bryant Park, Penny glimpsed a long line of people standing, waiting to enter a shop on Sixth Avenue called Bootsy. For the most part, the same consumer demographic that had gone nuts for Beautiful You was now swarming to buy a new style of shoes. It was a trend Penny couldn't understand. To her, the shoes were clunky and ugly, with wide straps across the arch and thick heels, but some group dynamic had taken hold. The same block of women, nationwide, was making a banal romance novel about vampires into a megabestseller.

The president ended her conversation and pocketed her

phone. Her attention drifted to the crowds of women waiting to buy shoes. "My relationship with Maxwell started like any other addiction," she reflected. "It was fun. I was your age. At the time I thought Max was everything I'd ever need in the world."

There was something tragic in her face as she talked about her younger, naive self. Her voice was heavy with self-disgust. "I trusted him."

Penny shifted uncomfortably in her seat. As the president talked, the younger woman's body was responding to some sexual cue. Whatever the stimulus, her nipples were almost painfully hard, so erect that even her silk lace bra felt like sandpaper against them. Perhaps it was the motion of the car, or the smell of the leather seats, but she felt a warm wetness collecting in her crotch.

President Hind asked, "Have you tried to have intercourse with anyone since him?"

Penny thought of the rapist, but shook her head: *No.*

"He thinks he's protecting us, but he's controlling us. To Maxwell it's the same thing."

By Lexington Avenue, Penny's breathing had grown so slow and labored that she had to open her mouth and gulp for air.

President Hind looked at her with sad eyes. "I asked him not to." For an evil conspirator she did something odd. From where she sat facing Penny, she leaned closer and took the trembling woman's feverish hand. "Just breathe. Just keep breathing," she said.

Clarissa Hind's voice was hypnotic. "Pretend it's like the weather, like a sudden storm. You can do nothing about it, so just be with it. Let it pass." She placed two warm fingers against the side of Penny's neck and counted silently. "There," she said. "You're returning to normal."

Cupping Penny's hands in her own, Hind entreated, "Listen!" She said, "Only one person can save the women of the world.

That person lives in a cave, high on the slopes of Mount Everest. Her name is Baba Gray-Beard, and she's the greatest living sex mystic." The president tugged Penny close and wrapped the younger woman in a warm hug. Cheek-to-cheek, Hind whispered in Penny's ear, "Go to her! Learn from her! Then you can fight Maxwell on a level playing field!"

Hind broke the embrace and sat back.

Whatever had come over Penny, the arousal was receding. She was confused, but had fully recovered by the time the car arrived at its destination. Accompanied by President Hind, she breezed through security. To Penny, the secret servicemen at the United Nations were interchangeable with the bodyguards who'd escorted Alouette on the day she'd given her deposition. They took the two women backstage. There, a makeup artist sat Hind at a mirrored dressing table and began styling her.

Reflected in the mirror, she addressed Penny. "I've told you everything I dare. If I told you more, he'd kill us both." Her eyes steely, she lifted her Dooney & Bourke purse to the counter and took out a bottle of pills. After she'd swallowed two, she replaced the bottle in the bag and zipped it shut. "Someday you'll understand." Her eyes shifting to see only her reflection, the president said, "You'll understand that what I'm about to do is my best and only option."

Madam President didn't say another word until it was time to take her place in front of delegates from every nation in the world. The chatter of the press corps fell to silence as she was introduced, and she strode confidently out from the wings to take center stage.

Growing up, especially through the arduous years of law school, Penny had all but worshipped this woman. As reported in the tabloids, Clarissa Hind had been the plucky community organizer who'd battled to improve funding for impoverished public schools in Buffalo. She'd spearheaded a drive for corporate sponsorship and gone straight to C. Linus Maxwell for a big-money donation. They'd been an immediate item in gossip columns. He'd recognized some innate quality in her and groomed her for greatness.

As Penny watched, here was the fearless international leader she'd always idolized.

"Citizens of the world . . . citizens of the United States," the president began. "I humbly stand before you. Three years ago I took the oath of office and promised to serve and protect."

Her amplified voice echoed around the vast council chamber. "I have failed."

The reaction to her words was a shocked murmur that grew as dozens of simultaneous translators delivered the equivalent message to the earphones of everyone present.

"My failure and cowardice are mine alone." As if facing a firing squad, the leader of the free world held her head high. "I only pray that the disaster I fear will never take place."

She unbuttoned her suit jacket and slid a hand inside, next to her heart. "In closing, I ask God to forgive me." She glanced at Penny standing in the wings, then cast her gaze out over the audience as if looking into eternity.

"The mistakes we make in our youth," she said solemnly, "we pay for with the rest of our lives."

There was no debating what occurred next. With the television cameras delivering the sight to viewers around the globe, Clarissa Hind, the forty-seventh president of the United States, withdrew a .35-caliber pistol from the inside pocket of her jacket. She placed the barrel of the gun to her head. And she pulled the trigger.

In the product liability department of BB&B, a disquieting pattern had begun to take shape. Over late-night cartons of Chinese takeout, Tad described how 70 percent of women who'd originally joined the proposed class-action lawsuit had withdrawn their participation. Of the remaining 30 percent, not a single potential plaintiff had filed a statement. This left them with a pool of zero women seeking damages for pain and suffering. From millions to zero.

In fact, as Tad told it, the situation was just the opposite.

Chopsticking a cold eggroll, Tad said, "It gets even weirder. All of our original respondents have purchased replacement Dragonflies from Beautiful You."

Penny dipped a sliver of barbecued pork in some spicy mustard and nibbled it, listening.

"Their brand loyalty," Tad continued, "crosses all consumer categories. These same ladies now flock to buy the same cologne for their husbands and boyfriends. They all buy the same novels from the same publisher." Microwave ovens, dog food, soap, it didn't matter. As he explained, all the products were manufactured by DataMicroCom.

Penny almost choked. "Maxwell's company!"

Tad nodded. "This tectonic shift in buying habits has made each subsidiary of DataMicroCom the sales leader in its niche."

Now Penny was confused. How did selling personal care products to 150 million women affect whole industries?

"These women in particular," Tad said, "control ninety percent of the consumer spending in the industrialized world." He sipped at his carton of egg drop soup. "The hand that rocks the cradle decides how almost all household income is spent."

Playfully Penny shook a deep-fried prawn in his face. "Oh, whatever work they do, believe me, those gals earn that money."

Tad's teeth snapped, biting the tasty crustacean and plucking it from her fingers. That was just as well, seeing how Penny had a severe shellfish allergy. Chewing, he said, "Wait until you hear *this:* According to our family law department, divorces are up by four hundred percent since Beautiful You launched. Gals are choosing gizmos over men!"

Aghast, Penny laughed, "I'm not!"

"Prove it!" Tad shot back.

Tad wanted to take their relationship to the next level, but Penny couldn't risk it. She'd been rejecting Tad for weeks. After what had happened with the attacker in the subway, she still worried that something inside her pelvis might be amiss. Tad was such a nice guy that he didn't press the issue. He was open and genuinely honest with his feelings for her. The polar opposite of Max. The last thing she wanted to do was to slash the genitals of the only serious boyfriend she'd had since college.

To change the topic of conversation, she asked, "So we have no class-action lawsuit?"

Tad shrugged. "No plaintiffs, no lawsuit."

Penny licked almond gravy off her chopsticks, thinking. "But we could still file my patent-rights brief?"

Tad sighed. He looked at her, his eyebrows arched with concern. "The deposition process might be humiliating for you. Brillstein won't pull any punches. He'll want to know the kinky details of every experiment you submitted to."

Brillstein. Penny hated him. But she knew that he'd argue her case. The firm stood to make a fortune if she won even a fraction of the profits from Maxwell's sex-tool empire.

Tad's eyes drifted to the huge ruby pendant on her chest. That souvenir. To spare his feelings, she could leave it at home. Beautiful or not, Penny resolved to stash the gem in the safety deposit box where her diaphragm resided.

She leaned over the desk and began to gather the statement forms for the product-liability case. "Let's not give up on the class-action case." She wrapped the forms with a rubber band

and headed for the door. "If you'll give me the day off tomorrow, I promise I can get us the plaintiffs we need!"

The next day Penny set off from her town house on foot. Gucci-booted, she cheerfully strutted down Fifth Avenue juggling a clumsy armload of clipboards. The pockets of her short-short Donatella Versace trench coat were stuffed to bursting with ball-point pens. Beneath the coat she wore a fun, rainbow-colored Betsey Johnson microminiskirt.

The birds chirped. The morning sun felt delectable on her smooth, bare legs, as did the appreciative, pop-eyed stares of handsome male strollers. Being at the center of such ego-boosting attention, it was hard to not get sidetracked from her legal fact-finding mission. Inevitably the warm weather lured her to take a detour through Central Park, where changes in the city's social fabric were impossible to overlook.

The usual legions of efficient British nannies and trim Swiss au pairs, those willowy young helpmates who shepherded the privileged children of wealthy Manhattanites, those girls were painfully absent. In their stead, packs of grimy, sticky-faced urchins roamed Sheep Meadow like feral coyotes. Also missing from the pastoral scene were the steadfast ranks of female third-world economic refugees who normally served as dutiful nurses and caregivers. A few elderly wheelchair-bound patients seemed to have been abandoned on the spot. Clearly these hopeless cases had been left to fend for themselves along the fringes of the park's paved pathways. As Penny sauntered past their slumped, blanket-clad forms, the odor of full diapers and colostomy bags goosed the already brisk pace of her cheerful steps.

It sounded crazy, but the few females around were either unattended prepubescent girls or drooling geriatrics. Aside from the very young and very infirm, the only women seemed to be pictures smiling from countless sheets of paper that, overnight, had been pasted up everywhere Penny looked. Lampposts . . . bus stop shelters . . . plywood construction barricades, every vertical surface in the Big Apple was covered with photocopied posters, each dominated by a photograph of a different woman. Captioning each photo were the words *Missing: Beloved Wife* or *Cherished Daughter* or *Adored Mother. Treasured Sister.* "Have you seen this woman?" the posters asked. "Missing since . . ." followed by a date within the past two weeks. To Penny they suggested tombstones, fields of headstones, as if the city were becoming a vast cemetery of women. It was really depressing. Scary, even.

Dark rumors already circulated that the new Beautiful You devices were somehow responsible. According to whispers, the early adopters had retreated to live like reclusive hermits under bridges or in unused subway tunnels. They'd left behind families and careers. Homeless now, their only allegiance was to their new personal care products.

Penny considered this frightening possibility as two overly groomed fellows jogged past her elbow. The joggers' immediate presence, so close, almost made her drop her load of clipboards. To her Midwestern eye their running shorts fit far too snugly, crassly displaying their hypertrophied buttocks and their constantly shifting, poorly supported man-parts. In the fey up-speak of a ten-year-old girl, one man commented to the other, "Let the gals have their fun!" His hale running partner replied, "I don't care if they never come back!" And the pair trotted away in a cloud of expensive cologne.

Watching them recede into the distance, suddenly Penny found her path blocked. Dead ahead stood a stranger. His short, neatly cut hair was disheveled, and the two ends of an untied necktie flapped down the front of his wrinkled suit coat. His coat, his trousers, and his shirt, they all looked as if he'd worn them to bed. "Can you help me?" he begged. His face was dark with stubble. In one hand he offered a sheet of pale-green paper. In the crook of his other arm he held a ream of the same. "Her name is Brenda," he whined, "and she's my fiancée!"

Balancing her armload of clipboards, Penny accepted the paper. It showed yet another smiling woman, a grainy head-shot enlarged and enlarged on a copy machine until the finer details were lost. She wore a Jil Sander blouse and gave the camera a dazzling grin. Below her picture were the words *CFO Allied Chemical Corp.* There was a phone number and the words *To Report a Sighting, Call Anytime, Day or Night.* Below that, the word *Reward.* Penny quickly stashed the flyer in her coat pocket, deep among her cargo of pens.

This unshaven stranger grabbed her around one wrist. His grip was painfully tight. His fingers sweaty. "You're a female," he marveled. "You've *got to help me!*" He was almost shouting. "As a woman, *you've got to take care of me!*" He barked a quick, hysterical laugh. His gaze swept hungrily up and down her remarkable body. "Oh, I haven't seen a real woman in so long!"

To escape required a swift, well-aimed kick of her Gucci boot. Her pointed toe connected with the man's groin, and Penny was able to pull away. Even before she'd landed her crippling blow, she'd noticed one final detail about the stranger. His face, his cheeks in particular . . . His skin was shining, wet with tears. He was crying.

Terrified, Penny didn't risk a second look. She took off in a mad dash toward the tapering pink tower on Fifth Avenue.

Lately, Beautiful You customers had started to call the mirrored pink building the "Mother Ship." Every dawn, the faithful patrons were out in full force. Although the doors were still locked, a line of antsy women stretched away for two city blocks. Impatiently shifting their weight from foot to foot, they all wore the same ugly, clunky shoes. Just as Penny had once waited outside the locked doors of Bonwit Teller, they waited. To a woman, they carried the same vampire romance novel. Many carried their lunches in bright pink bags to signal that they were repeat customers. Some among them looked exhausted, with lank hair and sallow faces. They made her think how Monique's pretty face had shrunken in recent weeks to a skull-like mask. Oh, and the unwashed smell that wafted from the poor girl's room . . . These days Monique didn't even call in sick, and Penny felt compelled to save her housemate's career by making excuses.

Midway down the line a middle-aged man wearing a Promise Keepers T-shirt was accosting a woman. Penny recognized the T-shirt because her dad had one exactly like it. Like an uncouth caveman the man held the woman by a fistful of hair, trying to drag her toward a taxicab that sat idling at the curb. The woman had lowered herself to a crouch, using her body weight to retain her place in the queue of early morning shoppers.

As Penny neared the struggling couple, she could hear the man saying, "Please just come home!" His words were broken by his sobs. "Johnny and Debbie miss their mommy!"

The woman, Penny guessed, was his spouse. For her part in the marital spat, the wife repeatedly clubbed her husband with something bright pink. Her weapon was floppy, flexible, and very long. On closer inspection Penny realized it was product number 6435, the Honeymoon Romance Prod. Normally it held six D batteries, and Penny could hear the weight of them slamming into the man's ribs like a bludgeon while his wife yelled, "This hunk of plastic is more of a man than you'll *ever* be!"

Gingerly, Penny sidestepped their quarrel and hurried to

the head of the line. In her arms she carried her stack of clip-boards, each already loaded with a registration form and a pen. She started her pitching with the most drained-looking women. These dead-eyed wretches stood at the locked doors as if they'd been waiting here all night. To judge from their body odor and sleepy, slouched postures, Penny thought that perhaps they had.

"Excuse me," she chirped, offering a clipboard form to the first woman. "Have you experienced a catastrophic failure of any Beautiful You product during use?"

She felt like a sex-toy ambulance chaser, but her ends would justify her means.

Shivering despite the morning warmth, the woman's ema-ciated hand accepted the pen. No intelligence shone in the stranger's expression as she turned her glazed eyes to the legal paperwork. Penny could see that she was young, but something had sucked the vitality from her. The bones showed beneath the papery skin of her face.

Penny recognized the look. After grueling rounds of ecstasy she herself would see this ghostly wretch in the mirror. Reduced to this level of exhaustion she'd been massaged and plied with hand-squeezed fruit juices. Max would order acupuncture and aromatherapy to aid in her recovery. These girls had nothing. They were dying from pleasure.

Their eyes glittered, glassy and sunken in deep hollows beneath their brows. Their clothes hung limp and heavy with dried perspiration. Their lips were slack. These had been the confident, relaxed gals who'd been striding around Union Square only a week before. It was obvious to Penny that their new toys had become a dangerous compulsion.

Jumping the gun, she told the woman, "We're organizing a class-action lawsuit to charge Beautiful You with malfeasance."

The woman croaked a response. Here, too, was a condition

Penny recognized. Often, after long bouts of testing, loud moans of ecstasy had left her own throat parched and useless.

Others edged closer, swaying, unsteady, craning their thin necks to see what Penny was up to. These curious zombies, Penny could see that their hair was breaking off at the roots, no doubt from malnutrition. Bald patches shone on their scalps. It wasn't lost on her that an earlier sexual revolution had created walking skeletons so similar to these. Not long ago, these staggering skeletal waifs would've been the victims of AIDS.

To rally them, Penny said, "You don't need another sex toy." Thrusting clipboards into every pair of hands, she said, "We need to make Beautiful You accountable for their crimes against women." By now she was shouting. "We need to shut down their business and demand reparations!"

The cadaverous girl at the head of the line swallowed. Her thin lips moved with the effort to form words. "You . . . want . . . to . . . *close* . . . them?" Her voice was a thin whine of terror. A murderous grumble echoed back along the line.

A voice called, "Wait until after I get my new Dragonfly. *Then* sue them."

Another voice charged, "Whoever she is, she's against a woman's right to own her sexual fulfillment."

A clipboard sailed through the air, barely missing Penny's head. It clattered to the sidewalk. A chorus of catcalls followed:

"She's a self-hating, body-hating antifeminist!"

"Loosen up, sister! And get your fat ass to the back of the line!"

"We've got to protect our right to shop at Beautiful You!"

A painful hail of clipboards came at Penny from every direction. The air was thick with hurled ballpoint pens and vituperative screams of female anger. This army of frustrated women was stoning her with vampire-themed paperbacks. In another minute they'd remove their clunky shoes and beat her to death. Helpless, she called out, "Maxwell is only manipulating you!" Her arms raised to ward off the hurtling books, she yelled, "He's making you into his slaves!"

As the crowd surged at her, countless hands seized Penny's hair and colorful Betsey Johnson micromini. Enraged fingers clutched her around the wrists and ankles, and she felt herself being pulled apart. Subjected to cries of "Oppressor!" and "Prude!" she was being painfully rent limb from limb. Torn to shreds.

A wild voice shrieked, "Beautiful You helped me kick my drug addiction!"

Another shrieked, "Thanks to Beautiful You I've lost seventy-five pounds!"

Almost inaudible against the animal screams of the mob, a lock clicked. A key turned, and a bolt snapped open.

Almost inaudible. "The store," Penny gasped. Faint with the effort to save herself, she gasped, "They've opened the store. . . ."

The announcement rescued her, as thousands of frantic shoppers turned en masse and stormed the big pink building. Dropped to the sidewalk, Penny curled into a protective fetal ball as countless ugly, clunky shoes stampeded past her to embrace their ultimate fate.

That night Penny slipped into a comfy pair of flannel pajamas from L.L.Bean. She went to bed early, nursing a glass of pinot gris and not a small number of clipboard-shaped bruises. After the day's aborted mission to collect plaintiffs, she'd arrived home crestfallen. She ached. Her smart micromini was grubby with handprints, and the crowd had shredded her Versace coat. She'd decided it was beyond repair and had searched the pockets for coins and chewing gum before consigning it to the trash bin. Crumbled in one pocket was the pale-green handout given to her by the frantic man in the park.

"Call anytime, day or night," it read. "Reward."

In bed, Penny smoothed the paper. She set aside her wine and retrieved the phone from her bedside table. A man's voice answered on the first ring. "Brenda?" It was the stranger. Her wrist still tingled from where he'd held her so tightly.

"No," Penny told him sadly. "I met you this morning."

"At the park," he interjected. He said he remembered because she was the only normal woman he'd seen all day. Actually all week.

"Every day," he wailed forlornly, "I pace that waiting line along Fifth Avenue, searching . . . searching . . . but Brenda is never there."

Choosing her words carefully, Penny encouraged him to talk. "Her disappearance, how did it happen?"

The man poured out his anguished tale. Feeding his grief was guilt. He had been the person who'd bought the initial Beautiful You item for her. It was supposed to be a birthday gift: product number 2788, the Instant-Ecstasy Probe. Brenda had blushed with embarrassment when she'd opened his gift in a crowded restaurant, but he'd gently encouraged her to use it. "Not right there in the restaurant," he added, insisting, "Only a tramp would submit to using a sex toy in a public restaurant."

Penny's mind flashed on her own French eatery episode with the Peruvian married stones. She squelched a twinge of embarrassment with a deep swallow of chilled pinot. Lying abed, she watched the fresh bruises on her arms shift in color from pink to red to purple. She reflected on her time in Paris and thought how it seemed as if she'd spent half her life drinking wine in bed and covered with contusions. This, it occurred to her, was how it must feel to be Melanie Griffith.

"One day," continued the man on the phone, "Brenda was the most influential power broker in the chemicals industry, and the next day . . ." His words trickled off in tired resignation. "She was gone." He'd searched her duplex co-op on Park Avenue and found that the only thing missing was the Instant-Ecstasy Probe. That was two weeks ago. Since then people had phoned to report a few sightings. One was under the rotting piers near Hoboken. Another time, security cameras in a bodega caught her shoplifting batteries in Spanish Harlem.

Listening to his account, Penny gulped her wine. She reached to where the bottle stood on the bedside table and poured another glass. She'd finished every drop by the point the lonely man's mood evolved from hopeful to fearful to savage.

His fury was audible over the phone. Even soused as she was, Penny could sense that he was red-faced and that his entire body was trembling. "If I ever meet the person who invented those demonic sex playthings . . ." He paused, choked with rage. "As God is my witness, I'm going to strangle her with my bare hands!"

The ugly shoes and fantasy novels were just the tip of a newly emerging trend. Day by day, Tad tracked the swing in shopping habits. One Monday almost sixteen million housewives abandoned the laundry detergents they'd been buying for decades and switched to Sudso, a brand introduced only the previous week. Likewise, an entire generation of female music lovers flocked to concerts by a new boy band called High Jinx. They fainted. They screamed. Watching these girls on television, Penny observed that they didn't behave very differently from the convulsions that had seized Alouette on the night of the Academy Awards.

Behavior and marketing specialists couldn't make heads or tails of the phenomenon. It was as if vast blocks of female consumers were responding to the same impulses. In the shadow of the president's self-assassination, the stock markets were a roller coaster. Share prices tumbled for almost all publicly traded companies. But, as Tad pointed out, every subsidiary of DataMicroCom was rocketing in value.

"Especially Henhouse Music," he insisted.

When the people around him responded with vacant looks, he added, "That's the record label that represents High Jinx. They've got songs in six slots of the weekly top ten."

Investors with forethought, Tad explained, were flocking to the commodities market. Manganese and potassium, specifically. Zinc, also. All the ingredients that went into the production of alkaline batteries. Speculators were bidding copper through the roof. Battery shortages had sparked riots, and a robust trade on the black market was prompting burglars to swipe half-depleted batteries from flashlights and children's toys. In the same way car break-ins had once prompted drivers to post "No Radio" placards in their windshields, now homeowners tacked highly visible "No Batteries" signs on their front doors in the hope of deterring thieves.

The whole world was struggling to make sense of what popular culture called the "Beautiful You effect." On television, pundits and analysts bantered about something known as arousal addiction. Prior to now, no one paid it heed, because it had hampered only the lives of boys. In recent decades it had been primarily young men who'd fallen victim to the crippling pleasures of sustained arousal. They'd been seduced by the soaring levels of endorphins generated by playing video games and perusing sexy

Web sites. A generation of young men had become entranced by the lure of loveless release and had fallen through the cracks of society. They were hunkered down in basement rooms heavy with the reek of their dissipation, oblivious to maintaining real relationships with actual love mates.

Penny tried to dismiss the reportage as male hysteria, but the concept was hard to ignore. According to experts, the trouble arose when our primal animal impulses were manipulated by breakthroughs in modern technology. Butter brickle ice cream was an excellent example. Its sugary, fatty goodness was exactly what our animal selves craved to survive. That was why Penny could never stop eating until the pint was empty. Her own evolutionary instincts were being used against her by product marketers. To date, arousal addiction had come to men visually, via fast-paced video games and high-speed Internet pornography, but Maxwell's new product line seemed to be having a similar effect on women.

It made perfect sense! The constantly changing stimulation was gradually rewiring their female brains. The limbic portion of the mind was awash in surges of dopamine. The hypothalamic regulation of rewards was foiled, and the prefrontal cortex was no longer in control. Oh, Penny thought as she pored over the medical studies—it was so complicated, yet so obvious!

Once addicted, ladies would binge on pleasure. The Beautiful You effect. Ordinary leisure activities would bore them. Regular pastimes would fail to hold their interest. And without the constant arousal of Maxwell's personal care products, women would lapse into severe depression.

Social commentators were quick to point out how advertising had long ago exploited men's natural sexual impulses. To sell a certain brand of beer, the media needed only to display idealized female bodies, and male buyers were hooked. This age-old tactic looked like it was exploiting women and pandering to men, but savvy observers had recognized how the minds of intelligent men were constantly being erased—their ideas, their ability to concentrate, their ability to comprehend—by each glimpse of enticing breasts and taut, smooth thighs.

It was the same way Max's Beautiful You tests had wiped Penny's mind clean of dreams and aspirations . . . of plans for the future and love for her family. The general culture had been blithely using sex to attack the brains of young males for so long that society had long ago accepted the evil practice.

Perhaps that was why the world was so quick to accept the disappearance of women into the same abyss. Artificial over-stimulation seemed like the perfect way to stifle a generation of young people who wanted more and more from a world where less and less was available. Whether the victims were men or women, arousal addiction seemed to have become the new normal.

On a rare evening outside the office, Penny and Tad had gone to a mixer at the Yale Club. Surrounded by Bucks County blue-bloods, he seemed to be immersed in his element. No, he wasn't ready to drop the class-action lawsuit, despite Penny's bruising failure to rustle up some plaintiffs. He'd adopted a sensible wait-and-see attitude. Given some time, he was certain more women would materialize to file claims. Until then, he was ready to move forward with her suit to contest the ownership of Beautiful You patents.

That was another reason to venture out tonight and have some fun. Tomorrow Penny would be confronted by the senior partners of BB&B and she'd be compelled to give her deposition.

At the Yale Club, Penny admired the casual way Tad wore his tuxedo. He greeted some of the wealthiest people in New York as old friends. He was a keeper for sure. If only he didn't keep pressuring her for vaginal intercourse. They'd done pretty much everything else, but Penny couldn't risk hurting him. Nor did she care to explain her growing fear to him.

Lost in these thoughts, she collided with another guest. A few drops of champagne were spilled, but no permanent damage was done. The tall, bearded man looked familiar.

"You are Penny Harrigan, no?" He offered his hand. "I am Pierre Le Courgette."

It was the prizewinning novelist who'd been dating Alouette at the time of her death.

"It was very sad," he said.

Penny squeezed his arm. "You must miss her very much. She was so lovely."

Wistfully, he replied, "Do not be mistaking me. We were not intimate lovers."

Penny waited for him to say more.

"We tried many times," he admitted, "but I could not know her in that way."

Dread washed over Penny. She pictured the blood gushing from her attacker's erection in the subway.

"Something . . . inside my Alouette," he began, but his voice trailed off in misery.

Penny risked finishing his confession. "Did something jab you?"

"Jabbed?" he asked, confused by the word in English.

"Like a harpoon," she coaxed. "Something impaled your penis."

His eyes flashed with understanding. *"Oui!"* he cried. *"Mon dieu!* It was hidden there, inside her *chatte.* She was convinced that Maxwell had left some tool inside her, although the doctors could find nothing." He reached to grip her by the elbow and steady her, saying, "My dear, what do you know of Alouette's condition?"

Penny reeled. The room spun. Was this the secret Alouette had planned to tell her over lunch?

At this Tad materialized and slipped an arm possessively around her waist. "I think it's bedtime for somebody." He held her so close she could feel his erection through the thin fabric of his tuxedo pant leg.

There it was again. He was pressuring her for sex. Just out of her growing irritation Penny was almost ready to let Tad take that dangerous chance.

The following day, on the sixty-fifth floor, seated in a conference room where she'd delivered so many extra chairs in the past, Penny gave her deposition. The only employee of the firm not present was Monique. Poor Monique was still barricaded behind her bedroom door. Otherwise, Penny faced associates and partners on all sides. Their expectant eyes scoured her for traces of falsehood. Any nervous tic might suggest she was lying. A microphone collected her words as she described the first night Maxwell had filled her with the pink-champagne douche. A stenographer scribbled notes as quickly as Max had.

The majority of her coworkers listened, spellbound. Their jaws hung in disbelief as she haltingly described the process by which Maxwell had battered her cervix to racking spasms of fulfillment.

Periodically, Brillstein fired off questions to challenge her. "Miss Harrigan, you said earlier that Mr. Maxwell placed a hand inside your vaginal orifice. How is that possible?"

The memory shocked and excited Penny. With the entire firm watching, she stammered, "I don't know."

"Take your time, sweetheart," Tad assured her. He gave her a wink and a quick thumbs-up. "You're doing great!"

Relentlessly, ruthlessly, Brillstein continued. "Would you say, Miss Harrigan, that your anatomy was especially suited for such extensive exploration?"

Penny bridled. "Are you asking if I'm a slut?"

"I'm inquiring," Brillstein sneered, "whether you contributed any unique abilities to the research process." He said *unique* as if it were a dirty word.

"There were times I almost *died*," Penny shot back. She tried not to fidget under his penetrating gaze.

"From the pain?" Brillstein hated her.

"Not exactly." With eyes in every direction, the only safe place for Penny to look was the floor.

Brillstein redirected. "You mentioned how Mr. Maxwell had made an exhaustive study of all things erotic. . . ."

In turn Penny told them what she could remember about the various swamis and courtesans Max had mentioned. She described Baba Gray-Beard, Max's primary mentor, and how the great woman lived high in the Himalayas in a hermit's cave, where he had sought her out. Penny related how the ancient teacher had mentored her billionaire student in erotic techniques that dated back to the dawn of human evolution. Penny did not mention Clarissa Hind and how the doomed president had urged Penny to also seek out and study with the fabled crone. Why drag the tormented president's memory through this?

Again, Brillstein interrupted her. "If my questions seem antagonistic, Miss Harrigan, please understand that I'm doing you a great favor. The counsel defending Mr. Maxwell won't be any easier on you."

Penny steeled herself. Shoulders squared, chin held high, she waited.

His eyes leered. "You're saying that you allowed Mr. Maxwell to anally stimulate you in a posh French chow hall?" Brillstein was grilling her with relish. His gaze was dissecting her body the same way so many wealthy strangers had tried to analyze her sensual secrets at Parisian parties. His clear assumption was that she was a deranged nympho in the sack.

In icy tones she replied, "Maxwell and I were coresearchers." She sensed he was preparing to fire his big guns. Despite the steady incoming rush of air-conditioning, the conference room felt like a sauna. Men pulled at their collars and loosened their ties. The few female associates seemed to swoon in empathy with her, fanning themselves with whatever legal documents were at hand.

"Is it true"—Brillstein consulted his notes—"that on the date of April seventeenth, between the hours of seven and eight p.m., you affirmed to Mr. Maxwell that you'd enjoyed forty-seven distinct orgasms brought on by what you now refer to as 'research'?"

Penny stiffened. It was true, but there was no way Brillstein could have those numbers. She hadn't mentioned them. He could only know those details if he'd conferred with Maxwell himself. The realization chilled her: Brillstein was secretly allied with Max.

Emboldened, Brillstein pressed his point. "For one full hour your heart rate averaged a hundred and eighty beats per minute." Referring to his notes, he read, "Your respiration was a hundred and ninety-one breaths per minute." These facts were clearly gleaned from Max's little notebook. "Doesn't that seem like sufficient reward for your participation in this so-called experiment?" He smiled a self-satisfied grin, his beady eyes daring her to deny his implication.

Not waiting for her reply, the senior partner clicked a button that was installed in the conference room tabletop. A projection screen quickly lowered from the ceiling. Another button brought a video projector to life, and screams roared from unseen speakers. Monstrously enlarged, the shape of a nude woman filled the screen. She rolled on her back amid white satin pillows, her fingers clutching white satin bedsheets. The hilt of something bright pink protruded from between her thighs. When her frenzied thrashing threatened to dislodge the pink instrument, the hand of an unseen man entered the shot. It pressed the tool fully into place. One of the fingers wore a ring set with a huge ruby.

It was Max's hand. It was Penny on-screen, heaving like a sexed-up Hottentot.

"Miss Harrigan," asked Brillstein, sneering at the video, shouting to be heard above the torrent of her recorded grunting, "how do you explain *this?*"

Penny looked to Tad for support, but he'd turned away. Resting his elbows on his knees, he was covering his face with his hands, shaking his head in despair.

It was one thing to discuss the testing process using lofty verbal legalese, but to actually see Penny wallowing, near-insane with wild animalistic release . . . spitting vulgar obscenities . . . she didn't look like a dedicated, hardworking scientist. During that scorching moment of humiliation, with scores of legal minds wondering whether she was a wronged coinventor or just a wanton harlot, Penny heard a familiar racket. A loud thrumming rebounded from the office towers around their building. A helicopter was preparing to set down on the roof two floors above them.

Penny didn't need to ask. She knew who was arriving.

The video stopped. The screen disappeared up into the ceiling.

"Gentlemen," Brillstein announced, "should we move on? We've got another lengthy deposition to take this afternoon."

As the weary attorneys rose from their seats and began to vacate the room, Brillstein offered Penny his hand. "If you don't mind a little advice, young lady," he said, "I think you'd be very foolish to pursue this claim."

Penny let him steer her toward the door.

As they parted company in the hallway, he asked whether she'd perform a favor for him.

Stunned, mute, she nodded.

"If you'd be so kind," he asked, his voice dripping with contempt, "please tell your little friend Monique she's fired!"

"Please don't be mad at me, honey." It was Penny's mom calling from Omaha.

Penny had been at the kitchen table, reading the newspaper when the telephone rang. All the day's news was about the late president. Officially the White House wasn't offering any explanation, but a fact-finding commission had issued its report. According to the security protocols the commander in chief was seldom searched or directed through metal detectors. It was always assumed that she would be the target. Not the shooter. Hind had been both. The vice president—a man, of course—had been hastily sworn in. Talk radio's bombastic pundits were blaming the self-assassination on menopause.

With the gun so close to the microphones, the noise had been deafening. Penny's ears were still ringing, and she had to concentrate to hear her mother speaking from Omaha.

Weighing her words carefully, the Nebraska housewife said, "I bought some of those Beautiful You doohickeys."

Penny held her breath.

At that confession, her mother's voice changed pitch, rising to a girlish squeal. "Why didn't you tell me?" she exclaimed. "The feeling is incredible! This is why God made me a woman!"

Penny tried but couldn't get a word in.

"Your father had been sulking in his woodshop all week." More bashfully, she offered, "They're not made to last, are they?"

Penny interrupted: "Which one broke?"

Her mother's blush was audible. "God only knows how those engineers product-test the durability of those things. I really gave it quite a torture test. Worse than John Cameron Swayze used to give to Timex wristwatches."

Vaguely, Penny remembered the watch's advertising slogan: *It takes a licking and keeps on ticking.*

"Until it broke"—her mother gasped—"I was having the time of my life!"

Penny crossed her fingers. "Which appliance was it?"

Please don't be the Dragonfly, she prayed.

"It was the Dragonfly."

"Mom!" Penny protested.

Oblivious, her mother prattled on. "Have you got a pair of those new shoes everyone is so crazy for?" With the chatty enthusiasm of a teenager she said, "Well, call me crazy, too. Those shoes are so ugly, but the TV commercials give me a little tingle inside. Just seeing those shoes on television, I'm tickled pink."

Earlier that day, Penny had knocked on her housemate's bedroom door. She'd not had the heart to deliver the bad news about Monique being fired for absenteeism. Instead, she'd stood in the hallway and rattled the locked doorknob while repeating, "Open up." She'd put her ear to the wood and listened to the ominous buzzing sound that emanated from within. "Open up," she'd demanded. "We need to get you some help."

Finally, the door had opened a crack. The stench was appalling. The crack was just wide enough for Penny to see a skull-like face framed in untidy braids. "Girlfriend," the skull had said in a rasping voice, "you need to go fetch me some batteries." The door had slammed. The lock had snapped shut. Once more, Penny had heard the muffled sound of humming.

It was maddening that now her own mother was threatened by the same terrifying obsession. Trying to redirect the older woman's attention, Penny asked, "Have you checked out those back issues of the *National Enquirer* like we talked about?"

Automatically, Penny's fingers rose to her own neck. Her pulse was 127. Time with Max had made her compulsively aware of her own vital signs.

Her mother didn't respond, not right away. It might've been Penny's imagination, but she thought she heard a distant humming over the phone. "Mom?" she asked, "is Dad using the chain saw?"

"I keep meaning to tell you," her mother said, "your father might be calling you." Her voice dropped to a whisper. "He wants to put me into a straitjacket and trundle me off to a loony bin." Exasperated, she hissed, "Just because I'm fulfilling myself so much."

"The tabloid research, Mom?" Penny persevered. "You were going to find out about Maxwell's childhood?"

Her mother changed the subject. "What are you up to tonight?"

Penny counted 131 beats per minute. "Tonight?" She needed to test something. "I'm inviting a friend over for the evening."

"Someone special?" her mother asked.

"Yes," Penny replied, without a trace of irony in her tone. "I'm spending the evening with someone very special."

Brillstein must've seen her name on his caller ID, because he answered on the second ring. His voice hushed, husky with desire, he breathed, "Yes?"

In the background, a matronly woman's voice asked, "Honey? Who's calling so late?"

"It's no one," he shouted away from the receiver. "Just work. I might have to run into the office for a few hours."

After she gave her address in a breathless purr, Penny hung up and ran to her wardrobe. She ransacked the enormous closets, looking for the most scandalous negligee. On a shopping spree in Paris she'd collected dozens of lurid teddies and nighties, hoping one would spur lust in Maxwell. None had. But this evening she selected a narrow strip of marabou feathers which had been artfully dyed dark purple. The way it was worn, it trailed down her otherwise nude torso, leaving her breasts exposed and only partially obscuring her vulva.

With moments remaining before Brillstein arrived, she turned on the chandelier in the town house foyer and took a position that would allow its light to throw her shadow against the inside of the frosted-glass front door. Waiting there, she undulated her hips in a way that would make her shadow look enticing from the street.

She stood undulating in ludicrously high heels—another purchase she'd hoped would pique Max's lust. Her trap was set. The doorbell rang: *ding-dong*.

"It's open," Penny called in as sultry a voice as she could muster.

Brillstein shouldered his way inside, panting as if he'd run every step of the way. Catching sight of her in her marabou splendor, he smacked his wrinkled lips with great gusto and said, "Well, just as I suspected . . . It is a spicy little whore, after all."

Penny sidestepped his lunge. Luring him through the spacious rooms, she allowed her hands to roam up and down the silken curves of her body. "Oh, Mr. Brillstein, oh!" She giggled and dodged another grab. "How long I've wanted this to happen!"

The foolish lecher was already discarding his overcoat, his

shirt, his pants. He trailed her around sofas and tables, always a step too late to snatch at her young, supple skin.

Baiting him, Penny asked coyly, "Are you working on behalf of Maxwell?" She giggled and flitted away.

Brillstein smirked. He wiped drool from his lips with the back of one discolored hand. A cat ready to munch on a very sexy canary.

Sulking, pretending to be offended, Penny evaded yet another grab and asked, "How did you know so many details about Max's notes?"

His Brooks Brothers boxer shorts were tented in her direction, and his porcine, hairy hips were already bucking in helpless anticipation. His withered buttocks clenched, thrusting his engorged groin. Frustrated little growls rose from his throat. "Let me catch you," he promised, "and I'll tell you everything."

She led him upstairs to her bedroom. There she feigned arousal, mewing and wriggling in the same counterfeit way that had enraged Maxwell. Brillstein didn't seem to notice that her heart rate remained flat. Neither did she sweat. He climbed atop her on the bed and bullied her legs apart. Shucking his undershorts, he made no pretense of giving her pleasure. A trickle of clear slime dripped from his erection as he stroked it against her. Smearing this discharge against her hairless skin, he crooned, "So smooth! So *smooth*!"

He merely spit on his hand and applied this sickening gob of saliva to her. He was having some difficulty hitting a moving target, so Penny stilled her loins a moment as he entered.

Giving a single shove, he drove his full length into her. She gripped handfuls of his wasted flesh and tightened her hold in preparation for the worst. All this time, she was praying that her theory was correct.

It was. Before he could withdraw for his second thrust, Brillstein began to bellow like a knife-stuck Nebraskan hog. He thrashed to escape, but her strong fingers held his flesh firmly between her legs. Whatever it was, something within her was hurting him, and Brillstein begged to be released. His spotted hands pushed and slapped at her, but Penny held tight.

"Tell me!" she demanded, driving her hips upward to keep him well inside her vaginal torture chamber. "Tell me what Maxwell is doing!"

Brillstein howled. Whatever Max had planted within her, it was doing its guard-dog duty.

"Did he have anything to do with Alouette's death?" she demanded. "Did he kill her because of the palimony suit?"

"Yes," Brillstein screamed. "You're hurting me!"

Shouting directly into his red, straining face, Penny demanded, "Does this have anything to do with Beautiful You?"

"I don't know!" He sobbed, twitching as if swarms of hornets were stinging his buried manhood.

If he was bleeding inside of her, Penny didn't care. Her best friend and her precious mother were in danger. Millions of women were threatened. Continuing her inquisition, grilling him the way he'd grilled her at the deposition, she demanded, "What is Maxwell's evil plan?"

"I don't know!" he wailed piteously.

At this, she released her deathlike grip on his sweat-soaked butt, and the weeping senior partner threw himself from her embrace. Bleeding copiously, through gritted teeth he said, "Maybe your IUD or something's slipped."

Stepping to the bathroom for rubbing alcohol and cotton swabs, Penny couldn't help but feel vindicated. Brillstein's small confession had confirmed her worst suspicions. There actually was a conspiracy. When she doused his damaged privates with the harsh antiseptic, her boss screamed and screamed. His blood still streaming down the insides of her thighs, she yanked a suitcase from her walk-in closet and began packing it with Vera Wang. At the same time she ordered her phone, "Siri, lease me a jet from JFK to Nepal, with one connection through Omaha, Nebraska. For when? For tonight!"

Before fleeing her town house, Penny had shoved her boss out the front door naked and bleeding, his clothes bundled in his arms. She'd also gone to Monique's locked door and knocked, saying, "Mo? Can you hear me?" She began sliding blueberry Pop-Tarts through the crack at the bottom. "Eat something," she urged. "Try to stay hydrated. I'll be back as quick as I can."

Her only answer was the familiar muted buzzing that had resonated from the bedroom for days.

As she raced through the concourse at JFK she noted, distractedly, that she saw no other women. From the ticket agents to the travelers, everyone was male. By all appearances women had ceased to exist in the public sphere.

To avoid drawing the focus of hostile men—New York City was turning into a sexual powder keg!—she'd prudently dressed in a vintage Yves Saint Laurent pantsuit. The look was a touch mannish, especially when paired with a ribbed white turtleneck that minimized the appearance of her stunning bustline. She'd coiled her abundant hair beneath a knitted watch cap, and wore no more than a smudge of sparkling lip gloss. Walking, she rolled her shoulders and affected a brusque swagger. If she caught the eye of a passing stranger she'd look like nothing more than a hip young sailor on shore leave.

Whoever it was at BB&B who had leaked word of the pending lawsuit to President Hind, that same source had apparently slipped the news to the tabloid media. At airport newsstands, the headlines blared: "Cinderella Penny Harrigan Invents Sex

Toys!" Front-page stories detailed her claims that her eroge-nous zones had perfected the Beautiful You carnal gadgetry. To accompany the story, each newspaper ran a photo of Penny's head sunk into a white satin pillow. Her crossed eyes and the slack tongue hanging out of her mouth confirmed that these photos were screen captures from the video Max had shot in Paris. The images were astoundingly sexy, but they hardly made her look like the ergonomic genius the tabloids claimed her to be.

Seated safely in the plush cabin of a chartered jet, Penny propped open her laptop and began to surf. It took only a few headlines to buttress her worst fears. For the first time in its history the National Organization of Women was canceling its annual conference due to lack of participants. Six weeks ago the roster had been almost filled, but in the days since Beautiful You had launched, all of the delegates had canceled their plans to attend. Some cited more personal interests they wanted to pursue. The rest claimed to be exploring alternative avenues to self-fulfillment. Whatever the case, with no active members and no conference, NOW teetered on the brink of nonexistence. Likewise, when Penny phoned the national office for the League of Women Voters, a recorded message told her that the organization was experiencing a temporary staff short-age and would be closed for an indefinite period of time. The female members of the Senate and House of Representatives had missed roll call for almost a week.

Fear bloomed in Penny's heart, but she kept on surfing.

In a seemingly unrelated story, all of the female members of the U.S. Olympic team had resigned. Every great female athlete—from field hockey players to gymnasts to figure skaters—was choosing to stay home and eschew a chance of winning the gold. Another news feature described how all of the altos and sopranos were AWOL from the Mormon Tabernacle Choir.

Almost 100 percent absentee rates were being reported among women in all the helping professions.

Meanwhile, according to the Web sites that reported business, the stock of DataMicroCom was sky-high. All of its subsidiaries, Beautiful You in particular, were reporting record sales.

In Omaha, a plain white van waited on the arrivals level of the airport to collect her.

"Penny," a voice called from the driver's seat. It was her father. His expression was puzzled as he asked, "Pen-Pen, why are you dressed like a sailor?"

The door on the side of the van slid open. A stranger crouching within shouted, "Get in, quick." He motioned for her to hand over her suitcase, saying, "We need to go rescue your mother!"

The stranger's name was Milo, and he was the leader of the local chapter of Promise Keepers, the chapter her dad attended. The van was Milo's, and the back was mostly empty except for a first-aid kit, some folded blankets, and an ominous coil of nylon rope. As her father drove them through the silent late-night streets of Omaha, Milo and Penny scanned the sidewalks and alleys for the missing woman. Milo plunged the needle of a syringe through the rubber cap on a bottle and drew it full of some clear liquid. In a seedy neighborhood, they spied someone wearing a bathrobe and pushing a rattling chrome shopping cart. Her hair hung in her face. Her runny eyes were swollen. The woman's bare legs were streaked with dirt. In the basket of the cart jiggled an assortment of soiled, dulled pink Beautiful You products. A cardboard sign was taped to the side of the cart. Hand-lettered in black felt-tipped pen, it read: "Will Work 4 Batteries."

"Pull up here," Milo whispered. "Don't spook her."

He rolled open the side door before they'd come to a complete stop. The woman standing near the shopping cart hardly had time to register their arrival before Milo was charging toward her with a blanket spread open between his hands. He threw the blanket around her and the pair fell to the ground. The woman was screaming now, fighting Milo as he held her wrapped. He shouted, "The rope! Bring me the roll of duct tape!"

Penny cowered in the van, but her father leaped from behind the steering wheel and grabbed the coil of rope. Together, the two men trussed up the woman in the bathrobe and carried her quickly back to their vehicle. Through all of this, she was screaming, "Not without my playthings! Let me have my toys!"

Milo slid the heavy door shut and Penny's father hit the gas, peeling rubber. Behind them the abandoned shopping cart and its sad cargo receded into the distance.

The entire abduction had taken less than ninety seconds. In the dark back of the van the kidnapped woman continued to shriek until Milo plunged the syringe into her arm.

Still breathing hard, but driving slower, her father said, "I'm sorry you had to see that, sweetheart."

Only now did Penny recognize the sedated wretch wrapped in rope on the floor.

It was her mother.

"Look at her, the poor woman," Milo said compassionately, as he sealed her mouth with duct tape. "We need to deprogram her." They drove through picturesque streets and neighborhoods Penny recalled from childhood.

Her dad described how her mom had quickly spiraled into madness. He and fellow members of their church had staged

146

an intervention and confronted Penny's mom about her Beautiful You compulsion, but she denied she had a problem. Tonight they were taking her home, where they could keep her tranquilized while she'd undergo a series of hypnosis and aversion therapies to help manage her self-destructive behavior.

Penny wasn't surprised that she'd failed to recognize this ranting maniac. Her mother's face was jaundiced and lined with exhaustion. At the family home they carefully carried the trussed body up the porch steps and through the front door. Once the patient was safely stripped of her clothing, and her wrists and ankles were tied to the bedposts of an attic bed for her own protection, Penny ventured to the basement, where her mother's collection of *National Enquirers* filled floor-to-ceiling shelves. Each shelf was labeled with years and months which corresponded with the back issues, but Penny didn't have to look far. Set aside in a stack were issues that contained the facts pertaining to C. Linus Maxwell. Bless her mother, Penny thought. The beleaguered wretch had gotten this far in her research, winnowing out these precious copies from the thousands she'd hoarded over the past half century.

After fixing herself a well-deserved cup of cocoa, Penny carried the tabloid newspapers to a favorite overstuffed chair near the fireplace in the living room and began to read.

There wasn't much new information to be gleaned. Maxwell had been born as Cornelius Linus Maxwell, January 24, 19— at Harborview Medical Center in Seattle. There was no record of his father. His mother had raised him by herself. She'd had no other children.

He'd attended the University of Washington, but dropped out his junior year when his mother had been killed. It was

rumored that he'd abandoned his studies in order to apprentice to some mystic in the Himalayas. Less savory gossip
placed him in far-flung brothels and covert medical facilities,
where anything could be bought. Debauched sex . . . designer
drugs . . . whatever the case, Corny Maxwell had disappeared
for six years. Within a few months of his reappearance he'd
allied himself with the youthful, ambitious Clarissa Hind.

In an issue dated ten years ago the business section of the
Enquirer contained a ten-part series about DataMicroCom's
ongoing research projects. Over the following ten installments,
the tabloid detailed how Max had become a pioneer in the
field of tiny-robot technology. Called "nanobots" or "nanites,"
these were robots so small they were measured in millionths of
a meter. They were hardly larger than molecules. Science had
always bored Penny, but she found the reading fascinating. The
primary application for nanobots was in medicine. More cor-
rectly referred to as "nanomedibots," these robots were so infinitesimal that they could travel freely through the bloodstream
or neural pathways and repair damaged tissue on a molecular
level.

An in-depth feature in the science section of the *National
Enquirer* filled in the picture. Some nanobots were designed
to scour veins and arteries, removing dangerous buildups of
plaque. Other swarms of nanobots sought out cancerous tissue
and killed it with heat or targeted chemotherapy.

A faint voice in Penny's head whispered, *And some nanobots
leak out of personal care products and hijack the crura of your clitoris!*

She searched for more news about nanobot development,
but the newspaper articles arrived at a dead end. Following a
decade of groundbreaking work in the field of miniature robots,
DataMicroCom had apparently dropped the entire matter. A
small follow-up article quoted Max as saying that nanobots

weren't cost-effective. He'd closed the bot division and redirected those resources toward the development of the more lucrative Beautiful You line of products.

Shocked, Penny remembered the episode in the president's limousine. Without any apparent stimulus she had felt herself becoming aroused. And not merely aroused—she'd been building toward an orgasm. Her entire awareness had been reduced to the tips of her erect nipples and clit. Only the president's gentle assurances had coaxed her through the tidal wave of erotic frenzy.

She thought of Alouette's breakdown onstage at the Kodak Theatre. And of her own bedeviled mother, bound to the bed upstairs. It was the broken item: the Dragonfly. The idea sounded crazy, like some conspiracy that a frothing-at-the-mouth women's libber might propose. But it was possible that the toy hadn't broken so much as it had *hatched*. Its body had split, releasing swarms of microscopic robots small enough to navigate upstream through her cervix into her uterus. Small enough to pass through the blood barrier in her ovaries and travel throughout her nervous system. Even to her brain. Who knew how they might be affecting her behavior and perceptions?

On her flight from New York, Penny had read about a crowd of twenty thousand female shoppers who rioted in Times Square, fighting one another for the chance to buy a new perfume. Likewise, in Rome, female shoppers were battling to lay their hands on a new face cream that was being heavily advertised.

That X-ray Penny had had after her attack on the subway platform, of course it'd shown nothing. Nanomedibots were smaller than anything a diagnostic tool could detect. And now, Penny realized, now they were implanted in tens of millions of women throughout the industrialized world.

If Brillstein was to be believed, and Max had caused Alouette's death, then perhaps the nanobots could do more than bring pleasure. Perhaps they could also kill.

Penny finished her mug of cocoa, then slowly climbed the stairs to the attic. In the darkness her father and Milo stood over the nude form of her mother writhing in bondage, moaning and gagged with duct tape.

"We can't cure her," Milo was saying bravely, "but we can curtail her self-destructive habits." The men knelt on either side of the bed and began to pray quietly into clasped hands. Fresh syringes and bottles of tranquilizer crowded the top of a bedside table.

Looking on, helpless, Penny wondered whether she might be correct. Nanobots might be behind her mother's wild sexual acting-out.

"Dad," she said. "I have to go."

Her father looked up, stricken. "You know, Pen-Pen, back when your mother and I lived in Shippee, the doctors warned us that she could never have children."

Penny listened. She'd never heard this. She checked her watch. The jet was already waiting on the tarmac.

Gazing down on his wife's dazed, helpless form, Penny's dad said, "Every expert we saw said she'd never have a baby. That's why you were such a miracle."

Penny stepped closer and hugged him around the neck.

Still kneeling, he smiled up at her. "You were our little gift from God." In a hopeful tone, he said, "If God can give us a daughter as wonderful as you . . ." He reached up and mussed her hair. "Then maybe God can deliver your mom from this hideous affliction."

Milo looked on, beaming with simple faith. Penny's naked, deranged mother was in good hands. "Stay," Milo insisted brightly. "Stay and bake us something!"

Penny checked her text messages. "The pilot says the weather is getting thick. We'll need to take off within the hour."

"Where to?" her dad asked. The poor man. His whole world was falling apart.

Her voice cold and resolute, in the voice of a stranger, Penny said, "To Nepal." She repeated, "I have to go to Nepal."

The yak would only carry Penny so high up the rocky slopes of the Himalayas. After the remote hamlet of Hop Tsing she was forced to ride the narrow, bony backs of Sherpas the last three almost-vertical miles. And even they would not take Penny the full way. As a distant cave came into view, the Sherpas trembled with fear. Muttering oaths to ward off evil, they lowered her to the sun-baked ground and began to retrace their steps. When she protested, one stout fellow pointed toward the distant cave and babbled in his native talk, hysterical.

Penny had no other choice but to continue on alone.

As she scaled the crumbling stone face of the mountain, she could picture Maxwell making this same pilgrimage as a young man. In Paris, he'd described spending years with this strange, aged mystic. He had presented himself to her as a willing apprentice, and she had agreed to mentor him in the most esoteric ways of the tantric. Despite his youthful vigor, Maxwell said those years practicing sex magic with the crone had almost killed him.

In fact—and this detail frightened Penny—he said the cave where the mystic dwelt was littered with the skeletons of men and women she had sexed to death. Their bones frozen in Kama Sutric positions of unbearable erotic contortion.

With her Louis Vuitton roller bag strapped to her back, she inched higher, clinging to toeholds in the sheer stone wall.

Remembering the tales of orgasmic agony Max had told, she almost hoped the mystic had died. It had been a decade since anyone had seen her. The dry, icy winds threatened to pluck her fingertips from the thin cracks at which she clawed. Native birds dived at her, pecking and scratching to protect their nearby nesting grounds. The stench of guano was overpowering.

What choice did she have? Even the president had sworn this was the only means to counter Maxwell's plot. By murdering Alouette in such a public fashion, he'd proved he could murder anyone, anywhere. He held millions hostage whether they knew it or not. Even if they discovered the nanobots, it was too late.

Only Baba Gray-Beard might offer an antidote . . . a treatment . . . a training that could counteract the legions of implanted microrobots.

A gust of wind tugged at Penny, tearing her grip from the rocks. In desperation, she unbuckled the Prada belt that held the suitcase to her back and watched it plummet into the void below her. It seemed to fall forever, turning in the air slowly before exploding in a burst of vividly colored Anne Klein separates. Unencumbered, she climbed faster. By midday, she felt exhausted as she hauled herself over the lip of the cave. It was unoccupied.

According to Max, Baba Gray-Beard spent most of her lonely days creeping about the steep cliff faces, gathering the lichen and mosses that constituted her meager diet. She subsisted on pillaging the eggs of cliff-nesting birds. Many of her aphrodisiac salves and poultices were formulated from the wild fungi she foraged. Her nights, Max said, she spent alone. For two centuries she'd lived in such solitude, exploring new, ever more powerful ways to pleasure herself. These were the techniques the Baba had schooled into Max and that he was co-opting in the mass-produced products of Beautiful You.

Just as he'd described, the cave was populated by skeletons and desiccated cadavers of people who appeared to have expired in the grip of extreme climaxes. Among the deceased were other items. Man-made items. These were the crude prototypes of what Maxwell had perfected and tested on Penny. Here, crafted from dried reindeer antlers and lashed together with animal sinews, were the erotic inventions of the solitary Baba. To endure innumerable nights of isolation, she had crafted and perfected these many devices for stimulating herself. Her boundless solitude had yielded this treasure trove of sensual tools.

Penny crossed the cave and examined them. Some, carved of living rock and polished to a glassy smoothness, were obviously designed to abrade the perineal sponge. Others were fashioned of bird bones and wrought to excite the clitoral legs that encircled the vagina. Still others had clearly been used rectally.

Evil Maxwell. With a single glimpse of these ingenious sex toys, the inventions of this aged hermit, he must've known that their power would overwhelm and enslave the civilized female. Each was astounding, and Penny marveled over them, not noticing that a stooped figure had climbed into the cave's entrance and was shambling toward her.

A creaking, quavering voice said, "I have a guest."

Penny spun around and caught sight of a hag who strongly resembled the surrounding devices and skeletons. Baba Gray-Beard was herself sculpted of bones and tendons, a knotted tangle of dried muscles and gray hairs. Her eyes shone like two moonstones, entirely white with thick cataracts. Her wasted body was unclothed, and her namesake abundance of ratted, off-white pubic hair had grown so long that it swept the ground between her bare feet.

Maxwell had said she was blind. The Baba, he said, found her way along the cliffs, climbing and hunting entirely by touch and smell. She knew the feel of every cleft and crevice in these mountains. She knew the distinct scent of every dirty crack.

She lifted her nose and sniffed the dank air. In a weathered voice, she said, "Do I detect a young, fresh pussy?"

Penny held stock-still. She quieted her breathing.

"Do not try to hide your smell," the crone chided. "It has been many years since I have had a student." She lowered a ragged pack from her back and began to remove clumps of moss from it. Carefully she lifted out small bird eggs, while saying, "From your odor alone, I know you arrive here from New York City, and that you come by way of Omaha."

Maxwell had warned that the Baba could tell a person's entire sexual history from the taste of his or her genitals.

"Expose yourself," the hag beckoned. "Let your flavor tell me all the truths that you cannot." She took another step closer, but waited.

Penny knew that she had no choice. Her mother and her best friend might be dying. A vast segment of the population was implanted with a power they refused to believe existed. Slowly she slipped off her Christian Louboutin shoes. Followed by her DKNY slacks and blouse. Lastly she lowered her Agent Provocateur panties. Each item she folded and carefully laid over a large rock.

When Penny was nude except for her Victoria Secret Miracle Bra, she stood and waited.

Baba Gray-Beard waddled up to her. The spotted crone petted between Penny's thighs with a trembling hand, croaking, "Ah!" Marveling, she whispered, "You have no hair. Is this Maxwell's malevolent doing?"

It was, but Penny was too frightened to speak. She nodded. It was the Uzbek tribal method with aloe and pine nuts.

The Baba proudly tapped a wizened fingertip on the cracked skin of her own chest. The constant tug of dry, icy winds had stretched her breasts until they flapped like leathery dugs. She nodded and smiled to herself. "It was I who taught him that technique."

Without hesitating in her caresses, the hag lifted the same bent finger toward Penny. Inserting just the gnarled tip of the finger, she said, "Little one, your vagina is so juicy!"

Like a dried twig, knobby and brittle, the rest of the finger slid inside as far as the knuckle. The old woman cackled. "So receptive, too! You will make an excellent student, my dear!"

As the centuries-old recluse probed her, Penny tried to remember all the things she loved in the world. Things like the carriage ride she and Tad had taken through Central Park. And butter brickle ice cream. And Tom Berenger movies. She thought of Fendi purses and summer carnivals with Ferris wheels and cotton candy. Wistfully, she recalled how much she'd admired Clarissa Hind, and how excited she'd been to see the first female president sworn into office.

When she could no longer dredge up pleasant thoughts, Penny squirmed in futile resistance to the old witch's finger. It seemed to be exploring the deepest recesses of her psyche.

After much poking about, the finger withdrew. It glistened in the dim light of the cave for only a moment before it disappeared between the hag's puckered lips. Sucking at it, the Baba groaned with understanding. She pulled the finger from her craw and licked it several times with a gray tongue before she spoke. "C. Linus Maxwell, he *is* the one who taught you." She was reading everything about Penny from this one sample. "He instructed you in all the arts which I taught him. He was my greatest student. A teacher craves such a student. But modern persons are too impatient; they seek only the fastest route to orgasm. They have no time for an old teacher. Maxwell had time."

The thorough examination sated the old mystic's curiosity. As her coarse red hands continued to stroke Penny, she said, "Yes, I trained Maxwell in the erotic ways of the ancients." Her voice creaked like the rusty hinges of a door opening onto someplace truly awful. "Those practices are almost lost to humanity. No one will devote the copious time and diligence required to acquire the sensual arts." Maxwell did. She was glad to have a student to mentor after all these years. "Before Max, my last apprentice was sixty years ago. His name was Ron Jeremy."

She continued to lick the finger, savoring it as she spoke. "Maxwell learned everything that was mine to teach. Those centuries of self-stimulating my loins, he benefits from all I've discovered." Dismay clouded the hag's expression. Even her blind, pale eyes darkened. "Now Maxwell has used the sexual wisdom of the ages to hurt many women and benefit himself."

Penny was shocked at the mystic's comprehension. When the hag again extended her twig of a finger, Penny gladly mounted it and rode it with excitement.

Tasting this new sample, the Baba intoned, "You feel a great guilt. You betrayed your sister women. You helped him to calibrate his weapons of control. Numerous are Maxwell's slaves due to the work you performed."

Hearing this, Penny wept. It was true. It was horrible, but it was so true that she'd never allowed herself to admit it.

The Baba sucked the finger in her mouth. She pulled it free and smacked her lips. "You, Penny Harrigan, have come to me for training so you can fight against him."

The gray tongue stroked the finger. Savoring whatever truths lingered in its wrinkles.

"You know my *name*?" Penny asked incredulously. It was the first time she had spoken in the cave and her voice echoed shrilly. "Just from the taste of my *juices*?"

Baba Gray-Beard's withered lips smiled. "I know many things." She motioned to a mat woven from dried lichens and her own shed hairs. "Come and sit. You will need strength for your erotic training. I will brew us some tea."

In the same way Penny had submitted to Max's experiments, sequestered in his lofty penthouse, now she gave herself to the Baba in the cloister of the old woman's stony cavern.

Penny had never been with a woman, but this was different. She never felt as desirable as she did when her tender, supple flesh was juxtaposed with the wizened hag-flesh of the ancient. The Baba was teaching her, instructing her in the greatness of sex magic. The crone fingered her relentlessly until Penny cried out, screaming as if these words would be her last on earth. The witch seldom asked her to reciprocate, but when she did Penny went about the task of pleasuring the wrinkled elder with the utmost respect. And when Penny wrested from her teacher even a modest cry of pleasure, it occurred as the greatest triumph.

When she embarked upon her hunts, the ancient teacher encouraged Penny to utilize the many bones and rocks available to build her own pleasure tools. Brandishing an armature of feathers welded to sticks with thongs of stout leather, the Baba boasted, "These may seem like the crippling versions that Maxwell has bastardized. But they are meant to enhance a woman's energies. They will make you stronger, not weaker." With a wink of one cataract-eclipsed eye, she assured the girl, "They will not exhaust you." Leaning closer, she leered. "But you must be *disciplined*!"

The Baba warned, "The erotic wisdom of the ancients is too much for most who seek it." She grinned wistfully. "The students trek here to acquire these skills. Many die from the hardships of the journey, but more die by their own hands." She explained how she would bring them eggs, but they would not eat. She'd invite them to her bed of moss and feathers, but they'd refuse to sleep. "So it goes." She shrugged with resignation. "I introduce them to a few rudimentary sensual practices, but they are soon consumed by self-pleasure."

To her own surprise, one night Penny brought her mentor to prolonged, strenuous release. Dabbling expertly with her lips and tongue, she teased the wily crone to a full-pitched fit of fevered yelping. The scrawny sex witch bounced violently atop their bed of twigs. Her toothless gums yammered incoherently.

Penny sustained the sweet torment to the verge of cruelty before she gradually lessened her campaign on her mistress's private parts. At last Penny lifted her drenched face from its task. She swiped her dripping chin with a clump of absorbent moss. Playfully, she caught the Baba's eye and demanded, "Tell me a secret, old one. Tell me a secret, or I will return to my licking until you go mad."

Penny knew her mistress was well pleased. The old woman looked drunk with pleasure. Breathless, the Baba shook her head to stave off the onslaught of orgasms.

"A secret, then!" Penny demanded.

"A secret," the Baba agreed. Lying on her back, she lifted herself to her elbows. "Did Maxwell tell you why he sought me out?"

Penny shrugged. "For instruction?"

No, the Baba shook her head sadly. "For distraction. To help him forget a great sorrow which had visited him."

"His mother's death," Penny ventured. This was hardly a secret; it had all been well documented in the *National Enquirer*.

Again, the mystic corrected her student. "Max launched his journey for sexual training in order to forget his *wife's* death."

It was Penny's turn to be confounded. Nothing could've surprised her more. "His wife?"

The Baba nodded in silent confirmation. Maxwell had once taken a wife. In college he'd met and courted a wholesome girl who was studying prelaw. The two of them had been deeply in love. This wasn't the cold, clinical Max with whom Penny had dallied. This younger man had been utterly devoted to his new bride. They were two lovers on the threshold of a blissful life together.

The sex witch sighed. "The details of the girl's death are unimportant. A severe allergic reaction. Without her, Max's life was also ended."

He'd arrived at the Baba's cave a recent widower. Embittered, his only goal was to squander the remainder of his years in hedonistic cavorting.

Penny craved more of the story, but this hardly seemed like the best time to pump her mentor for details. She asked, "What was her name?" She slid her fingers gently against the older woman. Playfully, she prodded the fragile tissues of the witch's bunghole. She spit generously to lubricate the worn orifice.

The Baba replied, "Her name?" She slowly succumbed to the stroking. Her voice softened as if she were lapsing into a dream. "Her name was Phoebe."

Phoebe. The name echoed for a long time in Penny's mind. Phoebe Maxwell. It was likely that Maxwell's people had excised every mention of Phoebe from the newspapers he owned, from the Internet, from history. She would be Max's Achilles' heel. She'd been proof that his heart could be broken. As Penny pondered this new aspect of his life, she lowered her face to the waiting thatch of off-white hair that even now thrust itself upward, eagerly nudging her for attention.

As Penny returned to her studies she yearned to ask how long Max and Phoebe had been married. Yet even without asking, somehow she knew.

They had been married for exactly 136 days.

For respite the Baba rubbed unguent into Penny's raw membranes. The sensual mystic lovingly tucked her into a bed of dried mosses and went out to forage for eggs and mushrooms. She brewed invigorating teas and prompted the girl to drink them from the wrinkled palm of her hag's hand. She taught her student how to grind spiders between rocks to produce a soothing ointment that would enhance Penny's anal sensitivity. So tranquil was her life and so deep their bond that Penny forgot about the legions of evil robots that might be swimming in her bloodstream. She wasn't to forget for long.

As if Max were testing his power, one day Penny felt her nipples grow hard and begin to vibrate. Her nipples and clitoris, they began shaking violently. The old woman had prompted her to orgasm many times that morning before leaving to scavenge eggs and lizards, so the last sensation Penny expected was this. So strange was it that she knew instantly that it was Max's doing. At the time she was sitting alone, cross-legged on the cave floor, sipping a cup of lichen tincture. The next wave of excitement struck her before she could even struggle to her feet.

What felt like a demonic possession overcame Penny. She wasn't in sole control of her body. A separate force seemed to bloom and expand between her legs. Her breasts ached with desire. Her pulse began to accelerate as goose bumps pebbled her skin.

Max had described the physical process so succinctly. Her aroused vagina was extending, growing in length as if to accommodate an erect phallus. It would balloon until it formed a pocket above the opening of the cervix, ideally to trap and hold sperm until they could successfully fertilize an egg. In nature, this was a natural and beautiful process, but what was happening to Penny now was Max's evil remote-controlled handiwork. It was easy to picture teams of microscopic robots ravishing her nerve endings. Even here, with her sequestered in the Himalayas, he could activate them. He was sexting—but with *real sex*. As if arousing her were just an application on his phone! Whatever his method, he was stimulating her the way he'd attacked Alouette onstage. This was some savage satellite-relayed rape.

Moments later, when the Baba returned to the cave, Penny was still wheezing and convulsing with unasked-for pleasure. The aged lamia flung aside her pack of moss and rushed to comfort the figure rolling on the floor.

"Fight it," the Baba urged, kneeling. "What is done to you, you can do in return." She wetted a thin finger in her toothless mouth and began to slide it between the girl's engorged labia. "You are not merely a receiver," the Baba cried. "Return the energy to its vile source!"

At that she shrieked and pulled back a finger that was already bleeding. "What is this monstrous thing?" She peered at a hole lanced in the tip of her shriveled digit. The flow of blood was channeled by the wrinkles and cross-hatchings that centuries had carved in her palms. "What has that devil installed within you?"

Even now Penny's sane demeanor had been displaced by the spirit of a slobbering madwoman. Delirious, she spread her legs and arched her back, pumping her thighs into the air. Her hands roamed her own nude body beyond her rational control, her deranged fingers tweaking and diddling in a frenzy of self-stimulation. Her head tilted back, her mouth hung open, and her tongue lolled thickly around her groaning lips.

The Baba cried out, "Vomit the pleasure or allow it to pass through you as you would excess food or wine."

She grasped the girl's arms and shook her. "A mirror is not burned by the sun!" She screamed, "Reflect back his evil!"

As Penny slipped deeper into an erotic coma she could still hear the old woman's urging. "You would not try to hold all of the water of the world inside your bladder." Muffled by sensation, the aged voice continued. "You wouldn't eat to hoard the entire world within your belly. Pleasure, like food, must pass through you. If it accumulates it leaves room for nothing else. You explode. Your only hope is to replace one pleasure with another. The way food drives waste from your body, you must use love to displace the sex magic Max is practicing. Focus on what you love, and you can deflect his erotic spell."

In desperation, Baba Gray-Beard seized a cluster of antlers and began to gently work it between the suffering girl's loins. "Do not fight the sensations," she urged. "My child, let them pass through you, or you will be killed like so many of my students whose skeletons you see around you."

Penny's eyes rolled. Spittle flew as her lips disgorged a furious stream of obscenities.

"That's it," the Baba exhorted. "Say the words! Release the heat!" Working the antlers gently, rhythmically, she pleaded, "Do not harbor the energy within you!"

Her voice guttural with lust, Penny brayed profanities. Her body intoxicated with pleasure, she rasped and squawked foulness.

"Allow the pleasure to overflow you!" the hag crowed.

Penny gasped. Her torrent of lewdness ceased. Slowly she came back into herself.

The witch tenderly withdrew the antler. "Your torments

will not end," she said. "You will find no peace until you have defeated Maxwell, or he has destroyed you." She began to apply a cooling balm of crushed centipedes to the bruises that were already forming between Penny's legs.

"What I teach you," the Baba said, "you must teach all women in the world so that they might defend themselves against this evil force."

Baba Gray-Beard spoke without bitterness. Nude, she lay back in her commodious bed of moss and feathers, and she parted her legs, shamelessly exposing the wrinkled flesh of her sex. This she began petting, softly flogging herself as she reminisced. Every stroke seemed to elicit memories, as if she were reading the stories from her own gray folds of skin. "I was orphaned at such a cruel age. At dawn I found her—my mother's body lay broken at the foot of a high cliff where she must've been gathering plover eggs." Her blank eyes stared into history. "I lifted my mother's cold hand and placed it against myself, pleading." In this way, the bereft child had eked out a few final hours of nurturance from her lost parent. "For a short while I did not allow the sex energy to leak from me through screams or thrashing."

It didn't take long before the heartless sex seekers of her village discovered that a helpless, unprotected child was theirs for the taking. The first night the young Baba was alone in her hut, they'd attacked.

Her voice husky with nostalgia, the Baba said, "They mapped for me my inner womanhood. With their every violent thrust they taught me about my body." She described how any number of savages might enter her in the night. Many took their wicked pleasure with her tender child's body, but the Baba resolved that she would take something from each of them in return. If she could not stop them, she could learn to control them by increasing or decreasing their pleasure. In her girlhood, she took on a thousand such attackers and used them to her own advantage. Those cruel encounters were her education. From her suffering she gleaned a wealth of incredible sex practices.

"I grew to be eager, my eyes shining with anticipation as they flopped out their meaty penises. I knew each was an opportunity to experiment and perfect my developing sex craft." She closed her eyes in dreamy remembrance. "Among my brutal mentors were women who palmed the back of my head, their fingers interlaced to hold me in place as they bade me lap at them until I neared suffocation." She spoke in a voice without misery. Outside the cave's mouth, a whiteout blizzard raged. Inside, a small campfire warmed a bubbling broth of stewed skinks. The Baba stirred the pot, saying, "This was my childhood, but those were but a handful of years. As my strength grew, the strength of my aging teachers began to fail. By then I'd enslaved them with my erotic skills, for I'd become a rich repository of sensual techniques. They could find satisfaction nowhere else, and I'd learned all they had to teach me. They brought me gold and jewels, things for which I'd no use. Finally, in scenes tinged with mercy and vengeance, I brought each of my former abusers to an ecstasy so great that he or she died."

The Baba's saga continued as she rose and began to pace the floor of the dripping cave. "My reputation as a sex crafter was such that students young and old, male and female, sought me as their guide." As a young sex witch, she was besieged by suitors yearning to acquire the secrets she'd accumulated, her real treasure, earned over countless grappling nights of pain. "To winnow their numbers I retreated to this cave. Here, only the strongest and most youthful can endeavor to reach me. The weak, the old, they die in their pilgrimage, and their bones almost pave the trail to my door." She laughed.

"The Sherpa will not approach me or my home," said the Baba. "The Sherpa believe that I kill my would-be lovers, but those who die do so by their own hands. . . ."

Only the healthiest aspirants reach the cave. There are no cripples among the skeletons. No deformed. These are the skulls of the beautiful with shining straight teeth. They came seeking pleasure for themselves, the Baba explained. "Only Max arrived with the purpose of providing pleasure to others. But once he recognized the power of supplying such pleasure, he was seduced to use it for his own gain!"

She gestured toward the skeletons, her voice windy and hollow. "They waste away and die." Starvation and exhaustion stripped the flesh from them and soon the young apprentices looked more aged than their bemused master. Not long after, the Baba would stagger back from her day's hunt and find them expired.

If she fancied a novel curve in the dead apprentice's iliac crest, the Baba might scavenge it for a new project. Nothing was wasted, for she used the vocal cords and sinews and dried entrails to lash parts together. Thus the young beautiful lovers brought her more pleasure once they were dead. With luck she'd fashion a new pleasure tool before the next student presented herself at the cave opening.

Aghast, Penny asked, "You used them, these bones?"

All Beautiful You products were based on the designs of the Baba. The arc of one tool was that of a rib. The diameter of another toy was based on a human femur.

Pointing to a tangle of ulnas and tendons, her eyes dancing with excitement, the Baba said, "Max once tried to murder me with that one! So great was his skill that he wielded my own creation to spur me to paroxysms of ecstasy so glorious that I almost died!"

She described how Maxwell had challenged her to an erotic

duel. He'd stood, nude, an arrogant young male animal, with his bare legs wide apart. He'd pressed his erection downward, toward his knees, and then released it to spring upward and land a great thwack against his taut belly. A waggish glint in his eye, he'd swiveled his hips to make his member swing from side to side, saying, "Come, old woman, impale yourself. Take your pleasure from this meat you've trained so well!"

Penny asked, "How did you save yourself?"

Smiling at the memory, the old woman said, "The weapon he used flew from my body and shattered. It blasted from me like a cork from a bottle, and the force threw me backward, where my head struck the cave wall. When I awoke Max was gone. He'd absconded with much of my sex-craft technology."

"But how did you free yourself?" Penny demanded.

The Baba touched herself solemnly. "I replaced one pleasure with another. I thought of how beautiful my mother was and how much I adored her. I screamed."

Penny gasped. "From your vagina?"

Almost shouting, the Baba responded, "Child, you can expel energy from any opening of the body!"

Penny sipped her lichen tea and considered the idea.

"This," the sex witch said, plucking something from her wet depths, "this is all I have remaining from my mother." The object she held was brownish, like polished wood, like an unvarnished pencil, and she withdrew it slowly. The extraction made a faint slurping sound. "It was her longest finger," the Baba explained in a hushed voice. "I cut it from her even while the wild animals devoured the rest." She offered it for Penny to examine. The finger gleamed damply, its surface fluted with wrinkles. The narrow end was scabbed with a discolored nail. The blunt end sprouted a shattered, yellowed stub of bone. It felt warm and alive, heavily scented with the Baba's natural oils. Even in the cavern's dim light, it was lovely.

Penny weighed the relic in her palm. It saddened her to think of her own mother nude and spread-eagled, struggling against her bonds in a gritty Nebraska attic. Gibbering in the throes of sexual cold turkey, she'd be writhing against the sweat-soaked sheets like a feverish wild animal. The image filled Penny with despair.

When the girl reached to return the treasure, the Baba did not extend her hand to accept it. Instead she arched her back and pushed forward her ancient pubis. Sensing what the sex crafter desired, Penny spit on the finger to moisten it, and she aimed its gnarled tip at the center of the snowy thatch. As she boldly pressed it home the older woman gasped with enjoyment.

"This is what I must instill in you," vowed the ancient. "I saved myself by channeling Max's contempt back to its source. When I awoke he was gone, the devil, and many of my favorite instruments were missing with him." What Max hadn't stolen he'd re-created from memory—the herbal recipes, for instance, for his unholy salves and enemas. "The way a bullet ricochets off a rock. The way an echo resounds off of a canyon wall. You must redirect his energy."

On one of her last dwindling days in the cave, Penny set aside her tea and searched among the meatless bones and castoff eggshells that covered the stone floor. The Baba would be away foraging for some time, and Penny needed to right a grievous wrong. After rooting through the litter, Penny located what she needed: her mobile phone. An icon on the screen showed that a few moments of power were left in the battery. She dialed a New York City number stored in the phone's memory.

On the first ring a man answered. "Brenda?" He sounded hoarse, as if from months of weeping.

Sadly, Penny replied, "No." Compassionately, she explained, "we met several weeks ago—"

"In Central Park," he affirmed. He sounded crushed, the poor wretch. His fiancée was still among the millions of women who'd dropped out of society.

Penny had to remind herself why she'd called. She'd wanted to apologize and to accept at least partial responsibility for the scourge of Beautiful You. And to promise that she'd do everything within her power to remedy the crisis. She wanted to assure this suffering, lovelorn stranger that she was almost ready to do battle with Cornelius Linus Maxwell. Soon she'd be a full-fledged sex witch, powerful enough to confront and expose Max's nanobot conspiracy. She wanted her kind words to wrap this pitiful man in a comforting cocoon. But at the crucial moment, her courage failed. Instead, she asked, "What's your name?"

Over the phone, the man sniffed. He said, "Yuri." His quavering voice calmed and he asked, "What's yours?" Suddenly his question had an odd, pointed quality to it.

Penny considered saying her real name. She stared guiltily out the cave's mouth, her eyes following the graceful path of a bird against the blue Nepalese sky. Eventually, she said, "I'm Shirley."

A longer silence followed before the man repeated, "Shirley." His voice now had a hard edge to it. "Shirley, why does my phone's caller ID say 'Penny Harrigan'?"

Caught in a lie, Penny froze, speechless and mortified. Her heart rate sped up to 165 beats per minute.

"Don't fool yourself," the man, Yuri, cruelly taunted. "I read the *National Enquirer*!" His tone was steeped in bitterness. "I know Penny Harrigan is claiming ownership of the Beautiful You patents! I saw on the news that you're appearing in court next week!" He brayed a hysterical laugh. "You stole my Brenda from me! You stole the wives from millions of husbands and the mothers from millions of children!"

His ranting had grown so loud Penny was forced to hold the phone at arm's length. The cavern echoed with his threats. She could hear the murderous scorn in his voice. It was unmistakable.

Enraged, Yuri screamed, "Every red-blooded man in New York dreams of killing you!"

Penny's phone beeped to signal that its battery was failing.

"If you dare to show your face at the patent-ownership trial," Yuri vowed, "we will tear you limb from limb. Tonight . . . tonight we will go to burn down your house—"

His threat knocked the wind from Penny. *Monique,* she realized. Monique was alone, incapacitated in her bedroom, equipped with only Pop-Tarts and bottled water. Penny needed to call and warn her. If an angry mob set fire to the town house, Monique would be burned alive.

That was when the telephone battery chose to go dead.

On her long flight from Nepal back to New York, Penny thought of her best friend. When she considered Monique, once so vibrant, now slavishly diddling herself in a darkened, locked room, using a human coccyx modeled out of some space-age polymer, she wanted to cry. Poor Monique with her abused, blistered privates, she was no doubt hovering in some twilight where pleasure yielded to death. Penny prayed silently to the ancient tantric gods that her lovable roommate still drew breath.

To pass the time during the lengthy trip, she practiced the self-satisfaction exercises the Baba had relentlessly drilled into her. She coaxed her hindquarters to the brink of an orgasm, and then replaced that thrilling sensation with thoughts of sincere love for her dad. By tweaking her nipples, she brought herself to the verge of hyperventilating, and then quickly redirected that mounting passion to dreamy thoughts of Abyssinian kittens.

Throughout their days together, the crone had selected erotic weapons seemingly at random from those strewn around the caves. Those rude assemblages of bone and stone and feathers, each she used as a wedge or lever to breach even Penny's most inaccessible tantric hot spots. Once she'd gained access, the witch had repeatedly stimulated Penny to lunatic arousal, always encouraging her to vent the enjoyment in physical thrashing and joyous shouts of vile language. Following each session, she would sponge the sweat from Penny's body using handfuls of fragrant mosses.

Together they would drink lichen tea, and Baba Gray-Beard would expound on the theory that pleasure was a deathless energy that can be directed and channeled. Pleasure, she explained, was attracted to those people who'd trained their receptive organs to welcome it. But, she warned, pleasure could not be held or collected. It must flow through its target, or that target would die.

Brandishing a ram's horn, which she had augmented with many thrill-inducing pebbles and herbal oils, the witch motioned for Penny to lie back, saying, "Shall we recommence your lessons, my dear?"

It was true. Penny's 136 days in Paris with Max had taught her about pleasure without love. But her weeks cloistered in the Baba's dank cavern had taught her that such profound ecstasy could coexist with an even stronger affection. The depth of her attachment to the witch-woman surprised even Penny. She had no idea of it until the final morning she awoke in their shared bed of dried plant matter and realized she had to return to the outside world.

That morning, Penny had quietly breakfasted on a porridge

of coarsely milled snakes. She'd packed her few belongings into a commodious sheep's bladder. Penny had lived day-to-day naked for so long that her Norma Kamali pantsuit felt strange against her body. She'd knelt to kiss the sleeping Baba good-bye. Then she'd begun her harrowing predawn descent down the sheer cliff faces of Everest.

Now, seated alone aboard a chartered private jet, attired head to toe in scrumptious Versace, Penny sipped tea she'd steeped using twigs and yak milk the lamia had gathered. She'd checked her e-mail and found that her patent-rights trial was set to begin in a few days. Her first step in her war against Max would be to contest his exclusive ownership of the Beautiful You designs. She'd force him to confront her, and they would do battle in a public court of law. If she lost, she would be dead. Death held no fear for her, only the hope that she'd someday be reunited with Baba Gray-Beard in an eternity of pleasure.

And if she, Penny Harrigan, won her audacious battle? If she won, and the world was truly liberated from the conspiracy of C. Linus Maxwell, then she would return to live as the old hag had lived: in that isolated cliff-side cavern, inventing endless means to pleasure herself and instructing those students who sought her guidance.

Returning to her Upper East Side town house, Penny found the frosted-glass front door marred by hooligans. Using bright red spray paint, someone had written, "Penny Harrigan Sucks Cocks in Hell!!!" in foot-high letters. The words stretched to deface the elegant stonework facade on either side of the doorway. Long drips ran down from each letter like horror-movie special effects. As she mounted the porch steps she saw that the white-marble stoop was cluttered with stuffed dolls. Roughly the size of baby dolls, each effigy wore miniature Salvatore Ferragamo pumps. Their facial features were stitched and quilted to closely resemble Penny's face. Careful embroidery had given them her warm brown eyes and pink pouting lips. It was unsettling to see how all the dolls were mutilated and bristling with pins. Penny gasped and shuddered, chilled by a realization: These were voodoo dolls.

Heaped among the evil artifacts were a number of decomposing chickens, their throats messily cut, their feathers splashed with gore. Their glassy avian eyes stared back at Penny accusingly. They'd clearly been sacrificed on the spot. The threshold of her home had become an altar for intense hatred. Drawn to the spilled blood were her old nemeses, black houseflies. They hovered above the stubs of burned candles.

Around her, the wail of fire engines echoed from every direction. A pall of black smoke blocked the sky, the stench of it making her cough. A rocket screamed by overhead, like military ordnance, tracing a low arc in the direction of Midtown. It disappeared behind some buildings. A muffled blast followed. The city had become, inexplicably, a battlefield.

Instantly, Penny thought of Monique.

Her roommate and best friend would've been upstairs when whoever had laid siege to the town house. A rush of loving concern displaced Penny's fear, and she quickly kicked aside the elements of the grotesque still life. She fitted her key into the lock.

Inside, broken glass crunched under every step of her Kate Spade kitten heels. The vandals had broken the panes of several windows. Their ammunition—rocks wrapped in paper scrawled with angry messages—lay in the shards. Thank goodness stout security grilles of ornately cast bronze had prevented the attackers from bodily entering.

Rushing up the stairs two steps at a time, Penny shouted, "Monique? Monique, are you okay?"

She wielded a fire ax to bust down the locked door of her roommate's bedroom. Within she found her once free-spirited friend lying across the sodden mattress of her bed, near death. The room stank of drool and stale blueberry Pop-Tarts. Penny nursed the girl, holding a cup of lichen tea to her chapped lips. If the batteries in her Beautiful You products had not failed from overuse, Monique would've died of exhaustion and dehydration long ago. As it was, the once sassy girl responded with hardly a whimper as Penny wiped her frail limbs with a salve made from eagle glands and rich reindeer tallow.

Penny spoon-fed the crippled girl a broth of plover eggs and fermented marrow. When her fallen comrade tried to speak, Penny hushed her. "You mustn't feel ashamed of your hideously degraded circumstances," she said. "You were the victim of primitive pleasures no untrained female could resist."

Penny carried her famished, unresponsive housemate to the media room and arranged her limp form in a comfortable lounge chair. As the two young ladies had done while watching the Academy Awards, Penny popped popcorn and lavished it with salt and butter. She hand-fed Monique kernels, slowly, placing them between the girl's chapped lips as, tonight, together, they watched CNN coverage of the world news.

Spread before them on the high-definition, seventy-two-inch plasma flat-screen was a panorama of global unrest. War and natural disasters were no longer the top stories. The Beautiful You effect had trumped every misfortune. Some men were fast forging new roles for themselves in this rapidly evolving world. Most were not.

Among the first group were slimy lotharios. Self-proclaimed intimacy coaches warned that women who succumbed to Beautiful You products would be unhappy with the ordinary machinations of a human sexual partner. However, any male who could wield a Rotating Relaxation Rod, product number 3447, such a man was never lacking for the companionship of the fairer sex. The cunning pickup line was no longer, "Would you like to see my etchings?" For a successful come-on, a would-be lover need only mention that he possessed one of the rarer BY products. Any laborer who could utilize a power drill or chain saw, he could easily operate the Jiggle Whip or the Trembling Love Snake. Thus, displaced workers from all the construction trades were finding new careers demonstrating Maxwell's personal care tools. In the retail shops. Or selling them door-to-door.

The CNN cameras panned across the showroom inside the Fifth Avenue store. Business was brisk as suave salesmen plied the female shoppers with products. And not just products, there were pricey warranties to sell. And financing schemes, the newscaster explained. Analysts claimed that DataMicroCom was making big money on the financing charges that customers accrued using their bright pink charge cards. Any desperate, libidinous lady wandering into that den of unscrupulous cads, Penny realized, she wouldn't stand a chance! It was the career that every male in the city hotly coveted.

On television, the scene changed. The cameras displayed the miles-long line of shoppers outside the flagship store. Among them, Penny recognized the sales associate from Bonwit Teller, her elegant good looks gone, replaced by a gap-toothed, slack-jawed zombie woman. Likewise, Kwan Qxi and Esperanza, Penny's former roommates, were there, bleary-eyed and clutching well-worn bright pink credit cards.

In recent weeks, according to CNN, the gender composition of the shoppers had shifted. Now an almost equal number of men stood waiting among the women. These were the profiteers.

Among the fastest to adapt, these usurious men sought to buy as many of the new products as possible. They were scalpers who, in turn, sold the toys to females at an astronomical markup. For rich women, crippled women, impatient gals, anyone who couldn't or wouldn't wait in the out-of-doors, it was an expensive godsend. Vibrators and dildos had become the world's new form of underground currency. No day passed without reports of Beautiful You trucks being hijacked for their valuable cargos. Warehouses were looted. Security guards assassinated in drive-by shootings. Deliveries of new stock arrived at stores by armored car. Recent purchasers were targeted by street thugs, who openly stole the merchandise at gunpoint for resale on the black market.

Rival gangs fought over turf. Slave-labor sweatshops flooded the market with counterfeit products that failed to satisfy.

To Penny, the whole situation seemed almost as crazy as Beanie Babies or those Michael Jordan shoes had been. Almost.

As Monique began to listlessly gum her mouthful of calorie-rich corn, the CNN reporter ascended in a helicopter from midtown Manhattan and slowly made his way northward toward a huge plume of black smoke that rose from the Bronx. The New York below them looked, to Penny, like some contested third-world killing field. Mortar rounds seemed to jet across the neighborhoods, igniting fires in high-rise buildings. Police cars and ambulances bathed the streets in flashing red lights. Traffic was gridlocked by burning vehicles.

The camera shot hovered above East One Twenty-second Street, moving steadily toward the Harlem River Drive, slowly crossing into the Bronx. Suspended high above the grid of streets, the helicopter swooped and tilted, dodging some kind of rocket or missile that came jetting directly at it. The weapon looked to be about the size of a bazooka shell. It blazed with flames and trailed an arc of black smoke. Another projectile raced directly at the chopper, and the pilot dived to avoid it.

On the media room television, the skies of the city were crisscrossed with these flaming warheads. Wherever they landed, each burst like an incendiary bomb, igniting buildings, cars, and trees. Turning the island into a war zone. By following the black arc of each, Penny could trace them all back to the source of the black plume.

The smoke rose from the center of Yankee Stadium. There, a massive fire appeared to be raging on the pitcher's mound.

The aerial shot cut to a ground-level news crew broadcasting from the infield. The scene was chaos as mobs of people caroused. Everyone within sight was male, and most wore Promise Keepers T-shirts. Penny could discern long chains of men. These chains snaked toward the bonfire from every direction, spreading to fill the stadium like the spokes of a wheel. They were all-male versions of the customer lines that snaked away from every Beautiful You retailer in the world.

The frenzied men were singing a song Penny recognized from childhood. It was the religious hymn "Kumbaya." Their measured, chain-gang movements were timed to the rhythm of the melody while they passed objects hand to hand. As each item reached the fire it was tossed into the flames.

The cameras drew closer, and Penny witnessed what looked like any male's vision of hell. Innumerable multitudes of severed penises were writhing in the conflagration. Phalluses squirmed in the intense heat, blistering and twisting as if in prolonged torment. Aflame, some suffering man-parts crept, inchworm-like, from the fire as if attempting to escape to safety. They flopped. Flipped. Jumped and twitched. As if in agony. These were caught by the surrounding men and summarily flung back to their doom. Still other dongs erupted in the heat, spouting pink molten lava.

They were all Beautiful You products, Penny recognized. The figures who capered and sang like savages around the inferno, they were men sacrificing their common rivals. As generations before them had torched books and disco records, these men yelped in cathartic abandon, passing the prods and love wands man to man, until they were heaped onto the bubbling, spitting flames. The stench and black smoke of this pyre hung over the streets, acrid as the poisonous reek of an unending tire fire.

Among the phalluses were withering Dragonflies and exploding douches. No product was overlooked. Batteries burst with a high-pitched squeal like butchered baby rabbits.

Other phalluses blasted off like skyrockets. They shot straight up from the bonfire. These, these were the airborne torches that had almost taken down the CNN helicopter. Like incoming missiles, they rained fire on the citizens of the metropolis.

The CNN reporter explained that these pleasure toys had been bought, borrowed, and stolen. Regardless of how they'd come to Yankee Stadium, none of them would leave intact. In every stadium around the world, from huge coliseums to bare-dirt soccer fields, the reporter intoned that hordes of enraged men were fanning the flames of similar love-tool pyres.

Without warning the camera jerked. It veered away from the CNN reporter. Someone, some unseen thug, had commandeered it, forcing the lens to focus on a single bedraggled man. His face was blackened with soot from the burning latex. A scraggly beard hid all of his features except his bloodshot eyes. Only when he spoke did Penny know who he was.

It was Yuri.

"Penelope Harrigan," he ranted from the plasma flat-screen

of her luxurious media room, "soon we will drag you from a courtroom and burn you on this fire like the witch you are!"

The Manhattan that Penny had returned to was a cityscape of men. Only men roamed the sidewalks. No one but men drove the cars and trucks or rode the subways. Every seat in every eatery was occupied by male buttocks. And walking among them, Penny attracted much attention. Her near-starvation diet of organic fungi and her long hours of strenuous self-pleasuring had left her body beautifully sculpted. Every muscle twitched enticingly beneath her thin, smooth skin as she confidently traipsed the streets.

To prevent being recognized she'd donned oversize sunglasses and a baseball cap worn backward. The glasses were by Fetch, and their stylish frames offered the perfect balance of "look-at-me" versus "go-away." She forswore wearing the huge ruby pendant that had become her signature accessory as the Nerd's Cinderella. Despite being incognito, she could too easily imagine a flood of livid vigilantes pouring from the skyscrapers. Men like Yuri. A world of furious, obsolete penises. The same men who had sacrificed chickens on her front steps, they would come streaming down the sidewalks. She pictured them all carrying torches and nooses. If they knew who she was, this all-male lynch mob would hound her as if she were the Frankenstein monster.

The smoke from Yankee Stadium hung over Greater New York like a pall. Blazing dildos shrieked across the sky, and ash fell like black snowflakes. The soot burned Penny's eyes and throat with its acrid stench. Smut, trickling down, clung to the pink flanks of the Beautiful You building. Enshrouding it. Making the tower look like nothing less than a dark parody of the snowy paradise Penny had so recently left behind.

The photocopied posters of missing women continued to paper every available public surface in the city. They climbed like kudzu up telephone poles and walls. But the harsh daylight had begun to fade the smiling photos—these beloved wives and adored mothers. These successful CFOs and CEOs, rain was washing away their career accomplishments. Their names were gradually disappearing. Already, they were half forgotten.

With them, the hard-won political and social progress of all women seemed to be eroding. Vanishing.

On the corner of Broadway and Forty-seventh Penny glimpsed a familiar face. A woman lay splayed on the sidewalk, leaning back against the base of a lamppost. From closer up Penny could see the afflicted stranger wore a gold-and-diamond Paloma Picasso brooch from Tiffany. Her hair was expertly high-lighted although it hung in rank tendrils around the smudged ruins of her once expensively made-up face. She wore the tat-tered remains of a pink Chanel suit, the jacket hanging open, her breasts bared to passersby. Her skirt was wadded up around her waist as she stabbed at her exposed self with a Beautiful You toy. Her legs filmed with grime, she gripped the hilt of the toy in both hands. Her fingernails rimed with dirt, she stirred the smut-stained tool in circles, plunging and withdrawing it. Like an inmate in a Victorian asylum, she giggled and stammered to herself, oblivious to the crowds who passed, averting their eyes.

Approaching this unfortunate spectacle, Penny ventured, "Brenda? Is your name Brenda?"

Without slowing her carnal machinations, the woman looked up at Penny with a faint glimmer of comprehension in her eyes.

"You're engaged to marry Yuri, remember?" Penny held out

her open, empty hands as if she could give the woman back her former life. "You were the CFO of Allied Chemical Corp." The pleasure tool, Penny recognized as Beautiful You product number 2788, the Instant-Ecstasy Probe. Its silicone-and-latex casing was worn and stained almost beyond recognition. Even Yuri would struggle to identify it as the special birthday gift he'd once given so innocently. Penny quickly found Yuri's number in her phone's history. She dialed it and listened to his phone ringing at the other end.

Simultaneously, she went to Brenda's aid, pulling at the remnants of the woman's jacket in an attempt to cover her bared bosom. Trying desperately to save her dignity, Penny insistently tugged the hem of the skirt down Brenda's legs while offering soothing assurances. No one stopped to help. Everyone scurried past. All were men, and they cast furtive, mortified glances at the scene and kept walking. Yuri's phone continued to ring.

"Someone call nine-one-one," Penny pleaded while she tried to match buttons with buttonholes. "Please." She couldn't help but notice that this slathering, maniacal creature wore a double strand of beautifully matched pearls. After her own 136 days among the glitterati, she could recognize that the ice-cube-size sparklers in this stranger's earrings were flawless two-carat diamonds.

In response, Brenda clung tightly to the phallus, bringing her knees to her chest, curling into a ball as if to protect her prize. She bared her teeth in a ferocious snarl.

"Help me!" Penny begged a pin-striped businessman who stared in horror and quickly darted in another direction. She was gently trying to yank the woman's fingers free of their task when she felt a sting in the side of her hand. This crazed stranger had sunk her capped teeth into Penny's skin. Her cheeks smeared with blood, she gnawed at the tender flesh near Penny's thumb like an enraged animal.

A bicycle messenger paused only long enough to say, "Lady, I hope you're current with your tetanus shots . . ." before jetting away.

Shocked and in pain, Penny dropped her phone, but not before she heard a voice on the other end say, "Hello? Brenda?" It was Yuri, but the phone clattered into the gutter, out of reach.

Penny wrestled to escape, but the woman's teeth held fast. Her panting sprayed Penny's blood from the corners of her mouth. Only when Penny launched herself away did she escape the madwoman's toothy grip. Even as Penny fell backward, the lunatic leaped to her feet and scuttled a zigzag retreat. Blood still streaming down her face, Brenda lopped along Broadway, her soiled hands grasping the pink-plastic object of her insatiable obsession. The all-male crowds stepped aside as she scooted past.

The only other females to be found were those haggard zombies standing in the miles-long line that stretched from the doors of the tapered pink tower on Fifth Avenue. The bedeviled wretches looked interchangeable. Their stringy hair had fallen out in clumps, and their fingernails were bitten down to the quick. To a woman, they each carried the same purse, wore identical shoes, dressed in look-alike outfits. These articles of clothing weren't attractive or well made, Penny noted, but they were all products manufactured by DataMicroCom and its subsidiary companies.

A defeated crew of stoop-shouldered men wearing Promise Keepers T-shirts were staging a protest march and vigil near the store's entrance. They trudged in a ragged circle, carrying picket signs that read, "Personal Fulfillment Doesn't Make a

Family!" Other signs declared, "Babies Should Come *Before* Orgasms!" Around and around they shuffled, beleaguered and ignored.

To confront the mob of ladies outside the flagship store, Penny stood with her feet planted wide apart and her shoulders thrown back. Her arms akimbo, she rested a fist on each hip. "Sisters," she shouted. "Hear me, my sister women! You must quit abusing your loins!"

The women squinted, observing her through narrowed, hostile eyes. They clutched bright pink shopping bags to their chests like talismans. No one spoke, but many hissed loudly.

"You're accessing a power you do not understand," Penny called. "An ancient practice of self-stimulation that requires decades to learn and utilize safely without resulting in permanent harm to the user." Penny stared boldly back into their slavering, snarling faces. "Most of you," she continued, "have also been infected with legions of tiny robots."

In response, many heckled. Others spit. In their uniform weakness none could launch an outright attack.

"Tomorrow," Penny decreed, "I shall make public the heinous scheme with which C. Linus Maxwell has plundered the sex secrets of the past in order to enslave all women." In response to their growing catcalls, she shouted, "Beautiful You squanders your endorphins. We must boycott all products made and sold by DataMicroCom." She urged, "I will school you in how to craft safe rudimentary personal care tools from the raw materials provided by nature." She offered, "I bring unguents to soothe your inflamed, overtaxed vulvas!"

Instead of joining her or attacking her, this time the mob turned away. Their jeering dropped to general grumbling. The gambit had failed.

Clearly Penny had misjudged the crowd. Their only interest lay in returning to the mother ship store and acquiring additional products. Reevaluating her strategy, Penny redirected her offense. "Sisters," she cried. "Pleasure is a human right! We must storm the bastions of pleasure and take what is due to us!" She shook a fist in the air, the teeth marks still visible, her hand stained red with her own dried blood.

This drew a positive response. Many in the crowd now cheered.

"Do not wait like passive sheep for your corporate masters to dole out dribs and drabs of ecstasy!" she railed. "Take it! Batter down those doors and take it all!"

Thus Penny rallied the ragtag queue into a rioting army. She whipped their hunger into a frenzied rage. Those thousands of desperate women surged forward and crashed against the pink-mirror facade of the building, hammering at the glass with the clunky heels of their ugly shoes. They wielded their worn erotic tools as truncheons. They beat with their fists until ominous cracks raced in every direction and the windows and doors bowed inward, ready to collapse.

Unnoticed, a black limousine had arrived at the curb near Penny. A rear window of the car rolled down, revealing the high cheekbones of a pale, almost reptilian face. Inside sat Maxwell. Speaking only to Penny, he said, "Get in."

"Hah!" she laughed, indicating her mob. Even now the store's crumbling exterior was crushed underfoot as the angry rioters swarmed inside to loot the shelves and display cases. "You cannot control our numbers, Max!" Victorious, Penny gloated, "We will take what must belong to us!"

In response, the figure seated in the back of the limo lifted a small black device. It was square and could easily be mistaken for a telephone or a gaming system. It was the device he'd been fingering in the audience the night of Alouette's death. He thumbed a few buttons as if composing a text message. He thumbed a few more.

"Go ahead," Penny challenged. "Call in the police. Call your thugs. Even they cannot stem this revolution!"

"Get in, bitch," Max repeated. "This is the last time I'll ask you *nicely*."

"Fuck you!" Penny screamed.

"No," Max said flatly. "Fuck *you,* my dear." At this he pressed a button and the looters all hesitated in their actions.

Some, including Penny, clutched themselves. The knees of most buckled and they fell, gripping their crotches in both hands. Soon all were writhing on the ground, making voracious noises, without human dignity. The army of the revolution broke ranks and collapsed into hedonistic wriggling. In place of the valiant rebels, here was an undulating carpet of human bodies. Their cries of victory dropped to a chorus of sensual moans. These occurred in synch with violent pelvic thrusts skyward.

With the push of another button more women frothed at the mouth and twitched in spasmodic convulsions. They were about to die as Alouette had died, of cardiac arrest or brain aneurysms brought on by too much erotic stimulation.

Even as the crippling spasms of pleasure rippled through her, Penny beseeched, "Set them free!" She began to crawl toward the car. Within her body, she tried to block the erotic force, to block it or redirect it back toward Maxwell. She made an angry, clenched fist of her pelvic floor. She meditated as the Baba had taught her. She tried all the tantric methods, but none seemed to work. Dragging herself across the concrete sidewalk, she arrived beside the car. Defeated, she whispered, "Release them, Maxwell. Spare their lives, and I will go with you now."

The car's door opened, and Max said, "Get in, or I will press another button and they will all die."

Pulling herself into the car's interior, Penny saw her face reflected in Max's polished shoe. *Reflect his power,* she told herself, but nothing happened. Once she was fully incapacitated, shivering and depleted on the car's carpeted floor, Max pulled the door shut and instructed the driver to make a slow circuit of Central Park.

Gradually the unbearable pleasure lessened. Max dialed it back, using his small remote. To any onlooker it would appear he was merely thumbing the buttons of a computer game. No longer subjected to the full brunt of the stimulation, Penny pulled herself up to sit beside him. He poured a glass of champagne at the car's small bar and offered it to her. Pink champagne. She eyed it warily.

"Do not worry, my girl," he crooned. "I don't need to drug you. I already possess complete control over your body."

Penny accepted the glass. The wine tasted so foreign after the many cups of healthy lichen tea and pickled cliff rats. Her vaginal walls relaxed, exhausted. "I know about the nanobots," she gasped. "I know they were delivered inside the Dragonfly."

"Clever girl," Max said. "You'll make an excellent president of DataMicroCom."

"I will not serve as your puppet," Penny swore.

"Poor Clarissa," Max said. "She never wanted to be president. That was something I bullied her into."

He explained how he'd met Clarissa when she was a simple Avon lady selling lipsticks door-to-door. She was nothing to him. A cipher. But he saw how, with the power of life or death, he could bully her into becoming anything. After they'd had their 136 days of romance, it was too late. She was implanted. She no longer had any choice except to be what he wanted her to become—or to die. She'd never wanted to become a senator, much less the president, but if she refused—or if she'd failed in her bids for election—Max would've killed her and begun the process with another woman.

"It was the same with Alouette," he said wistfully. "She was a pretty face, happy to be nothing but a simple fashion model. . . ."

But after being implanted with battalions of nanobots, she had no choice. If she failed to give a brilliant performance, Max would punish her with debilitating levels of pleasure. He would drive her to the brink of insanity by blasting her clitoris with ecstasy for days so she couldn't eat or sleep. Failure ceased to be an option, and Alouette grew terrified of her own genitalia.

"To survive, both women became what I decreed. If either had told anyone about the hold I had over her," Max said, "I would have killed her."

"Is that why you murdered Alouette?" asked Penny.

"She was going to tell you," Max confirmed.

Max's chauffeur steered them in an endless loop through the smoky, war-torn setting. It seemed like centuries since she'd taken the romantic horse-drawn carriage ride with Tad down this same leafy route.

Through the limousine's tinted windows she could see the park. The unchaperoned packs of children still roamed, abandoned by their wayward nannies. The wheelchair-bound geriatrics were still parked like aged Eskimos left to die on arctic ice floes. Standing among them was Yuri, the jilted bridegroom deserted by his pleasure-obsessed fiancée. Bearded, alone in his anger, his clothes disheveled, he continued to leaflet the passing crowds with his pale-green handouts. His photo of Brenda, like his memory of her, would be fainter with every generation of photocopies. Penny yearned to leap from the car and rush to him. She dreamed of showing him the teeth marks on her hand as proof that his beloved was still alive somewhere. Those toothy scars would instill him with renewed hope.

Max followed her gaze to the bereft man. Dismissively, Maxwell shook his head. "I will not let some lunatic murder you." He waved his hand in a sweep that seemed to encompass the entire city. Perhaps the entire world. "Wherever you walk . . . every moment of your life since your birth . . . my security forces have been constantly watching over you. My guards prevented those ruffians from setting fire to your town house . . . once, they saved you from a tornado." Less warmly, he added, "You belong to me. If anyone ends your life, it will be me."

Penny sighed in resignation. "And what is to be my purpose in your grand design?"

Max smiled with a strange mixture of pity and affection. "You will serve as the permanent CEO of DataMicroCom. Every day for the rest of your life you will wear panty hose and carry a briefcase. You will wear your hair as a lacquered helmet and eat salads. You will sit through board meetings so tedious that they will test your sanity."

Max fixed her with a smug smile. "Every woman in the world dreams of becoming my wife."

"Are you hitting on me?" Penny asked, stunned.

"Don't be silly. I'm *proposing*." He shrugged as if to dismiss any argument. "You'll make a stalwart consort. There's no reason why either of us ought to spend our life alone."

The queen of England, the Chinese media baron, the steel magnate, all of his earlier conquests were living similar chaste lives of duty to him and only him. This network of powerful women gave Maxwell dominion over the entire human race.

"Through Beautiful You," Max said proudly, "I've successfully implanted nanobots in ninety-eight-point-seven percent of the adult women in the industrialized world."

This, he confirmed, was how he controlled their buying habits. During television commercials for certain products, those made by DataMicroCom, he'd broadcast a signal that triggered erotic sensations. Be it a shoe or a motion picture or a vampire novel, women quickly associated the stimuli with their aroused response, and they rushed to buy.

"Women are the new masters," Max boasted, "but now I am the master of women."

Penny knew he was telling the truth. At least his own truth.

"Don't reduce this to some playground contest," Max warned. "This isn't about boys versus girls. This is about power. We live in an age when women hold the bulk of the power. In government, in consumer purchase decisions, women steer the world, and their longer life spans have left them in control of the greatest wealth."

He marveled at the black control box in his palm. He turned the device in his hands so she could better see it. The surface was a mosaic of black push buttons, each marked with a letter or number. A keyboard. "Can you imagine if this controller fell into the hands of a thirteen-year-old boy?"

Dryly, Penny said, "It has."

Max's thumbs twitched over the buttons, and she cried out as a spasm of electric arousal ripped through her clitoris.

Suppressing her orgasm, Penny said, "You've created a very effective deterrent to people making babies." She was thinking of the injury done to everyone who'd tried to enter her.

Maxwell smiled enigmatically. "If your labors please me, I might allow you to reproduce. Human beings are incapable of controlling their numbers, so I must do so. In my utopia only the brightest, most productive females will be allowed to bring forth offspring."

Hearing this, Penny could understand why the president had killed herself. Maxwell planned to control the birthrate of the entire industrialized world.

"Overpopulation," Penny said. "So that's why you've placed a dog in the manger."

He nodded with obvious pride. "You're referring to the gatekeeper function. Certain nanobots can deliver a pulse of scorching plasma energy. It was invented to destroy cancer cells, but I find it works equally as well on male erections."

Wryly, Penny said, "You'll be happy to know that it works equally as well on the fingers of Himalayan mystics."

Max raised an eyebrow. "Ah, you sought out Baba Gray-Beard." He smirked, asking, "How is the old girl?"

"She despises you!" Penny countered. Despite how he tried to hide it, she could see the news saddened Maxwell. To press her advantage she added, "The Baba loathes you for how you've stolen the sex secrets of the ancients and used them for your profit."

Without speaking, Max wiggled a toggle on his control, and Penny felt a twinge of heady desire flutter through her.

She flinched but recovered her composure quickly. She narrowed her gaze. "Equipped with her guidance I might prove to be more of a challenge to master than your previous slaves."

Max spied her clenching and unclenching her hands in rage. "You are no longer the weak child whom I tutored in the ways of pleasure. . . . I sense that under the Baba's tutelage you've become something dangerous: a woman." His eyes gleamed with something like admiration. "If you ever consider doing me harm, please know that to kill me would be to unleash consequences beyond your wildest imaginings!"

"After tomorrow," Penny fumed, "the entire world will loathe you." She sipped at her glass of champagne. "In the opening arguments of my patent-rights trial, I plan to expose your entire dirty scheme!"

Max fingered his controls.

Penny felt a shiver of pleasure tease her anus. A warning. She ignored it.

Max toyed with another button, and she felt her nipples begin to enlarge.

"Surely," she taunted, "you can do better than that."

"And I promise I will," Maxwell swore. "If you attempt to expose me I will make you grovel and bark like a mad dog in heat on the courtroom floor. I will drive you insane with passion. And I will kill you."

That night Penny built an altar to the tantric gods of long-ago. She made an offering of tea brewed from a fistful of soil brought back from the cave of Baba Gray-Beard. Using a cool compress of damp lichens, she blotted the feverish brow of her best friend and housemate. This night might be Penny's last on earth, but even death would be better than living as a slave to Maxwell. She pictured the nanobots already massing for their attack in her brain and groin. She telephoned her father in Omaha. Her mother had not improved, but neither was her condition worse. She was heavily sedated and being force-fed through a stomach tube to keep her alive.

Only Tad seemed to believe her. In response to her call he raced to her town house, bringing the legal brief for the two of them to review. Over pizza in the kitchen she had explained about her trip to Nepal. She told him about the gatekeeper lurking within millions of women. That crippling pulse of malevolent penis-lancing plasma energy.

Penny explained everything. Now, only now could they fully and honestly consummate their romantic friendship. Drinking cups of the Baba's sacred dirt tea, they sat at the kitchen table and discussed taking their relationship to that next level.

Tad looked at her, the cooling pizza forgotten between them. His expression was that of a confused, frightened little boy. His eyes round with terror. For months, he'd seen Brillstein limping around the office, obviously in prolonged agony. He swallowed nervously. He didn't seem eager to suffer a similar fate. "I thought you couldn't have vaginal intercourse?"

As the Baba would tell her, Penny's vagina wasn't her only access to power. It no longer mattered whether she was pretty or ugly, thin or fat, young or old. She was already well schooled as a vastly accomplished sex witch. Hers were the skills passed down through a thousand generations of wily sex crafters. She wielded that amazing carnal magic in her hands and mouth. The knowledge was trained deep in Penny's every muscle. Her well-educated rectum alone knew countless methods of giving pleasure.

Penny boasted about none of these natural talents to Tad. Instead, she merely nodded in the direction of the Sub-Zero refrigerator. "There's a bottle of champagne chilling." Her voice furred with erotic suggestion, she said, "Why don't you pop the cork while I go upstairs and slip into something sexy?"

In her bedroom Penny retrieved the negligee of marabou feathers dyed dark purple. Many of the feathers were stiff with dried blood. Brillstein's blood. But the purple perfectly camouflaged that gory evidence from the night she'd seduced and interrogated her evil boss. Donning the plumage, she slipped her feet into her tallest pair of Prada heels and surveyed the results in her dressing room mirror. The memory of the aged senior partner lodged within her, weeping in pain, it made her giggle. The sight of her own magnificent, hairless vulva prompted the bittersweet memory of mounting Alouette's beautiful face in the restaurant toilet stall.

From downstairs, Tad called up, "Champagne's ready."

"Give me one more minute," Penny called down. She rushed to Monique's room. There, her roommate was sleeping soundly, too exhausted to hear Penny collect a sticky armload of much-used Beautiful You products. These she quickly carried into her own bathroom and flung into the shower.

Tad called up, "You ready? I'm bringing the champagne."

"I'm in my bedroom," Penny hollered. She was hurriedly using the shower's handheld attachment to rinse any accumulated residue of old lubricant and dried body fluids off of the various borrowed erotic tools. Now that she knew Max's design secrets she could easily recognize how one product was a plastic version of a human clavicle. Another was clearly a rubberized-fiberglass copy of a scapula. Each of these she blotted dry with a hand towel and flung onto her bed. As Penny heard Tad's footsteps mount the stairs, she had barely enough time to curl her eyelashes, wax her legs, and apply perfume behind her ears.

Doing so, she ransacked her memory for details about the male sexual anatomy. Max had taught her some. Baba Gray-Beard had taught her much more, but Penny had put none of this learning into practice. Her mind reeled with the effort to picture Tad's inferior rectal nerve and his tunica vaginalis.

As a finishing touch Penny walked slowly in a wide circle, scenting the love chamber. The Baba had taught her well how to express the powerful pheromones that naturally accumulated in her Howard gland, and doing so effectively filled the romantic setting with an unmistakable hormonal aroma.

By now Tad was standing in the bedroom doorway, holding the bottle of champagne and two Baccarat flutes. A winning combination of excitement and vulnerability filled his eyes. With a fluttering of marabou feathers, she led him to the bed and quickly undressed him, covertly reviewing his general anatomy. A few gentle caresses located the puboprostatic ligament. Subtly exploring, her fingers teased their way gradually deeper and deeper into Tad's rectum. She traced his inguinal canal to the bulbourethral glands and the ejaculatory duct. If he objected to the liberties she was taking he didn't say so. On the contrary, the virile, brash attorney squirmed with trepidation as he watched Penny combine the pink champagne with the premixed packet of Beautiful You proprietary secret ingredients. Under her touch his youthful flesh quivered with fear and anticipation.

Unknown to him, the blood of her thwarted, would-be lover still stained the mattress where they staged their lovemaking. Fortunately, Penny had thought to flip it over.

Penny savored his goose bumps. This was how Max had felt as he'd dictated her mounting ecstasy. This was power. Gone were the young blue blood's wordy declarations of love. For him nothing existed beyond the erotic sensations he was feeling for the first time. He shuddered with ill-concealed passion as she invaded his frightened sphincter with the syringe's nozzle and the doctored pink wine began to expand and invade his bloodstream. Penny was coaxing his body to a fulfillment which would strain the very framework of his reality.

If Penny herself felt aroused it was on an intellectual level. Tad's groaning and squirming were proof she'd attained a mastery of human pleasure centers. She'd seen so many women acted upon. Grossly manipulated. It felt wonderful to see that she could have an equal effect on a man. Max was right about one thing: This wasn't a battle of boys versus girls. This was about how insight into your own body gave you power over others. Penny had once been the groveling, drooling test subject. Tonight she became the master. She controlled.

Deftly, she compressed his seminiferous tubules in order to suppress spermatogenesis. Penny Harrigan was no longer the shivering slab of meat waiting to be acted upon. Despite her dyed-purple plumage, she was the peerless sex lamia. Her every caress monitored the young lawyer's heartbeat and temperature. He gasped. His heart rate was 197 beats per minute. Tad's pelvic floor surrendered, and she expertly inserted a bright pink phallus chosen from Monique's sizable hoard. Using product number 371, the Daisy Love Wand, she stirred and churned the intoxicating concoction in her boyfriend's bowels. Such machinations quickly sent him into an erotically induced coma—his core temperature dropped below eighty degrees Fahrenheit, his pupils became fixed and dilated—and Penny was compelled to resuscitate him using her own breath. Just as Max had stimulated her to the brink of death, then brought her back to life, Penny resurrected Tad, telling him, "Do not die. Now that you know the joy that is possible for your body, cling to your paltry life. . . ."

This wasn't sex the way Tad had always known sex. The way Sigma Chis knew sex. He didn't ejaculate. Penny's careful tantric touch had suppressed his spermatic artery. Instead of a full-out emission of hot seed, only a clear jewel of seminal fluid trembled on the tip of his exhausted, modestly sized erection. This droplet Penny gracefully collected with the tip of one finger and brought to her tongue. It had the usual fructose sweetness of seminal fluids produced by the Cowper's glands, but beneath that lurked more subtle shadings of flavor.

As she had seen the Baba do, Penny sucked and licked every nuance from the sample. In it, she could read the schoolboy affection Tad was harboring for her. She could discern his dreams of their marrying and quickly raising a large, boisterous brood of children. In that single drop of glandular secretions she tasted a suburban ranch house, a pedigreed Irish setter, a seven-passenger minivan. He was as trapped by his small-scale, gender-specific dreams as she had been by hers. Hidden behind all those details was something more elusive. She smacked her lips, savoring the final hints. At last her taste buds recognized the key flavor component. It was shame.

Spent, Tad sprawled on the disheveled bed and returned her

gaze with dread. Even now her hands were tenderly applying a soothing ointment of mashed leeches to the raw, inflamed skin of his scrotum.

The truth of his fluid shocked Penny. But it was unmistakable. Smiling sheepishly at him, she said, "I know your darkest secret. There's no need to hide any longer." As she said the words, Tad closed his eyes, mortified.

She promised, "I won't tell anyone . . . but you didn't go to Yale, did you?"

Hearing that, the ambitious young attorney-at-law dissolved into tears.

Under oath, Penny would speak the truth for those who could not, for Alouette and Clarissa. She would speak for the ragged hordes lining Fifth Avenue. Entering the courtroom, she surveyed the proceedings and panicked. There were no women in the jury box. There were no women among the reporters or spectators in the gallery. Everyone present was male. To be the only woman was thrilling and intimidating. She froze in the doorway a moment too long, just time enough for every eye to find her. Every voice fell silent. She knew she looked breathtaking, her every muscle toned. She lifted a manicured hand and ran her fingers through her lustrous hair, turning her head slightly from side to side so that the long, thick strands bounced and caught the light. Every man was looking at her, and she was looking at no one.

She willed herself to take a step, and the eyes followed. Their hatred felt like a heated fog that swirled around her limbs until she arrived at the plaintiff's table.

Brillstein limped heavily into the courtroom. Wounds like he had suffered were slow to heal in the elderly, and he was clearly still in agony. Wincing, he lowered himself slowly into his seat near Penny, his red-rimmed eyes glowering at her. Only Tad separated the two of them. The firm had agreed that a younger man should question Penny when she was called to testify. The list of witnesses who might be called was short, because Tad planned to subpoena Maxwell's notebooks.

Voices shouted in the hallway outside. Heads in the courtroom turned in the direction of the disturbance. Male voices were shouting, "Maxwell, did you still love Alouette?" A chorus of men was shouting, "How are you holding up in the wake of Clarissa's self-assassination?" It was a near-repeat of the scene Penny had witnessed in the lobby of the BB&B building, when Alouette D'Ambrosia had stepped out of the elevator. Now dozens of journalists and bloggers were fighting for Max's attention. They all held camera phones overhead to capture video of him as he entered the courtroom.

Penny couldn't see him. Max was too closely protected within his scrum of blue-suited bodyguards. But she could see the tiny camera screens that depicted him from multiple angles. He wore a muted Ralph Lauren suit, appropriate for a wedding or a funeral. His pale hands were empty; there was no sign of the control box with which he could torment anyone implanted with the fiendish Beautiful You nanobots. A bemused smirk flitted across his pale lips.

For her part, Penny had worn a durable, stylish Jil Sander pantsuit. She couldn't risk a skirt or dress. She had no interest in repeating the tragically fatal striptease that Alouette had been compelled to perform onstage at the Oscars. She had considered smuggling a gun in her Prada shoulder bag, à la President Hind, but it was too late to murder Max. Courtroom security would be too tight.

The gaggle of reporters trailed Max all the way to his place at the defendant's table. There, a member of his defense team pulled out a chair, and Max took it without so much as a glance in Penny's direction. Even at a distance she could tell that his demeanor today was as cold as his hands had always felt. Gone was the gently smiling, always attentive dinner date who had coaxed her to discuss all of her worries. It was odd to see him without either a pen or a notebook.

True to his word, C. Linus Maxwell had ceased the flow of interest payments from her fifty-million-dollar trust. If she was driven to, Penny knew she could always sell the hefty ruby that dangled from the slim gold chain around her neck. She would squander her last cent to see his downfall.

Everyone stood as the judge made his entrance. He gaveled the trial into session.

Tad stood. "As counsel for the plaintiff," he announced, "I call Penny Harrigan as my first witness."

Every eye was upon her as she stood. Being constantly inspected by the world's rich and famous had left her immune to such public examinations. A thousand strangers were judging her body, her hair, even her character. None of that mattered. She walked like a queen striding toward the guillotine. She placed a hand on the Bible offered to her. Only then did she allow her eyes to meet Maxwell's. He returned the look, his gaze calm, unimpressed. An expression of supreme boredom. His half-closed eyes suggested that he was suppressing a yawn.

As Penny took her seat behind the microphone and stated her name for the record, he reached one pale hand into his suit jacket and removed a small black object. This he held in the palm of one hand and began to manipulate as if he were keyboarding a text message.

Not a text message, Penny thought. This would be a *text massage*.

Whether the effect was psychosomatic or not, Penny couldn't tell, but a soothing rush of warmth flooded her breasts. The general effect was so loving, so nurturing that Penny guessed it was her imagination. It was nothing like the rude sexual assaults he'd menaced her with earlier. This light stroking sensation between her legs was more like the touch of Baba Gray-Beard. Penny squirmed a little. Perhaps these were the feelings which Max broadcast to prompt women to buy certain books and shoes. This was how he could deliver female voters to his choice of candidates. It tickled slightly. The effect reminded her of the phrase her mom had used: "tickled pink."

Rising from his chair, Tad approached. "Miss Harrigan," he began, "are you a virgin?"

Penny wasn't shocked. She knew his entire line of questioning. Their strategy was to make her look like a brilliant coinventor, not a young flower led astray. "No," she answered. "I am not a virgin."

"Were you a virgin when you met Mr. Maxwell?"

Penny shook her head. "No, I was not." The pleasurable sensations continued to course through her. Her heart had begun to beat so heavily that she could almost feel the ruby pendant bouncing against her chest.

Tad fixed her with a stern look. "Did you participate in sexual encounters with Mr. Maxwell?"

Max's fingertips hovered as if waiting for her to betray him. Penny nodded.

The judge interjected, "Let the record state that the witness answered in the affirmative."

Tad continued, "Did you freely engage in the use of tools intended to heighten erotic experience?"

The remote-controlled pleasuring ceased abruptly. The warm buzzing in her nipples and groin, it hadn't been her imagination. It had been a warning. In response to Tad's last question Penny said, "Yes, I permitted Mr. Maxwell to test many of his ideas on me."

Without taking his eyes off of her, Max nimbly touched a series of buttons.

Penny felt her underarms grow damp. Her clothes felt as if the fabric were smoldering, about to catch fire. A trickle of sweat crept down the cleft between her buttocks. A long, sensual moan rose up in her throat but she choked it back.

Tad asked, "Were you compensated for the labor you performed for Mr. Maxwell?"

At the word *labor,* Max laughed quietly, tucking his chin to his chest.

Angered, Penny replied, "No. He gave me specific gifts of a personal nature—haute couture clothes, for example—but I was not formally compensated or recognized as his colleague and coresearcher."

Max glared at her. It was easy to read the rage in his face. How dared she assume equal status with him? He tapped several keys on his control box.

In the same instant, Penny gasped. Her heart stuttered. Her body strained to be free of her snug garments. Every inch of her skin grew so sensitive that even her silken underwear became as binding as barbed wire. Her fingers struggled to subtly undo various buttons and zippers, to find relief without betraying her arousal. She couldn't give Max the satisfaction. Besides, wriggling like a revved-up pole dancer would hardly win her sympathy with the all-male jury.

Tad didn't seem to notice. He asked, "Are you aware of the defendant's alias, 'Climax-Well'?"

Penny quelled a fresh rush of passion. She rotated her hips against her chair in what she hoped was an inconspicuous fashion. She said, "The tabloids called him that. But he *owns* all those *tabloids*!"

Tad continued, "Strictly in your own opinion, Miss Harrigan, what would you say is the chief source of Mr. Maxwell's extensive sexual expertise?"

Here it was, the opportunity to denounce him. Penny quickly swallowed the hot saliva that flooded her mouth. She discreetly lifted a tissue to blot at the beads of sweat that were welling up on her forehead. With the entire world listening, she would explain about Maxwell's journey to Nepal and the apprenticeship he'd served at the knee of the Baba. She'd describe how his truncated tragic marriage had motivated him. And Penny would state for the public record how Beautiful You intimate care products were modeled after the desiccated bones of crazed pilgrims who'd pleasured themselves to death. The world would soon know how Maxwell had looted the sensual secrets of all human history in order to enslave female consumers and control their spending habits. Those degraded ladies were captive to an erotic power beyond their comprehension, and Penny would rescue them. Max would be unmasked.

Even as the words formed on her lips, her breathing grew slow and heavy. Penny's thighs wiggled to be free from her moistened underpants. Her feet kicked off the shoes that seemed to trap them. In subconscious response the male onlookers eagerly edged forward in their seats. Their lustful eyes devoured her.

"Tell us," Tad encouraged. He really looked yummy in his lawyer clothes. Penny couldn't wait to marry him once this ordeal was behind them. Their honeymoon sex was going to be fantastic.

She was only vaguely aware of how Max was pressing buttons, frantically trying to stem her testimony with a larger wave of ecstasy. He might even be trying to kill her with a pleasure-induced stroke or heart attack. He grimly punched keys, never taking his eyes off of her physical reaction.

The nanbots that were implanted within her nervous system, they were most likely feeding Max all of her vital signs.

The black box he held, it would be relaying her heart rate, blood pressure, hormone levels—everything.

His powers went far beyond what she'd anticipated. Max pressed one button, and she instantly tasted phantom chocolate. The best dark chocolate she'd ever known; her mouth was brimming with the delicious flavor. He pressed another button, and Penny smelled the heady perfume of a beautiful rose garden. The nanobots he'd delivered via the infamous Dragonfly, they rallied to stimulate all of her senses. Vast symphonies of violin music played in her ears. The thrilling effects of the pink champagne douche seemed to swell afresh within her.

Still, Penny fought to speak. Her hands roamed unbidden in her hair. Her back arched to thrust her breasts forward. "He's controlling the world . . ." she said in a quavering voice. She pointed a shaky finger. "Look! With his telephone!"

Noticing her distress, Tad cut in. "Your Honor," he addressed the judge, "it appears that the witness is falling ill."

"Please stop him," Penny wailed. "He's controlling my mind!" Of their own volition, her hands were stripping away her blouse. Her violent rubbing and shimmying made her slacks flutter down to collect around her ankles. A cacophony of savory tastes—foie gras and Grand Marnier and caramel lattes—tickled her palate. Deafening Mozart arias rang in her ears. Her sinuses were inflamed with the sweet odors of jasmine and puppies. To the world he looked like he was playing Tetris, but Maxwell was spurring all of these exquisite sensations to occur as his fingers fiddled with keys like a virtuoso concert pianist.

Helpless, Penny felt her body respond to an invisible attacker. Her orifices ached as if she were being violated by hundreds of erect penises. Her legs and lips were forced apart, and she could taste and feel a multitude of unseen tongues invading her. Phantom teeth nibbled playfully at her nipples, and she felt hot panting against her neck.

She screamed, but no one came to her rescue. The court stenographer recorded her pleading. The sketch artists drew her struggles.

Tad stared at her in shocked disbelief. She was no longer the accomplished sex witch. As before, she was the sweaty slab of meat under someone else's erotic control.

The paramedics arrived and lifted her onto a gurney. They asked her for the year, the president. They asked her name and recognized her with delight: "the Nerd's Cinderella."

All the way to the mental hospital one of them kept marveling, "You should've married him. . . ."

Despite a steady downpour of cold rain, a bedraggled line of shoppers stretched along Fifth Avenue. The drops flattened their hair into lank ribbons that hung over their faces, hiding their dulled, glassy eyes. Their ruined shoes stood, brimming, in puddles. Every few minutes a tragic scarecrow would stagger a step forward. One end of the line vanished through the pink-mirrored doors of a shop. The opposite end of the line stretched to the horizon. Here and there a shopper had collapsed, but even those feeble ladies continued to inch forward on their hands and knees.

Few if any of them looked up as a superstretch limousine carried a wedding party to the front of St. Patrick's Cathedral. There, a canopy protected the arriving guests. Among them were world leaders, the queen of England, a Chinese media baron, prizewinning lady artists of every ilk. Legions of journalists crowded the sidewalk. It was the news story of the decade. The world's richest, most powerful man was getting married.

En route to her nuptials, the bride was driven past the miles and miles of haggard shoppers. She kept her veils lowered, hoping that she wouldn't be recognized. She, Penny Harrigan, had failed to save anyone, and now she would pay the ultimate price. She would break no new ground for the next generation of women. She'd open no new frontier for feminism. Adorned in a voluptuous Priscilla of Boston wedding gown, she steeled herself to walk down the aisle and pledge her troth to C. Linus Maxwell.

On every corner, sidewalk newsstands displayed the day's banner tabloid headlines: "Nerd King Marries His Evil Queen." Another headline: "All Hail Queen Penny." Yet other tabloids trumpeted: "Climax-Well Plots to Take Over World" and "Corny Maxwell Builds Secret Sex Robots." Only Penny could recognize his strategy. He'd planted these stories in order to present the truth as a ludicrous joke. He was undermining the credibility of her discovery. Now no one would ever believe her.

Her vintage wedding dress was appropriately cumbersome. She was hobbled by its weight of petticoats and flounces. But it was necessary for the mythology taking place. To everyone else in history, this would look like a storybook ending: Cinderella wedding her Prince Charming. Max needed that to bolster the illusion he'd crafted for so many years.

Overall, the inky smoke of burning latex blanketed the city. Flaming dildos continued to pelt down, dealing random death.

The Beautiful You stragglers plodded along like an army in endless retreat from some distant battlefield. Wounded and dispirited. Their sodden clothes streaming, they had no idea that they were pawns in a worldwide plot. Penny had not only failed to help them, she'd been actively complicit in their defeat. It had been in her bed that the weapons of their downfall had been perfected. Penny's feedback had honed the tools that now devastated her gender. So it was only fitting that she must pledge herself to Max.

The most intelligent, talented, determined women in the

world were now subject to his whims. With the push of a button he could put incredible tastes in their mouths. He could make them hear glorious music that didn't exist. He controlled their reality. Today marked the beginning of a dark age for women everywhere, and Penny hoped it would last for only one generation. Once the truth came to be widely known, maybe the next generation would steer clear of Beautiful You products.

But, Penny thought, if the nanobots were self-replicating, each mother might pass the tiny masters to her daughters. Perhaps to her sons as well. Within a generation the entire industrialized world would belong to Max. Evil Max.

If, as he'd said, he'd had a vasectomy, there would be no one to inherit his legacy. Knowing him, Penny assumed the reins of power would eventually pass to a fully automated supercomputer. Soon some software program would be telling everyone what they felt and tasted, doling out artificial orgasms and sweet, faked music via the nervous-system robots.

By then, Penny realized that it wouldn't matter how anything tasted. DataMicroCom could put any ingredients in the foods they sold. Actual flavor and mouth feel wouldn't matter, because the nanobots would control how the consumers perceived all products.

Penny recalled the cab ride to her first dinner date at Chez Romaine. In contrast to walking that first red carpet ignored, this morning a dense wall of newshounds filled the sidewalk, vying to get a photograph of her in her wedding finery. Scores of Max's lackeys carried the train of her dress and held black umbrellas to prevent even a single raindrop from marring her appearance. A scrum of blue-suited bodyguards escorted her through the crowd.

Rushing up the steps of the cathedral, Penny tasted spicy barbecued ribs. She heard sweet birds singing. She knew none of it was real. Max was only putting the perceptions in her head.

To comfort her, she supposed. Her mind would never again be her own.

Entering the foyer of the church she caught sight of three familiar faces but dismissed them as more Max-induced hallucinations. They smiled. She smiled back, asking, "Are you guys for real?"

They were her parents and her housemate. Her mom and Monique looked fragile and emaciated, but apparently Max had given them enough strength to be here today. The two women were less wedding guests than they were hostages brought to ensure the ceremony would go through without a hitch. Penny might attempt another rebellion, but not if the people she loved were in constant danger.

It seemed ironic how not long ago her mom and Monique had been badgering Penny to throw away her birth control and trap Max into marriage. Now she was the one who was trapped. And this morning they looked like mourners at a funeral. They all four hugged warmly.

As the ushers stood ready to seat her parents, Penny's mother whispered, "Here, take this." She pressed something into her daughter's hand. "Read it."

Penny noticed with horror that her mom's wrists were raw with rope burns. Her bare arms were polka-dotted with the red scabs marking hypodermic injection sites. What she offered was a folded square of paper. Smoothing it flat, Penny found it was a yellowed page from an ages-old back issue of the *National Enquirer*. Nervously, she asked a bodyguard whether there was a toilet she could use.

Not one of the parish's pious cleaning ladies had reported to work in weeks, Penny noted with disdain. Maneuvering her gigantic hoop skirt into a filthy toilet cubicle took some doing. Every movement caused the elegant satin to wick up unclean water from the urine-stinking floor. Penny could hear the first strains of the "Wedding March" as her eyes furiously scanned the tabloid page. The headline of the article read, "DataMicro-Com Gambles Big on Cloning Technology." According to the piece that followed, Max's company had made massive investments in researching how to create a viable human embryo and clone it. This research had taken place during the same era as the nanobot research. According to the *National Enquirer*'s science writer, the company's stated long-term goal was to generate a microscopic clone. That clone would be sealed in suspended animation. It could be implanted and gestate to maturity within a surrogate womb.

Penny read and reread the article before flushing it down the toilet.

If Max could sneak mind-controlling nanobots into women, why couldn't he smuggle a suspended embryonic clone into them as well? Including her! Without a doubt this would be a clone of himself. That, *that* was his master plan. To control world population growth . . . to perpetuate his global corporate power . . . like some parasite, he planned to hatch thousands, possibly millions of identical Maxes in the uteruses of unsuspecting women. That was his scheme to bring peace to mankind. His perfect world would be populated by a billion versions of him!

Maxwell was standing at the altar. Her parents were sitting in the front pew, waiting with the hundreds of dignitaries and celebrities for the bride to come down the aisle.

Every woman in the church smiled raptly. Clearly Max was bombarding their senses with every enjoyable sensation imaginable. Penny's mom sighed as if lost in the rapture of fresh-baked brownies. Monique's eyes slowly closed as if she were carried aloft on a magic carpet of waltz music. Only Penny was exempt from whatever pleasures Max was using to keep the other women docile as the ceremony progressed.

Soon she'd become Mrs. C. Linus Maxwell. She'd found her destiny, or it had found her. From this day forward she'd be at the helm of the largest corporation in the world. She'd be wife to the richest man on the globe. Penny took her place at his side. Veiled. Implanted. To love, honor, cherish, but most important—to obey.

The bishop asked, "If anyone here can give just cause for why these two should not be joined in holy matrimony, speak now or forever hold your peace."

A murmur came from the rear of the church. The multitude of elegant necks swiveled to watch as a stooped figure slowly trudged down the center aisle. Its scraggly gray tresses were streaming with rainwater. Its withered body inched along, unclothed. A trailing abundance of gray pubic hair hung so far down it brushed the red carpet. To judge from his expression of surprise and fear, Max knew instantly who this uninvited apparition was. The approaching hag lifted her blind, whitened eyes in his direction and spoke. Her crone's nose sniffing the air, she cried, "Maxwell, I can smell your fear!" Her voice a rusty croak, her toothless mouth bade, "Stop this . . . travesty!"

Warily Maxwell dipped a hand inside his tux jacket and brought forth the black control box. His touch could torture or kill millions.

The ever-encroaching hag commanded, "Tell her, Maxwell!" The witch pointed a gnarled finger and ordered, "If you can wed the girl then tell her the truth! Tell your young bride the true nature of her existence!"

Max's eyes bulged in horror.

Now halfway down the aisle, the ragged cadaver-woman bade, "Tell her the secret which I could not. This knowledge must come from you. Tell her!"

Penny stood, confused, glancing between the ragged accuser and the man who was about to become her husband.

Of course this was the Baba, come all the way from Nepal to New York. Her lips parted and she said, "Tell her why you've dedicated your life to the service of pleasuring women!"

Max lifted his controller for all to see. "Take another step, old mother, and the death of a billion women will be on your head!"

The Baba quelled her progress.

Here Penny interjected. "Baba," she cried boldly, "I know the reason Maxwell stole the sensual secrets of the ancients. I know why he's wagered his lifetime to gain access to the world's best vaginas!"

The women present continued to swoon heavily in their waking pleasure dreams. The male guests seemed nicely surprised to have some unexpected interruption in an otherwise tedious wedding ceremony. If they were aware of the women's pleasure they were studiously ignoring it. These men, for the most part, appeared to be the scurrilous lotharios and black-market profiteers who were exploiting the Beautiful You effect.

As Max's finger hovered over the buttons of a global massacre, Penny announced, "I know about the cloning research. I know that Max has implanted cloned embryos of himself in every user of Beautiful You products, and soon he'll trigger them all to begin gestation." She had the attention of the entire cathedral as she shouted, "The same nanobots that bring pleasure and pain to Max's slaves, those same tiny robots will suppress the immune function that might otherwise reject these foreign fetuses. That army of microscopic robots will protect and defend those fetuses so that hundreds of millions of fertile women will give birth to exact copies of Cornelius Linus Maxwell!"

By the end of her short speech Penny was screaming her words. Wildly waving her wedding bouquet about. As she fell silent, the assembled crowds stared at her in disbelief. Penny, in her fluffy, flouncy gown, waited for the reaction of outrage. She readied herself for Max to begin tormenting her with a few keystrokes. None of that happened.

The Baba turned clouded eyes on her. The old woman tilted her head quizzically and said, "What are you talking about, my dear? That's not it at all."

Somewhere, someone in the cavernous church giggled.

"Another word," Max threatened, "and I'll deliver more suffering than you people can imagine!"

Heedless, Baba Gray-Beard ventured, "The dress you're wearing, Penny Harrigan, it was *her* dress twenty-five years ago. It's the wedding gown Max's long-dead wife wore when she was your exact age!" Her words echoed around the huge stone chapel. "Ask your groom why that dress is such a perfect fit!"

The dress had been an exact fit. From the first time Penny tried it on, the gown had felt as if it were made for her.

Before she could ponder this miracle another moment, Max fingered his device. Unseen, a satellite relayed the signal, and Penny felt a searing jolt of pain shoot through her. Likewise, every female wedding guest shrieked and slumped to the cold floor. Only the Baba remained upright, staring defiantly into Max's outraged eyes. "Tell the girl," she hissed. "She must know the destiny she was born to fulfill."

"Never," Max cried.

Penny was only vaguely aware that the Baba had closed the distance between herself and Maxwell. The two adversaries circled each other, the tuxedo-clad dandy and the emaciated skeleton. Maxwell stashed the control box in the inside pocket of his tux jacket and raised both his empty hands menacingly, ready to lunge at the hag's next words.

The bishop stood over Penny, blushing furiously as she wriggled at his feet, writhing in agony and sensual pleasure, near crazed, with a lunatic's guttural yammering streaming from her mouth.

"You, little Penny," the Baba shouted. "You must reflect his evil energy. It was no accident that you met Maxwell. Only you can defeat him!"

No sooner had she muttered those words than Max sprang forward, grabbing Baba Gray-Beard around her desiccated throat and saying, "Die, wicked sorceress!"

Even as she gasped for her next breath, the Baba said, "Look! Look in his notebook at a date nine months before you were born, Penny!" Her voice reduced to a garbled whisper, she said, "Look and see who he was seducing. . . ."

Penny rolled around in the fluff of her vast wedding dress. She could sense the nanobots scooting about in her veins. She wanted to slice her arteries open and strain her blood clean. The robots would never be at peace. She'd never be free of them. Maxwell's little sentries were alive and inflicting their pain from the inside.

Her neck crushed in Max's cold hands, the Baba was dying. After two centuries of coaching pilgrims to sexual enlightenment, the gentle yogi was expiring in the grip of her greatest pupil. Even as the hands throttled her windpipe, she croaked, "Child, you must rebound his energy. Channel it through yourself and return it with greater force!" She whispered, "No mirror is ever burned by the rays from even the hottest sun!"

To displace the assault of false pleasure, Penny concentrated on her close-knit family and their simple Lutheran faith. She savored the real friendship that had formed between herself and Monique. Penny's mind embraced everything she truly loved in the world. Butter brickle ice cream. Ron Howard. Richard Thomas. With steady meditating, Penny's consciousness began to deflect the signals from Max's control box. The teeming nanobots gradually trickled downward, crowding to a halt within her waiting pelvis.

Simultaneously, a shrill whistle filled the church. Faint at first, the sound grew in strength. The whistle increased to become a siren, a wailing of air-raid volume. The siren built to a bullhorn, so loud it threatened to scramble the brains of everyone present. The guests, the bishop, every person in the cavernous church clamped their hands over their ears and cowered in pain.

Penny was its source. Muffled only by her skirts and crinolines, the trumpeting sound was being emitted from between her legs. It echoed off the masonry walls. The towering stained-glass windows rattled. As trumpets had toppled the great walls of Jericho, thin cracks opened between the cathedral's stones. A dust of mortar drifted down. As the sound built to thunder it exploded through her satin and petticoats, spraying sequins and seed pearls like shrapnel. Shredded lace flew like countless flakes of white confetti, exposing the seat of the bride's power.

Penny focused on the love she felt for the great Baba, and the edges of her sex flared outward, blasting forth a huge noise. It blared, a sonic cannon. The blast extinguished the sanctuary candles.

Without warning, the cathedral's great rose window exploded. Not outward. The window burst *inward,* pelting the wedding party with razor-sharp fragments of red, blue, and green glass, shattered by something flying bullet-fast from the direction of Yankee Stadium.

Like a lightning bolt . . . a ball of fire . . . a molten flaming mass of latex and batteries shot across the vast length of the great sanctuary. With the force of a shotgun blast, this murderous rocket smote Max squarely in the tailored inseam of his designer formalwear. This searing-hot mortar round of burning personal care products, it tore into the groom's private man-parts, doubling him in half at the waist and toppling him backward.

The centuries-old lamia was dead.

Maxwell, he'd been mortally wounded by a weapon from his own arsenal of space-age pleasure tools—an immolating phallus that had launched itself from the Promise Keepers' bonfire! Blood flowed steadily from the torn crotch of his tuxedo. Penny didn't need to look closer to know his genitals were obliterated. Like a character in some Ernest Hemingway book she'd been required to read in high school, his private junk was blown to bits by the blast. Baba Gray-Beard was dead and Max was dying.

The nanobots within her ceased their torment. Slowly Penny and the other women in the church struggled to their feet, blinking dazed eyes. They shook their disarrayed hair out of their faces and opened their purses to begin the long, difficult task of repairing their makeup. And their lives.

The frigid fingers of a dying hand closed around Penny's ankle. It was Max, looking up at her with pleading eyes. His already pale face was bled paper-white, and his lips moved to form words. "Listen," he said. "Look." With his free hand he reached into his jacket pocket and produced a ragged scrap of newsprint. "For you," he said, and held it for her to take.

Penny knelt and accepted it: a newspaper clipping dated

exactly thirty years ago, to the day. It had been saved from the *National Enquirer*. Prominently featured was a black-and-white photograph. It was grainy and faded by the years, but it was like looking into a mirror. It was her face, wearing the same veil and gown she now wore. It was a wedding announcement. Cornelius Linus Maxwell was to marry Phoebe Bradshaw. Stapled to that was a second newspaper article, an obituary dated exactly 136 days later. The young Mrs. Corny Maxwell had died from an allergic reaction to shellfish.

Fear shadowed Penny's heart. She herself was allergic to shellfish. Their first dinner at Chez Romaine, when she'd almost ordered scallop sushi, Max had stopped her. Somehow Max had also known about her severe allergy.

"My wife," he said. Where his penis and testicles had once dangled, Penny saw that there was only a rude wound gushing blood. The same dying hand that had presented the articles now offered his ubiquitous notebook; holding it open to a specific page, he said, "'Test subject number eleven forty-eight, Myrtle Harrigan, March twenty-fourth, 19—. Place: Shippee, Nebraska...'"

Penny's mother sobbed quietly as Maxwell read aloud the details of their tryst. Twenty-five years earlier, she had been a small-town newlywed attending a pie social at the local grange hall. In untypically gallant language Max had recorded, "'The test subject seemed bereft as she confided in me about her inability to bear a child. A stranger in town, I must've seemed a safe person with whom to unburden her heart.'" A generation ago, this young Nebraskan woman had spilled out her secret fears to Max just as Penny would on their first date at

Chez Romaine. "'The woman was a hundred and sixty-eight centimeters in height, approximately fifty-four kilograms in weight—'"

A distance away from where Max held his notebook, recounting his past, Penny's weeping mother lifted her face from a handful of tissues and interrupted: "I was only fifty-one kilograms!"

Dying, Max continued. "'In my heart I knew I could do more for this poor, barren woman than provoke her to a gut-wrenching orgasm. It was within my power to give her the baby she so badly wanted.'"

He described how he'd seduced this latest test subject over a slice of pumpkin pie. Her husband was away, attending a Promise Keepers weekend retreat. It took very little charm to persuade this lonely young housewife. Max had consummated the evening in the backseat of his rented Ford Explorer.

"'When her heart rate reached one hundred and sixty-three bpms,'" Max announced flatly, "'I implanted a cloned zygote along with the latest generation of nanobots needed to ensure its survival.'"

Sobbing, Penny's mom insisted, "I've never weighed more than a hundred and twenty pounds, even after you got me pregnant!"

Nine months later, Penny had been born. A seeming miracle.

From his anguished expression Penny knew her father had no idea. Neither of her parents had suspected that they'd played a part in Max's plan to replicate his long-deceased wife. They'd innocently harbored the experiment of a fiend. He could've planted his embryo in any of the many women he'd romanced. He could've implanted embryos in all of them.

More troubling to Penny was the real possibility that she wasn't herself. It was bad enough that impulses were being beamed to her, prompting the arousal of her pleasure centers. Now her very DNA was secondhand, bequeathed to her by a madman genius who yearned to be reunited with his beloved. She, Penny Harrigan, was the genetically resurrected Phoebe Maxwell.

In that shocked, otherwise silent moment, one voice rang out. As spunky as ever, Monique squealed, "Omaha girl! Yikes!"

Farther back in the church, Esperanza, once more a Latin spitfire, shrieked, *"Ay, caramba!"*

"All your life my agents have kept watch over you," Max whispered, blood leaking from the ragged gash between his legs. The church had fallen so silent that everyone present could hear his confession. Penny had only to look at the faded photograph in the obituary to know this was all true.

Her guardian angels, she realized, weren't the helpful agents of Homeland Security. Since infancy, those suited and besunglassed sentries had protected her on Max's behalf. They'd allowed nothing to befall her before she could mature as a replacement for his long-dead wife.

"You are proof that my cloning technology will work," Max continued. "I've spent my life gaining access to every uterus in the civilized world."

As a gesture, even to Penny, it was really quite touching. Maxwell *had* loved her. He'd loved her enough to resurrect her from the dead.

Maxwell crowed, "You with your perfect genitals, my good girl, you will be my gift to all men!"

The Baba's battered corpse lay beside him, so close that his blood washed against it. As the flow of his living juices slowed,

Max's eyes fluttered closed. His lungs exhaled their final breath. "Oh, Phoebe . . . I've missed you for so many years. . . ." And Max was gone.

Alone in her Himalayan cave—nude, of course—Penny sprinkled seasonings into a stewing broth of chopped lizards. She stirred the simmering pot and brought a steaming spoonful to her lips. The taste filled her with a sad nostalgia for the dead Baba. Not an hour after the lamia and Max had expired on the floor of St. Patrick's Cathedral, Penny had boarded a private chartered jet and was winging her way to Nepal. She'd scaled the ragged cliffs of Mount Everest still wearing the tatters of her wedding gown. She'd told no one her destination.

Penny's parents were safe. Monique was delivered from her battery-powered obsession. Monique, to judge from the text messages she blasted on an hourly basis, was engaged to marry Tad. She'd continue to reside in the Upper East Side town house *and* have the adoration of a handsome spouse.

Penny reasoned that perhaps in due time a trickle of students would find her here, lured by the ancient legend of a mystical sex witch who could perpetuate the erotic legacy of the ages. A constant stream of physically perfect specimens striving for erotic education would deliver themselves to apprentice with her. Penny was the heiress to the collected tantric skills of all time, was she not? She, Penelope Anne Harrigan, would accept the torch passed to her by the likes of Baba Gray-Beard and Bella Abzug. She'd liberate women from having to go to men for fulfillment. This legacy—not clothes, not jewelry or practicing law—this was the destiny she had long sought. Hers was a power based on carnal pleasure. Her kingdom a realm beyond interpersonal politics.

Penny had learned what was important. Family was important. Love was paramount.

Slowly she stirred. Concocted according to the Baba's favorite recipe, the soup's surface was garnished with flakes of spicy guano. As Penny squatted beside the cooking pot she enjoyed the gentle warmth of the flames. In the stance of a sumo wrestler, she lackadaisically stroked herself with a short, knurled length of what looked like damp wood. It was the Baba's longest finger, the very finger with which the wise ancient had read all of Penny's secrets. As the old lamia had cut a finger from her own dead mother, Penny had severed this memento mori from her mentor's cooling corpse. Still, the keepsake, even well lubricated with stone-ground rabbit sebum, fell far short of slaking Penny's growing melancholy.

The words *arousal addiction* loomed in her mind, but she shooed them away.

As she dipped her spoon for a second taste, she worried that millions of ladies all over the world were likewise crouched, struggling to achieve fresh self-fulfillment. After the sultry ordeal of Beautiful You it was possible that they might never achieve comparable heights of release.

The rudimentary pleasure tools fashioned by the Baba . . . they were okay. But minus the high-tech vaginal stimulation of Max's hybrids, not to mention the salivating attention of the mass media, Penny felt down in the dumps. Perhaps the eggheads were right. Just as teenage boys clung to their precious video games and skin flicks, Penny longed for her bright pink products. Perhaps arousal addiction was real. Her limbic brain was thirsting for dopamine. Her hypothalamus was completely catawampus! She was suffering withdrawal from the Beautiful You effect. She redoubled her efforts with the desiccated finger but felt little reward.

Leaving the fireside, she waddled across the cave's littered floor in search of something. She cast aside the aged tendons and Prada handbags in her frantic search. At last, she found the object she so feverishly sought.

It was a small black box, no larger than a Game Boy. Max's controller. She'd pocketed it in the final moments of her botched nuptials. After Max had been fatally cut down by a flaming dildo projectile, she'd also made off with his precious notebook. Since then she'd spent the wintery hours deciphering these coded records of his sensual research. The mosaic of black push buttons was cryptically labeled, but she'd taught herself what combinations to press for the best results.

She'd begin with the blizzard winds outside the cave's entrance. Night and day they wailed, a constant annoyance. Quickly Penny utilized the controller to adjust her perception.

She keyed in the first code, and the satellite-relayed result was almost instantaneous. She tasted a flood of red velvet cake with chocolate icing and rainbow sprinkles sliding down her throat. No Swiss clockmaker could've picked out the codes with more dexterity and accuracy. To distract herself further, Penny punched another combination of keys and tasted delicious butter brickle ice cream. Regardless, her busy fingers weren't satisfied. Making quick work, she prompted the nanobots in her brain and bloodstream to create the overwhelming pleasure of Tom Berenger and Richard Thomas kissing her wetly on the lips and breasts.

In the next instant, something shocking occurred. A sound. Someone spoke, and the kissing stopped. It was a familiar voice. A female voice. Penny's eyes scoured the filthy cavern but found no explanation. The disembodied words were vague as a dream. But it was unmistakable: The speaker was Baba Gray-Beard. Hanging in the chill air was the odor of fermented egg yolks, the signature aroma of the lamia's labored sex panting.

Dared Penny hope? Might the great mystic's ghost return to make love magic to her while she slept? A darker possibility was that the nanobots were somehow continuing to shape her perceptions. Faint as a thought, the Baba ordered, "Destroy it!" In words as weak as an echo of an echo of an echo, the spirit warned, "Little one, such power will corrupt you as it did Maxwell. . . ." The spirit urged, "Mash the evil controller device betwixt two large rocks before it *seduces you!*"

In awed response, Penny whispered, "Baba, are you here?"

She waited, listening, hearing only the fierce wind. She sat and contemplated a future of solitude with only the hoary love implements hewn from bone and sinew. She counted to a hundred in fives. She examined the sorry state of her cuticles. After that, she counted to a thousand by twenties. The sex witch's ghost spoke no more. The youthful sex apprentice struggled with the decision of what to do next.

Immediately, inspiration struck. The DataMicroCom satellites were still in orbit. Why couldn't she deliver succor to the legions of gals worldwide who were sharing this same withdrawal from Beautiful You bliss?

Unselfishly, she toggled and keyboarded until these same amazing sensations were bombarding all the women implanted by Beautiful You products. Penny's mom in Omaha. Sassy, spunky Monique. Even Brenda—now Yuri's newlywed bride *and* the CFO of Allied Chemical Corp. Kwan Qxi and Esperanza, too! Wherever they were, they would all be savoring rich desserts and the heavenly bliss of ripe movie-star smooches.

Impulsively, she filled their far-flung nostrils with mango-scented breezes. Let all her sister women rejoice, Penny told herself. Through her they would achieve solidarity.

While their actual circumstances might be grinding poverty

and ignorance, she'd bestow upon them a rich surrogate reality. She'd deliver to their taste buds an unending banquet of gourmet delicacies. An unending repast without a single fattening calorie! She'd replace their mundane thoughts with snippets of inspirational poetry read aloud by the cultured mouth of Meryl Streep.

A few pecks on the right keys, and she'd carpet-bomb them with self-esteem and resolve problematic body-image issues for all time.

She cupped her breasts in her palms and lifted them, examining the nipples with growing awe and wonder. They were astonishing. Her heart, nay, every cell of her swelled in recognition of her own glory and beauty. Following suit, women around the world—tall women, crippled women, fat, old, young and skinny women, they rediscovered themselves. Wherever they were at that moment in their lives—dining at picnics or riding aboard buses or performing intricate brain surgeries— they paused and regarded their bodies with a new, powerful appreciation. Flat-chested, bowlegged, humpbacked, or balding, Penny would force them to recognize their innate beauty. At her satellite-relayed prompting, all women would begin to pet themselves, reveling in the quality of their skin. Penny's electronic urging would compel them to immediately celebrate their bodies with vigorous self-romancing.

This, this was power. She, Penelope Harrigan, would reign over the world, a benevolent lady dictator, awarding well-deserved pleasure to the multitudes. She'd surpassed the power wielded by even her heroes, Clarissa Hind and Alouette D'Ambrosia. To redeem Max's wicked technology, she would singlehandedly bring about world peace and order. She'd reward good behavior and punish the bad.

The generations of females trained too long to look for

insults and injustice, Penny would pummel them with joy and drive them to accept happiness. A happy ending. With stealthy, subtle manipulation of their pleasure centers, she'd gently bully them into achieving their full erotic potential. Lady political activists might bicker over their strategic goals, platforms, and agendas, but Penny would trump their catfighting by giving them tsunami waves of physical thrills.

An ancient truism had once decreed, "Self-improvement is masturbation. . . ." At last the inverse would also be true.

"Baba," she cried out, "rest easy, my guardian! I will not allow the power to overcome me!"

This, Penny whispered to herself, *this would be the best time in history to be a woman.*

She'd give ladies the ultimate zipless fuck. Erica Jong would be so proud of her. This—sex crafting, practicing carnal magic—would be the new frontier for the next generation of young female searchers.

Acting on a generous impulse, Penny pressed the buttons that would bestow a loving, sisterly, long-distance hug on Gloria Steinem.

That accomplished, she scuttled back toward the cooking fire lest her tasty lizards scorch.

Intoxicated with satisfaction, weak from joy, again she referred to Max's notebook of codes. Perfect as this moment was—the precious finger lodged deep inside her, the stewed skinks bubbling deliciously, the flames warming her nude, astonishingly beguiling body—even this scene could be improved upon.

With tired, trembling, happy fingers she punched a few more buttons on the controller.

What took place next was only a nanobot-induced hallucination, but Penny could see it, smell it, feel it.

A robust, strapping figure emerged from the snowstorm and stood brazenly unclothed in the cave's mouth. His dancing blue eyes filled with lust. His impressive, freckled-pink manhood swung heavily between his legs. And a handsome Ron Howard swaggered boldly toward her.

The author would like to acknowledge the following visionaries for their unflagging faith and support of the arts. May the tantric gods visit you with frequent, pulse-pounding, sweat-soaked episodes of full release as you slumber.

Mallory Moss
Katie Dodd
William Klayer
Kasey Bossert
Ian W. Arsenault
Halle Kasper
Megan McCrary
Mandy Boles
Kyle Becker
Adam Stratton
Donald Hugo III
Chuck Crittenden
Peter Wollesen
Stephanie Jean Ray
Nicole Doro
Valeriya Kulchikhina
Meghan Sherar
Angelena Bigham

Zachary Glenn Harbaugh
Andrew G. Gahol
Peter Osborn
Christopher Seevers
Kerstynn Lane
Michael John Silvin
Mandy Marez
Joe Wilson
Wessly Ford
Stephanie Wiley
Patrick D. O'Connor
Henry S. Rosenthal
Brian Manning
Parker Cross
Margaret Dennison
Sharon Leong
Kevin Stevulak
Charlotte O'Neil Golden

Michael Anderson-McGee

Katie McCartney

Jacquelyn Nicole Tawney

Gary Eaton

Mike Parkinson

Dustin Schultz

Gina Chernoby

Michele McDaniel

Jake Richard

Ryan O'Neill

George Washington Anderson III

Aysha Martinez

Trev Pierce

John Hardenstine

Bettina Holbrook

Michael Bowhay

Mark V. Paulis

Kevin Sharp

Patricia Scott Petey Wells

Mike Hardin

Thomas Wayne Harvey

Andrew Greenblatt

Elizabeth C. Nichols

Brian Foster

Bryce Haynes

Tatianna Abastoflor

Ronald Green, Jr.

Alisha Ohl

Cody Maasen

Bryan Kraig Ward

Jessica Dugan

Matthew A. Eller

Meredith Alder

Tiffany Joy Atencio

Kyle Adamski

John Michel

Quentin R. Voglund

James Bendos

Gabriel Cesana

Jason W. Bohrer

Shane Gollihue

Scott Trulock

Aaron Blake Flynn

Brett Kerns

Juliet Walker

Kristina Valencia

James P. Giacopelli

Karen Zacconi

Sean K. Smith

Rita Su

Will Tupper

Michael Pedrosa

Russ Robertson

Tag

Samantha Jade Schnee

Rubyann Baybo

Yassaman Tarazkar

Shereen Lombardi

Ashley Blaike Ralph

Mike Dyson

Lorne Sherman

Patti Vanty-McKinley

Shaun Sharma

Christine Strileckis

CHOKE

Victor Mancini, a medical school dropout, is an antihero for our deranged times. To pay for elder care for his mother, Victor has devised an ingenious scam: he pretends to choke on pieces of food while dining in upscale restaurants. He then allows himself to be "saved" by fellow patrons who, feeling responsible for Victor's life, go on to send checks to support him. When he's not pulling this stunt, Victor cruises sexual addiction recovery workshops for action, visits his addled mom, and spends his days working at a colonial theme park.

Fiction

DAMNED

Madison is the thirteen-year-old daughter of a narcissistic film star and a billionaire. Abandoned at her Swiss boarding school over Christmas, she dies over the holiday, presumably of a marijuana overdose. The last thing she remembers is getting into a town car and falling asleep. Then she wakes up in Hell. Literally. Madison soon finds that she shares a cell with a motley crew of young sinners: a cheerleader, a jock, a nerd, and a punk rocker, united by their doomed fate, like an afterschool detention for the damned. Together they form an odd coalition and march across the unspeakable landscape of Hell—full of used diapers, dandruff, WiFi blackout spots, evil historical figures, and one horrific call center—to confront the Devil himself.

Fiction

DIARY

Misty Wilmot has had it. Once a promising young artist, she's drinking too much and is working as a waitress in a hotel. Her husband, a contractor, is in a coma after a suicide attempt, and his clients are threatening Misty with lawsuits over a series of vile messages they've discovered on the walls of houses he remodeled. Suddenly, Misty's artistic talent returns. Inspired but confused by a burst of creativity, she soon finds herself a pawn in a larger conspiracy that threatens to cost hundreds of lives.

Fiction

HAUNTED

Haunted is a novel made up of twenty-three horrifying, hilarious, and stomach-churning stories. They're told by people who have answered an ad for a writers' retreat and unwittingly joined a *Survivor*-like scenario where the host withholds heat, power, and food. As the storytellers grow more desperate, their tales become more extreme and they ruthlessly plot to make themselves the hero of the reality show that will surely be made from their plight. This is one of the most disturbing and outrageous books you'll ever read, one that could only come from the mind of Chuck Palahniuk.

Fiction

LULLABY

Ever heard of a culling song? It's a lullaby sung in Africa to give a painless death to the old or infirm. The lyrics of a culling song kill, whether spoken or even just thought. You can find one on page 27 of *Poems and Rhymes from Around the World*, an anthology on the shelves of libraries across the country. When reporter Carl Streator discovers that unsuspecting readers are reading the poem and accidentally killing their children, he begins a desperate cross-country quest to put the culling song to rest and save the nation from certain disaster.

Fiction

PYGMY

A gang of adolescent terrorists, a spelling bee, and a terrible plan masquerading as a science project: This is Operation Havoc. Pygmy is one of a handful of young adults from a totalitarian state sent to the US disguised as exchange students. Living with American families to blend in, they are planning an unspecified act of massive terrorism that will bring this big dumb country and its fat dumb inhabitants to their knees. Palahniuk depicts Midwestern life through the eyes of this indoctrinated little killer in a cunning double-edged satire of American xenophobia.

Fiction

RANT

Buster "Rant" Casey just may be the most efficient serial killer of our time. A high school rebel, Rant Casey escapes from his small-town home for the big city where he becomes the leader of an urban demolition derby. Rant Casey will die a spectacular highway death, after which his friends gather the testimony needed to build an oral history of his short, violent life.

Fiction

SNUFF

In the crowded greenroom of a porn-movie production, hundreds of men mill around in their boxers, awaiting their turn with the legendary Cassie Wright. An aging adult film star, Cassie Wright intends to cap her career by breaking the world record for serial fornication by having sex with 600 men on camera—one of whom may want to kill her. Told from the perspectives of Mr. 72, Mr. 137, Mr. 600, and Sheila, the talent wrangler who must keep it all under control, *Snuff* is a dark, wild, and lethally funny novel that brings the presence of pornography in contemporary life into the realm of literary fiction.

Fiction

TELL-ALL

For decades Hazie Coogan has tended to the outsized needs of Katherine "Miss Kathie" Kenton, veteran of multiple marriages, career comebacks, and cosmetic surgeries. But danger arrives with gentleman caller Webster Carlton Westward III, who worms his way into Miss Kathie's heart—and boudoir. Soon, Hazie discovers that this bounder has already written a celebrity memoir foretelling Miss Kathie's death in an upcoming musical extravaganza. As the body count mounts, Hazie must execute a plan to save Katherine Kenton for her fans and for posterity.

Fiction

ALSO AVAILABLE
Stranger Than Fiction
Doomed

ANCHOR BOOKS
Available wherever books are sold.
www.anchorbooks.com